ULTRAMARINE

Pat Jourdan

Copyright © Pat Jourdan 2021

The right of Pat Jourdan to be identified as the author of this work has been asserted by her in accordance with the Copyright, Designs and Patents Act 1988. All rights reserved. No part of this book may be reproduced, stored in a retrieval system or transmitted in any form or by any means (electronic, mechanical, photocopying, recording or otherwise without the prior written consent of the author, except in brief quotations in reviews or articles. It may not be edited or amended, without the author's written permission.

patjourdan.wordpress.com

The cover picture is from the painting 'Coming Home' by Pat Jourdan *for*

Amelia Hull-Hewitt, Hunter Jourdan and Inigo Jourdan

The essence of deception is not the lie that's told,
but the truths that are told to support it.

Philip Kerr, *The One from the Other*

also by Pat Jourdan

Short Stories
Average Sunday Afternoon
Taking the Field
Rainy Pavements
The Fog Index
Hotel Curtains

Poetry Collections
The Bedsit Girl
The Bedsit
Ainnir Anthology
Turpentine
The Cast-Iron Shore
Liverpool Poets 2008
Citizeness

Novels
Finding Out
A Small Inheritance
Maryland Street
One Hundred Views of NW3

Ultramarine

Pat Jourdan

1

It was unbelievable. She was here, right in the middle of that picture. Right in the middle of the sequinned sea, here on board the white ship cutting like scissors across a dark blue ocean. Of course, the old dream version was that long-ago TV advert, engraved in sharp black and white. Here it was all in colour and Cora was on this brilliant white boat set in an ultramarine sea with waves the colour of sapphires.

There was always that advert on the television, with the stunning ship slicing through the water as she was struggling across the room, staggering from tiredness and hidden malnutrition It became a vision of hope, its calmness and promise; somewhere on the horizon was a sunset that the ship sailed towards. It shone across the living room and each time Cora stopped, staring at the advert, aware that there were still possibilities somewhere, however faint.

"You could use a cruise on P&O" it promised and taunted.

The café windows on board were frosted glass, a shame. Café Olivos was set with plump retro club chairs as far as anyone could see, huddles of olive green, coffee and plum-coloured tub chairs. They circled tables with legs set into the floor and fitted with one central pole to be seaworthy. Two couples sat un-talking over the remains in their waxed coffee cups. An elderly man hovered over a sheaf of papers like an off-duty accountant or a man plotting his escape from financial responsibilities.

Various vastly overweight women (and men

who also looked over nine months pregnant) called in for takeaway snacks of loaves crammed with cheese or ham, given fancy foreign titles. Only one table of teenagers were happily talking and – so far - of average size.

A mistake. The windows were not muffed or masked glass; a never-ending dimpled grey showed that there was grey sea placed at two thirds down the window. Haze had lifted though the horizon was still blurred, and the sea looked merely like moving wallpaper.

Another fat-bellied man strolled in with wife following; two obese people, they chose a window table to sit at beside the non-view. Then the woman, dressed in loose brown sweater and brown trousers, turned towards the counter and it was obvious that this time the high-thrown stomach was that of a pregnant woman about eight months ready.

Chatting expertly in English, the counter assistant, blonde and brown eyed, told a customer that the café opened at five, yes, five, she had to be up at four. Another customer commiserated, remembering he'd had a job that had also started so early.

"You ought to be going off to bed now, you know, it's getting on for one."

"I will, if you'd be going with me!" she answered and all three laughed at the ridiculous situation. "I cannot even go to bed early. In the evening I look at my watch, it is nine, ten, eleven – and I cannot go to sleep. I am all nerves!" She smiled brightly again. Beneath her eyes, brown smudges in the skin showed the nervy tiredness and all her face was striped with frown lines which lifted, vanishing with each smile. The job was eating her up alive. The

boss came round a pillar with a stack of some more clean trays to set on the shelf.

"You should try working with her! It is hell!" He returned and shot handfuls of clean cutleries into the containers along the counter.

The pregnant woman went off somewhere – perhaps to puke, as the ship was rolling constantly – or to pee yet again with a baby's pressure on her bladder. Squashed inside there, not much room to move; an extra cup of coffee meant more upset. Her husband stayed regarding the non-view seriously.

Back from wherever, the brown-clad pregnant woman went to sit beside her husband (who had done nothing while she was away, not ordering any drinks) at the window side where the sea was back at mist again, its non-view. She talked about the doctor's advice, rubbing the lump gently with both hands which were festooned with gold rings, as if over-married. He laughed at something she'd said and looked across the room as if to find other answers. But he continued to sit idly as if never intending to eat or drink.

Across from them a bunch of teenagers, probably the only ones on board, discussed in posh English accents about a couple splitting up; the parents of one of their friends.

"And he's adopted. Had to go to her sister's. There was nowhere else for him to live." They all murmured sympathy like a quick group prayer.

"James's lot split up lately too."

"It seems to go round a group quickly, like measles, families breaking up, it's all the rage." Then the tallest, a boy of about seventeen dressed in a red

T-shirt changed the subject with,

"Is anyone going to have another coffee? We've got just enough time before the next film starts."

"When James told me, I didn't know what to say, you get upset for them, or at least I do, for James and his sister. What's going to happen to them?" The girl persisted with the stories of all the couples of their parents' age breaking up. But the others changed tack. These were families they all knew, and it was an upsetting subject.

"I just hope my parents last out a couple more years together, the way things are going."

"Look, we're off to Bilbao, let's enjoy what we're doing right now, worrier. It might not happen."

"So, thinking about yesterday, when we were leaving, how would you describe Brad, then?"

"He's rangy."

"He's also astonishingly thick."

"And thin!" They all grunted in amusement this time and the conversation meandered onto other topics.

2

1967

Summer arrived with a flurry of blossom along the sides of garden walls all along Downshire Hill. White and cream-painted houses enhanced the clematis and wistaria set in front of the houses. Fallen cherry blossom petals drifted from the paths into the gutters, turning the road into a pink mass, a lovely early June morning, full of promise as Cora walked up to Fitzjohn's Avenue.

She arrived to clean at the Reitzmans as usual, to find both Mr and Mrs Reitzman struck with summer colds, although it looked more like flu. They were lying in their matching single beds, white lace coverlets neatly arranged, both propped up watching TV. A large television set was newly installed against the wall at the end of their beds. As they both coughed and spluttered, they followed the news bulletins and special broadcasts about the new war between Israel and the Arabs, sparked off by border disputes. Crashes and billowing orange and black clouds filled the screen. Glasses of Lucozade and various pills were scattered across the bedside tables. There had been a rally in the Albert Hall of 10,000 people in solidarity with Israel, organised by the Zionist Federation against Jordanian aggression. Roads to hospitals were destroyed. Children on both sides left dead. Israeli forces were capturing east Jerusalem and Palestinian territories, the West Bank and Gaza. The TV rattled with missile shots.

And now Mount Sinai, the very mountain where Jehovah had given Moses the Ten Commandments, right there in the start of the Bible, was also involved. The smell of war was in the air, even here in Hampstead. The au pair, Louvaine, was now in charge of both the children and the daily running of the house.

"This is really worrying, anything could happen," Mrs Reitzman whispered. "I've nearly lost my voice. Just do the usual but see that the dining room floor is specially polished, we had a dinner planned for the end of the week, but it looks unlikely now. Never mind, it will wait until next week." Mr

Reitzman looked glum and embarrassed to be found in bed like this by their cleaner. He needed to be upright and wearing his usual navy suit.

Cora attended to the bedside clutter first, took the tissue-stuffed wastepaper basket downstairs and brought up that day's The Times and The Guardian and the Daily Mail, then went off on her usual tour of hoovering the house from top to bottom. Four hours a day here; afternoons scattered elsewhere; lunchtime spent hurrying through the streets to wherever the Daily Maids agency had booked her.

For the rest of the week Mrs Reitzman remained in bed, red-nosed and sniffling, the TV control in her hand, switching anxiously from channel to channel, following the spiral of violence and suffering in what had been now called the Six Days War. Mr. Reitzman had managed to get up at last and wandered around looking rather lost. It was so convenient, obviously, that his office was just across the landing and he could go in there and dictate a couple of letters to his daily secretary, Audrey, in comfort, a green silk dressing gown over his pyjamas. His company imported cameras from all over the world, all of them bringing in bad news clearly in the future like this.

It was only Cora's social life that kept her functioning. A raft of parties each weekend helped to dull the drudge of weekday work. There was always going to be a better job, but once fixed into a daily work routine, it was impossible to afford time off to go off for any interviews. Weeks merged seamlessly into each other. And almost midsummer to the day, two sisters living over a dress shop in the High Street invited Cora to another party. Both Elston sisters came round the Rosslyn Arms on Friday evening and threading through the groups approached her, almost whispering,

"We've decided you're interesting enough to pass our test! We want this to be a different kind of do – more talking and meeting, not a loud bash. It's a sort of dual birthday party and we thought it was about time we did it, everyone else has parties these days. So, it's next Saturday night, but don't tell all the pub, we've only got a small flat!" Rowena and Daisy waltzed out of the Rosslyn and went off to spread their secret invitations in other pubs.

On Saturday evening, early, Cora rang the discreet bell at the side of the fashionable dress shop set at the corner of the High Street and Fitzjohn's Avenue. Daisy came down to the door, walking through the racks of exclusive clothes and ushered Cora past the models and rails and upstairs to their flat. The premises were so expensive that she would never have thought of entering the place or even spend time looking in the windows.

It was not a drink-and-dance revel, more a gentle sit-and-chat with added wine and eatables. Cora eventually sat on a settee and started talking to a boy who looked slightly like a young Prince Philip, with fair hair and slate-grey eyes. He wore a tobacco-coloured corduroy jacket although it was a warm evening. He said he was going to travel round the world next year with two girls,

"Those ones over there, we're not involved sexually, it wouldn't work, I'm their best friend anyway, it would ruin it all. My name's Mark. What's yours?" Cora felt he was interesting – he told her he was also writing a multifaceted saga of a mythical country, founded on Icelandic myths, "With a bit of King Arthur myths thrown in, too. It's complicated." He was planning on going to university eventually too but wanted to do this round-the-world trip first, not that his parents approved of it at all. But then, what else would you expect?

Meanwhile he had worked in a garden centre,

been an unqualified teacher in a private school, worked for a debt-collectors and almost been a milkman.

"But they said it was useless training me, it costs thirty pounds to train a milkman! Fancy that! They pointed out that I was an educated person and most likely would not stay working as a milkman for long enough, it was a job for a working-class type of man. I suppose they were right; they must protect their own. So now I'm working on almost rebuilding someone's house in Finchley, it's a bit awkward as they are living on the premises as well."

Luckily it was an old and rambling property with several floors. "There's absolutely ages of work to do there, they keep changing their minds. Husband wants more wide spaces; wife wants more smaller rooms." He asked her about herself, his name was Mark, what was her name and what she was doing and, incidentally, how old was she?

"Twenty-six! By the time I'm twenty-six I expect I'll be married and have three children." Cora felt a failure, not able to defend her latest bedsit and the writings and paintings and the past boyfriends and the non-marriages and the non-children.

At this point a very drunk Tom stumbled across the room and asked Cora to see him home, he was feeling rather out of it. It was a moral debt she owed him; he had rescued her once when she was in tears in the middle of the street having just learnt that the love of her life was a married man with an eleven month old baby. Tom had taken her into his arms and walked her home. He was warm, like a big teddy bear.

"Sorry, I've got to go now," she said, getting up and crossing towards Tom. They went out into the warm night and progressed gradually along to his flat in Frognal, where she placed him on his sofa, getting a bucket for him to vomit in if necessary and a jug full of water. Giving Tom these instructions and hoping he would not end up in too much of a mess, or even die outright, she let herself out of his flat, leaving his door-key on the table and dashed back to the party. But the interesting young man had gone, together with his two companions.

Telling Sophie in her bedsit upstairs about it the next day, in one of their usual Sunday afternoon inquests, Sophie was aghast she had not taken his phone number or address or even his surname.

"You know his name is Mark, that's all? Why don't you just call round there now at the girls' flat, it's the afternoon, and they're sure to be up by now, and ask them all about him? That would be a good way to find out and get in touch with him again." So, with fresh lipstick and a coat this time because the day was not as warm as last night, Cora went up to the dress shop and rang the secret bell set in the doorframe. Daisy came through the dress shop and opened the door. It was strange to be walking past the model dresses and coats in the daytime like this. They went through the hidden door at the back and up to the flat again.

"Oh, Rowena knows more than I do, she knows everyone, don't you!" She turned to her sister. Daisy sat down and kicked her shoes off. "These have been killing me since last night. We didn't go to bed until something like five, and we've managed to clear everything up quite well, don't you think?" There was no trace of last night. But Rowena was no help. It was embarrassing to be asking this question, they were both so nice about it.

"No, I'm sorry, I didn't know them at all, Joseph was coming out of the Grapes and I just said, oh, you can bring those other people too if you like. So, he didn't really know them either, they just looked all right. So, sorry you've gone and lost him now, it happens that way." Rowena looked pensive for a second then lit up. "We've got some rosé wine left over, would you like some? We've started again; Harry and Joseph are coming over this afternoon for a stiff walk across the Heath to get some fresh air for a change."

"They're trying to convert us to healthy living, but they depend on our parties for their social life," Daisy remarked cynically.

The week continued in its usual boring pattern. On Tuesday evening, however, Dorothea from the room next door came in to see Cora. Dorothea was of an uncertain age, she looked about fifty, but must have been thirty at the most. Her face was pitted with pockmarks, some outbreak that surely had been eliminated in her original Holland. Her job was as a translator in some publishing house; that was as much as Cora knew about her. For the most part, Dorothea passed by on the stairs like a grey mouse.

"I wonder if you would do me a favour," she said, sitting down on the spare chair. "I've got some – er - difficulty, and so I was wondering if you could help?" Cora was already hooked. Any plea for help had to be responded to, apart from its appeal to plain human curiosity.

"Sure, as far as I know, what do you mean, help?"

"I've got a problem... and it is going to get worse tonight, I've taken some pills already and I thought, if I knock on the wall later tonight, when the pain gets worse, would you go and phone for an ambulance? And I've got the phone number of a friend here, Mathilde, she will look after all the rest, you won't need to do anything else." Cora could see the details behind the faltering words. She had never had a conversation with Dorothea before; this was extreme, woman to woman stuff, a real crisis. She was involved now.

Dorothea gave her the friend's number and money for the call. "And here's the keys to give to her when she calls. I'll leave my door unlocked, so you can let the ambulancemen in," was the end of their confab, as Dorothea went back to her own room, adding, "I've got a bag already packed," her sad efficiency masking the torment.

About ten that evening, the knocking on the wall was quite clear, like a prisoner sending a signal. Cora leapt out of bed, dashed next door and found Dorothea in bed, writhing in pain, her face white with stress. Off to the payphone in the hall, luckily there was no one about. The ambulance arrived quickly and the two men carried the moaning Dorothea, wrapped in a red blanket, down the stairs, Cora carrying the overnight bag.

"It's all right now," Dorothea managed to say. "Just phone Mathilde."

"You're not a relative, are you?" one of the paramedics asked "So you wouldn't be allowed in the van. She'll be taken to St Mary's Paddington, though we might end up in Harrow Road, you'll have to check later, sorry." Their mix of efficiency and sympathy was astounding. Cora went back into the silent house, phoned Mathilde that the ambulance had taken Dorothea away already and to check with the hospitals to find out more.

Ian in the upstairs bedsit, however had picked up on the goings-on. He never missed anything. The next day he stopped Cora in the hall.

"Been a naughty girl, our old Dorothea, then, has she? Midnight ambulance and all!" He was triumphant and mocking. "Wouldn't have expected anything like that of her!" Cora said she did not know any details, it was just a pain, appendix, peritonitis, something like that. She had removed the blood-stained towel from Dorothea's bed, stuffing it into a plastic bag and had tidied the already tidy room. It was surprisingly anonymous, no books, no photos, no posters, no personal changes that anyone would make to any rented room; it was all exactly as it had been when she moved in, the furniture in the same place. It was the home of a nobody.

Dorothea reappeared a few days later, her friend Mathilde, also speaking Dutch, brought her back. Nothing much was said - a box of chocolates in thanks to Cora and then an unannounced departure. Such an enormous event and not a speck of evidence, all smoothed away except for Cora's remembering the events and how serious they really were. Obviously, Dorothea did not want to come back - why start her days with the broken pieces of yesterday?

The next Saturday night Cora got ready with the same weekly procedure, off to the pub, get news of an address or two and then off to a party. She felt lacklustre applying mascara for another night. It was like clocking into a late-night factory shift. A last spray of perfume and off downstairs, open the front door, and there, standing on the doorstep, was the lad from the party. They looked at each other, happily surprised.

"We were wondering which bell to ring; we haven't even sorted that out yet. There's supposed to be a party here tonight, isn't there?" Mark said. The two girls from last week's party smiled sheepishly at her from the lower step, with another, smaller boy, behind them.

"No," Cora said, laughing, "You've got the wrong house, there's nothing here at all. There was a big party last night next-door though, you could hear it all over the street. That must be the one you were told about. You're just one night too late." The little group had a conference and decided there was another address they could go to for a party, and she was welcome to join them. Off they walked to somewhere past Belsize Park station.

"It's a bit early yet, but we're saving money by not going into the pub first," the taller dark-haired girl told her. "I'm Rhona and this is Kirsty, we're both from the same village in Scotland. There was nothing to do up there, so we're staying in London and saving up to travel round the world." Then Mark told her again that the three of them were going to travel together, they were not intended as girlfriends that would make it far too complicated.

"It'll work better that way," he assured Cora. "But the two girls'll need me for security, you see. So, we are working at any old job to get ready and plan it all out for next year." The quiet boy with them, Bill, was not going to be joining them as he said he had a good job and a car and was saving for the deposit for a flat while still living at home. His absolute plain sensibleness made him immediately unattractive.

They sat chatting for most of the time, as the party was so crowded, there was no room to dance. As it got late Mark said he had to see the two girls' home, a minimum rehearsal for his future trip. But he said he would call in during the week.

And, sure enough, on Wednesday, Cora came home from work at half-past six, the sun still warming this side of the street up Parliament Hill, to find two glossy LPs leaning against her room door "With love, Mark"– Jimi Hendrix, *Axis Bold As Love* and the Beatles' brand-new *Sergeant Pepper*, as they had been talking about them, the latest and most exciting music that everyone in the pub was talking about.

He called round later that Wednesday evening and stayed the night. It was as easy as that. They relaxed into each other and the sex became better each time, a belonging that did not stop. Then the feather kisses of morning led to them grasping each other all over again for more.

He lay back on the pillow and started to confide in her,
" D'you know, the first time I had sex was with a woman whose house I was cleaning in, Yes! I'd started the hoovering and dusting and so on and then I saw a book in the shelf, *The Hidden Persuaders* and I sat down and started reading it right then and there. She came in early that afternoon and found me sitting there and we started discussing advertising and so on and then she said, what about a drink. We sat there drinking whisky and chatting and one thing led to another. I was a virgin, a complete beginner in the sex

stakes and it was awkward at first. But of course, she was a married woman, heaven only knows where her husband was. It was all really O.K.I can tell you! I was delighted, I can tell you! This great change in my status! I started laughing, I said, 'So, this is what D.H.Lawrence was going on about all the time! Why did he make it sound so complicated! I've been led astray all this long!'" The awkward part was having to ask her for the money afterwards."

"You really got away with it? What happened after that?" Cora was intrigued.

"Well, it sort of petered out after a couple of months. We had a weekly assignation if you could call it that, but that was all. It wasn't going to lead to anything more, I could see that. We couldn't go out together or anything. Then they stopped their booking as they went abroad or something. But she'd done me a welcome service and I'm still sort of thankful to her. Sandra, that was her name."

"And what happened then?"

"Oh, I had a sort of proper girlfriend, Amy, all the time though, right from schooldays. Nothing happened there at all, well, not really..." He told her that he had tried 'everything but' with his previous girlfriend, but no real complete sex.

"Oh, we drove each other mad, bathing together, rubbing each other to infinity but no real intercourse. We were saving it, sort of, until we both got to university, I think, or at least that was Amy's usual answer. Now, though, I think she was just afraid. It could have been easy, after all. Thank goodness, Sandra saved me from exploding completely."

"Then you wouldn't be here, would you, all of

our destinies hang by threads. Like meeting you at the front door here last Saturday, that was a real coincidence."

He put his arm around her, giving a warm hug.

"So, well, I'll go and get some of my things and we can start together here, I'll tell my parents I'm moving out." Cora was a bit taken aback at this abrupt start but how could she object; everything was working smoothly and to slow things down was to risk breaking this new link, this door into a new life. You did not start objections at this moment. The room was actually a double room: Fred had asked her if she could afford it and perhaps she had taken the risk with this sort of outcome in mind. Or perhaps she liked the extra space after so many cramped bedsits in Clapham or Brixton.

It was now a rush to get dressed and revert to the daytime Thursday routine and go off to the Reitzman's place. Mark went off to call back at his parents and leave for his work too.

He moved into her room on the Saturday with his clothes and a selection of more music that changed the surrounding. The stripped-down voice of Martin Carthy and his plangent version of *Scarborough Fair*, the longing of the lad who is waiting for his lover. *For once she was a true love of mine* – the lad who was lost in his love and unable to get out into ordinary life again. *"Tell her to buy me an acre of ground"*. If only. It was so stark that it scoured the room with its purity and scratched her soul. Mark told her that its first printing as street music was in 1670,

"But it's even far older than that." He said he used to go to Cecil Sharp's House as a follower of traditional music. She admired him for that. Mark said he also used to go to anarchist meetings at a pub in central London, an extra interest. He was interested and aware on all points, intelligence spread wide and omnivorous.

"I'll take you to one of their meetings at the Lamb and Flag, you'll learn a lot about politics, it's real discussions and inventive ideas. Some of them are absolutely barking mad, of course, but you're going to get that in all political parties."

Every day Mark put the Sergeant Pepper LP on the record player, as if he were trying to decipher it. The songs fell against the walls like invisible wallpaper. They were the only two people in Hampstead who were quibbling about the grammar in a line in *Strawberry Fields Forever.*

"It's about, hung up about."

"Yes. It's trying to be quick and trendy and American."

3

July brought mumps and strawberries. Cora lay in bed completely dizzy and feverish. Mark was kind and caring, he was immune, he boasted, he had already had mumps as a child. An accomplishment. Mumps in males over puberty was supposed to cause sterility. Cora asked him to phone the Reitzmans and tell the agency that she was really out of it. The week flew past in a daze. Mrs Reitzman kindly came round with the week's wages, a genuine bonus, and met Mark. Fred stayed out on the landing, as if the rent money was contagious too, but he left a punnet of fresh strawberries outside their door. After a few days ("I've got to do something," Mark said, phoning for help,) a young woman doctor came round to Cora's isolation. No one else would enter the room. After she gently examined the neck and looked at her throat. The doctor stood at the end of the bed,

"Any other pains, anything else you would like to tell me?" Cora thought this was a strange question and searched for something to say.

"Well, with all this upset, I've had no periods this week either, perhaps my insides have been affected?" The doctor gave her an internal examination, flexing skilled fingers up the private tunnels.

"All O.K. There's nothing serious to worry about now. And I am happy to inform you that you are also pregnant." The doctor looked round the large room, absolutely pleased. "It would be possible to have a baby here, it's a nice situation." The baby could sleep inside the fitted wardrobe, it seemed. There would be no other place to put it. Something inside Cora chilled, a leap into an uncertain future.

Mark, however, was delighted.

"My parents, well, they'll have to let us get married now. They can't stop us." The law was that anyone under twenty-one had to get permission from their parents, it was essential. Matters were moving along at a rapid rate, like a ball of wool unravelling. No, it was more like a runaway train, reckless and exciting and no way could either of them stall it now.

Her own two records, Procol Harum's *A Whiter Shade of Pale* and Jimi Hendrix's *Purple Haze* were now put aside. She had finally paid off the H.P. agreement to buy the record player. Fred had acted as guarantor, with his usual amused incredulity at someone like her, broke, wanting to buy something out of reach. But he knew Cora was honest enough to make the effort to keep up the payments and here was the finishing-line reached at last.

Luckily, he approved of Mark and did not object to his moving in; the room was usually rented as a double room anyway, so he could hardly object now.

From here on there were endless appointments at the doctor's, the first one being at 6p.m. on July 18th. It was rather a dash as work only ended at 6p.m. too, so she began by owing extra time to the afternoon people, a German family in Arkwright Road., plus the Plessiers and Bouvards in Arkwright Road. From here on it was a process of running two lives at once, balancing the pseudo medical one and the day-to-day routine.

Two steaks were left under the grill while Cora went off for some milk from the grocers near the Magdala pub. A normal late summer day; looking forward to Mark coming back from work. When she got back to the room, ready to start grilling the steaks, she found them covered with small, glistening white oval eggs. A passing bluebottle had found the perfect place to deposit her young. They were linked, two females, pregnant and needing a home for their offspring. All creation depended on this female drive to nest-make.

All those Giotto, Duccio, Fra Angelico, Botticelli, Raphael, and all the other Renaissance painters of The Annunciation celebrated this – the agreement of a young female to be impregnated and produce young. It was unclear if all animals, fish, and insects had great pain in the birthing process. But her friend Rita had told her, that sitting up late with a pregnant white rat, a discarded pet of her son, the poor female rat had heaved and writhed in pain. The anger of God, the casting-out of the two naughty ones from the Playground of Eden, surely did not go down the entire chain of species as far as a female rat or bluebottle.

The myth was a rationalisation of that pain of childbirth, dog, cat, rat-birth and so on, something that existed anyway in nature. It was men who had turned it into being seen as a punishment of women in childbirth. You hurt because you are bad. You hurt because Eve ate the apple. You hurt because Eve had sex with Adam. Now square that circle.

She washed the shiny clustered eggs off the steaks carefully and did not mention it to Mark. Grilling would disinfect them perfectly. The little pearls shone as she destroyed them, a lost future family cloud of flies.

They became more and more entwined, growing into each other daily. Mark was interested in whatever she was reading and wanted to share any book from the library she started, to match what was going on in her head. He said he did not like her reading any book without him. He would feel shut out. Their lives were parallel now, it seemed.

"Actually, I don't like your painting or writing really, especially the painting, because then you go into a place I can't follow you into and I get puzzled when you paint, as I can't enter there, I don't understand what you are doing."

He had to be there all the time, parallel - sometimes Cora glimpsed a hint of irritation behind the neediness, but she was intrigued, impressed, flattered to be held so important and dismissed the instant.

This week they were reading John Fowles's *The Magus* rabidly, almost fighting over the book. As soon as Mark had gone to work, Cora would pack it into her bag with her apron and, as soon as break-time arrived wherever she was cleaning, go on with where she had stopped. The lunch break consisted of dashing from the Reitzman's to whatever address the Daily Maids had given her for the afternoon, eating a sandwich in the street, and swigging cold coffee from a plastic bottle. When he came back from work, Mark continued to read on right away from where he had left a bookmark. A ripped piece of paper showed his place; they were both racing along, eaten up by the book.

It took over three weeks out of their life, going deeper and deeper into the trance of the narrative and its psychic adventures.

"It's drugs by any other name, other methods," he remarked. The complicated layers of deception both exterior and interior were exquisitely done. Layers of meaning blended into each other. "It's as if we are living inside the book, while living our real lives at the same time." Mark was entranced by it completely.

So, when the film of John Fowles' *The Collector* appeared at the Everyman in the High Street, they took it as a sign confirming that their enthusiasm was right and their taste impeccable. They got to the 7.30 showing, late enough to recover after work and have something to eat at home first and early enough to go for a drink after. The film even had shots of nearby Hampstead streets where the naïve young woman became involved with the introvert lad who trapped her into his house. It could have been set anywhere near here. While wrapped up in beautiful photography and well-chosen and designed settings, with the added glamour of Samantha Eggar and Terence Stamp, it was the age-old Bluebeard story of the ugly loner kidnapping the trusting young woman.

Afterwards there was enough time to go into the pub nearby for a drink. It had a strange clientele; glamorous blonde au pairs, usually Swedish, and ageing middle-class actors. The two groups ignored each other cleverly.

As Mark and Cora sat chatting amicably, recovering from the intensity of the film, she noticed there were two little boys standing outside the gents' toilets. They were looking apprehensive. Everything else was going on as normal - the long-legged Scandinavian beauties, all au pairs off duty, busy talking to each other while the rest of the pub was entirely gay men, with a large number of ageing actors in cashmere sweaters. They stood confidently. still acting as if on stage, posing and talking in booming voices, incredibly assured of their own worth even now that they were becoming old and superseded by younger men.

But the two boys, aged about ten and eight, remained standing there with a man behind them (their father?) The three all had red hair, the boys' hair excessively shiny as if it had only just been shampooed and they both wore navy gaberdine macs, a bit on the long side, as if it were some school uniform, although it was a warm late summer night. As she went on chatting to Mark, still going on about the film, she watched the three figures outside the toilets. If they were waiting for their mother, she had already been an unconscionably long time in the ladies. In fact, the two boys looked rather frightened. It was already gone half-past ten by now, long past their bedtime and no woman had appeared.

She did not like to think what she was thinking and had to remark to Mark about it, as he was sitting with his back to the scene outside the toilet door. He turned round and glanced at them.

"If it is what you think it is, well, we can't really do anything about it, right now can we? It could all be quite above-board, but they do look vulnerable and you're probably right, this time of night too, sadly." They agreed the pub was full of important and probably powerful homosexual men, and it was a very grey area, just their own assumptions filling in gaps and perhaps making up a story to fit. Even worse, the police station was only a few hundred yards down the hill. So near and yet so far. Mark and Cora walked home still discussing the film and its intricate link between freedom and imprisonment and distracting each other from any disquiet about the trapped boys standing by the pub toilets. They never talked about the situation again.

4 The summer raced on with perpetual sunshine and for the August Bank Holiday they went off to an old school-friend of Mark's. Pete's parents' house was out in the country, past Elstree and this was going to be a real house-party. The group had the house to themselves; Pete's parents were in the Maldives or somewhere exotic for a fortnight. Music became the lifeblood of the day and night. The

Foundations *Now That I've Found You* boomed out regularly and at full pelt. But Cora was at that part of pregnancy where she was tired all the time and at five in the morning she eventually went downstairs objecting to the incessant playing of *Itchycoo Park*, its teenage revolt clearly audible even through the thick carpet in the bedroom upstairs.

It made her unpopular; it was a drawback against Mark for choosing her with all her adult worldly worries like pregnancy and her needing to get back to work promptly at the end of the holiday weekend. Cora was the only one who had to go to work on the Tuesday morning and after bolting a cup of tea and her iron tablets, she walked off to the suburban station for the early train back from Radlett to London. All the others were either unemployed or working adjustable hours. The music could go on endlessly without her.

Iron tablets, however, should only be taken after food and a swooning nausea began right there and then as she stood on the platform. She could neither go back nor refuse to get on this train; there would not be another one for almost an hour. Public embarrassment for private experience; pregnancy made her a public fool, a disgrace. By creating life, you went through these stages of wanting to die, to just curl up and die right here on the platform, in front of bored commuters. The ladies' toilets were not clean but were a necessary haven. She managed a quick puke before the train drew in and hoped for the best, trying to concentrate on the landscape flicking past and wondering if she would ever have the time to paint again.

The pregnancy was causing more problems.

They had kept it secret so far. It was too much for his parents to handle just yet, Mark said. They were just getting used to the fact he had moved in with her. Now and again Mr Williams met them by appointment for a drink in the Magdala, which was near, where he always asked Mark to consider returning home, did he ever stop and think what he was really doing and how upset his mother was. All this was said right in front of Cora as if she did not exist. His father always ignored Cora as he brought their drinks to a table at The Magdala.

"He would have taken more notice of a dog," she moaned to Mark later.

"Give him time," Mark soothed. They also had to inform Fred now about their change in circumstances. He knew at once it was an accidental pregnancy but appreciated that they were going to keep the baby. He was not going to approve, however, a baby being on the premises. The house was a youthful Nirvana; babies would ruin the ambiance. As it was, tenants magically tended to move out as soon as their thirties hit, the noise, music and constant mix of visitors suddenly taking a trying tax of their energy.

Now Mark and Cora were preoccupied with saving money for a new flat and furniture. Trying to not go out and spend, they continued with library books; after all, the library was nearby in Keats Grove, and they moved on to reading *Cider with Rosie*. The descriptions of lush countryside were almost tangible and the magical eye of childhood showed riches that adults ignored.

"But it wasn't much fun for the poor cow, was it? It was all wonderful for the young kid, but he wouldn't realise what she was going through." Mark pointed out. He had benevolent insights like this. They both read the book at once, piece by piece, gulping it up like the cider itself.

It was time to buy some furniture for their new place wherever it might be. With two wages coming in it was easy to save and they could choose something interesting.

They spent Saturday night staying in and listening to the Saturday night play on the radio while sanding down the furniture just bought from Ron Weldon's second-hand furniture shop in England's Lane. A captain's chair, a chair made totally of turned wood and a large kitchen table to be delivered eventually when they got a new address; the future was becoming actual now. Mark also produced a new double sheet, bought in a sale, a strange light grey colour called Knights in White Satin, after the hit song. It just looked dirty and Kirsty, calling round remarked on it, was that a real colour?

There was more to consider – Cora thought that he had taken the old gold ring of her grandmothers to see if he could find a wedding ring for her birthday, but when she asked, Mark looked blank and said, surely it was somewhere else? And didn't she find it wedged behind the cupboard where it had fallen. But at least it had started them thinking about their own status apart from what Mark's father thought of them.

So, on the next Saturday they wandered from one jeweller's shop to another round Notting Hill. But to think that their love was somehow linked with the mass-produced rings in the windows of H M Samuels and Ratners made them worried. A smaller shop right at the end of Portobello was private enough, and Cora and Mark chose a plain gold ring. Being so proud and happy, she chose the thickest gold band to signal the new relationship in public and they paid half each, to signify how important it was to both. The jeweller gave them a box bound in imitation leather to keep it in.

"Not that you'll be placing it in this very often, if at all," he added, congratulating them. It was like an impromptu little marriage ceremony right there on her birthday.

By a few days later she found the new ring was often awkward, it constricted movement and squashed the bend of the third finger, but it shone as strongly as a neon sign, which was what its function really was.

5

A dull November evening and Mark blundered into the room, although the weather was not
bad; something had upset him. He plonked his bag of tools down heavily by the door.

"I need a cup of tea, right away." Cora turned round. He did not usually give orders out like this.

"What's wrong then? You upset about something?"

"I was not going to tell you, but ... well, I was walking down that cut in front of the hospital, you know where I mean. I'd just walked up from Belsize Park Station, and I'd nearly got to the hospital front gates at the bottom of the walk, where it slopes, and these two police dashed down after me. They pulled me back to their car, it was parked up near the taxi rank, and they told me to open my tool bag and wanted to know what my name and address was. I told them, *told them,* I'd been to work in Finchley, at the Friedman's place as a handyman, and I was going home, where my wife was pregnant, and we lived up by Parliament Hill.

I even said they could come and inspect us if they didn't believe me. And they could ring the Friedman's to verify my day's work if they wanted to." Cora stood silent, shocked. "When they realised, I was quite respectable, a good accent and all that, do you know what they said?"

"Well, it's all surreal so far, what did they say?"

"They said that a man like me, who looked poor, carrying a tool bag, wasn't likely to be living in Hampstead and was more probably a housebreaker."

"At six o'clock on a November evening? Bit early to start, don't you think?" She joked. "But seriously, has it really come to this? We are not supposed to be living here if we look poor?"

"You've got it. An ordinary tradesman, just going about his business, is not supposed to come from here, just allowed to work here in the daytime. I should have been going in the opposite direction according to them. We might as well be in a segregated area. They could issue day-passes. After all, Fred wants us out of here, he doesn't want any baby disturbing his Club Med playground for his 18-30-year-olds." Cora said no more, it was bad enough as it was.

"In police custody, I've always wondered about that," Mark said.

"It would be just as awkward to be sunk in custard," Cora joked, trying to be cheerful.

That week they were both reading Mary McCarthy's *A Charmed Life,* which gave several ideas on how to save money. Cheap ideas for presents - it was going to solve their first Christmas gift list together. Buying some lengths of red ribbon, Cora then bought several handfuls of oranges and a jar of cloves and happily made pomanders, which magically shrank and did not actually look as glamorous as their name suggested. Sophie's face gave away how awkward a gift it was. However it might be dressed up as something Tudor and vaguely to do with Queen Elizabeth I, it was just a shrunken orange, disguised by cloves being stabbed all over it. Sophie handled it as if it was a hand grenade, which was exactly what it looked like, it had to be admitted. Stripped of their literary or historic references, the dead and dying oranges, studded with bits of brown sticks were politely accepted by their friends and quickly put into the rubbish with the Christmas tinsel as soon as possible. Taking Sophie's reaction as a hint, Cora was left with half a dozen useless pomanders slung over their coat-hangers in their wardrobe, bobbing awkwardly each time a jacket or coat was taken out and leaving her wondering if any insects were going to be burrowing out in the spring.

But in the Magdala they encountered the same discrimination against the poor or whatever it was they were doing wrongly. When Cora had come in here previously, it was on her own, all dressed up, or with a group of regulars. But standing at the bar with Mark, the tacit selection was obvious. Time after time, customers appearing behind them were served –

sometimes over their heads. When they had been waiting long enough for the publican to have made his point, he gruffly served them the lager and lime and the beer that they usually had.

"You're not imagining it," Mark glumly commented as they walked to a table eventually with their begrudged drinks. "If we were anything else than ordinary white residents we could complain. But we're trapped." Cora felt ashamed as if she had led Mark into a trap. Perhaps she had been tolerated when she was single, to pad out an otherwise totally male set of customers. But ordinary poor couples were probably not the image the landlord wanted to encourage.

A December midday and Cora slipped and fell over outside Hampstead Station in the snow on the way to the ante-natal class. Passers-by kindly helped her to stand up again and she leant against the wall to calm down. The extra weight had altered her balance and that part of the pavement sloped anyway. But she did not tell anyone at the health centre, held at a church hall further up Heath Street. A nurse, in full navy dress and white pinafore and starched cap, was loudly admonishing a young blonde-haired woman in the next cubicle.

"This baby is going to get born. You can't go on pretending it is not going to happen. Time to take this seriously and put your mind to it. This little baby will need your attention – things like baby clothes, a cot, mattress, blankets, a pram." The girl looked blank. The nurse, tough love, relented slightly. "We can put you in touch with people who will help." Cora sitting nearby, saw all of this. The onslaught was unstoppable for all of them, any baby came with a list of demands and responsibilities, pink or blue. She was already collecting things from the new Oxfam shop each time coming home after work, a quick roundup of nightdresses, matinee coats, and shawls. And she had already bagged a yellow plastic baby bath which held the accumulating collection of clothes as well as an old copy of Good Housekeeping's Baby Book from 1959. Things must not have changed too much since then, though the babies in the photos already looked dated in their carefully knitted layettes.

6

Cora was eventually invited to Christmas dinner by his parents. She was already attending more hospital appointments regularly as soon as work finished or having to juggle cleaning times and staying later to make up lost time. Mark said he had told his mother that he would only come for Christmas if Cora could be invited too.

" I said that if they wanted me to come home (it was only as far as Kensal Rise) for Christmas, then they'd have to include you. Then I told her, by the way, you were pregnant too. So they said yes after all." He hugged her. The battle he had been nobly fighting had hopeful signs now. It had taken so long, with all the background troubles that he had carefully kept from Cora.

His father had not told Beryl about this and pretended he did not know and was as surprised as herself about the pregnancy.

Christmas dinner passed off well, Cora ate

everything in sight, and they were relieved she seemed polite and unthreatening after all. As Mark was under twenty-one, parental permission was necessary, a legal block they both had not realised would be such a problem. His parents disapproved of their precious adopted son (doubly valuable) having anything to do with this older adventuress. Earlier, Mr and Mrs Williams had been thinking of making Mark a Ward of Court and getting him out of the clutches of this evil woman in Belsize Park, not known as a family area, more a haunt of bohemians of all types.

Mark's previous girlfriend's mother had got in on the act quickly. Mrs Carter rang the Williams in panic and moral outrage, now that Amy had been ditched

"He's fallen for the oldest trick in the book."

"Yes. How do we know who the real father is?" Beryl agreed. "She probably saw him coming, took advantage of his inexperience He's a real innocent in all this. Who is she anyway?"

"You'll have to try and stop him living with her. Look up how to make mark a Ward of Court, that should do it. Try and get him back home, point out all the drawbacks of living away like that, too risky. Not got a proper flat, has she? Has she any money?"

"No money as far as George saw. He's met her twice with Mark in a pub. Doesn't have much to say for herself. I'd like to ask her a few questions all right!"

"You've got to get him away from her before it's too late," Mrs Carter insisted. "She's much older than him, you said? The rule-of-thumb is you take half the older one's age plus seven years, anything over that is not advisable. What does George say?"

"George's seeing him this Saturday."

"You'll have to move quickly." Amy, the former girlfriend was still a virgin and had been kept in waiting by conventions and a strict mother who now saw the entire situation unravelling.

But now Cora was sitting right there at the Christmas dinner table and was behaving quite well. She was not as outrageous as Mrs Carter - Mark's previous girlfriend's mother - had feared and Beryl was relieved. It might not be as bad as they had imagined. Perhaps they could patch something up and try to get all this sorted out. Going in for setting up a Ward of Court might be too much trouble and it was going to be too late now, if she was pregnant after all. Beryl took Cora into the small front room for a private talk. They sat on the settee, rather uncomfortable with each other.

"You can make arrangements, then, you better get married as soon as you like," Beryl said. "You'll have to get the banns sorted out at the Town Hall and all that, it takes three weeks, that does. And what about your family, what do they think?" Cora explained that she had virtually no family, having left home many years ago and she had been living with distant relatives in Sheffield before coming to London.

"My parents split up when I was a teenager and I didn't fit with either of their new lives. We are just not in contact anymore, it's useless to pretend. I went and stayed with another part of the family instead, an aunt and uncle, but I was always in the way, really, they were glad to see the back of me. I'm on my own here, there's no one else to inform, really," she told Mrs Williams. "There's no one to go back to." All her life these days was spent on page 70 of the

London A to Z. The Williams gave them some extra food to take home, generous slices of chicken and cake, plus two boxes of chocolates.

"We've got so many this year," Beryl said. "Cousin Doris always sends us a box of Black Magic." Mark could identify all the chocolates without reading the little diagrams and names, Truffle, coffee cream, orange, fudge. Cora was impressed.

"Oh, we usually had a box of chocolates every weekend, I soon got to know the contents." Cora was equally impressed at such a life of luxury, like a small Christmas every week.

After all the Christmas and New Year's parties in the house, Fred asked Cora to clean the downstairs flat. He had friends from abroad to stay in the extension and now it needed to be cleared out. There had obviously been a massive party there, the bins were full of assorted empty bottles. Used condoms slumped in wastepaper baskets, the residue of festive assignations. But any money was good money now, she was in no position to refuse work. Cora was on all fours scrubbing the kitchen floor because it was in such a mess, when Mark called in. Mark said later how ashamed he felt at seeing her like that. But their postcards left in local shop windows had produced no news of flats to let and they were being evicted, however politely it was being done and Fred had to be humoured after all.

The pressure mounted as Fred decided to decorate all the rooms in the house. In a giddy moment they had painted one wall in their room a mixture of blue and turquoise that they called Hendrix blue. It had both punch and tranquillity and became 'their' colour. But they got home from work one day to find the colour obliterated under a coat of ordinary cream paint. When Mark commented that it was an intrusion, they had not been told that Fred had given the decorator a key, Fred said they would be moving soon and anyway, the house style was now totally magnolia paint.

"And how's the flat search going? You haven't much time now, have you? When's the baby due?" It got worse. The next day when they got back from work, they found all the ladders had been left in their room after the painter had finished. At seven the next morning the decorator, already in his paint-spattered overalls, looked across at them as he calmly let himself into their room with a passkey, waking them up as they lay naked in each other's arms. It was hard to protest adequately from the pillows, and they were both in a mix of anger and fear.

"This isn't decent! It's harassment, that's what it is!" Mark protested from their lumpy bed.

"Boss says it's got to be done." The man looked at his watch. "Start work at seven really. It's already ten past. Got to get on." He clattered both long ladders out onto the corridor and went downstairs to fetch new tins of magnolia paint.

"It's a posh upper-class form of what Rachman or the Krays do, to get rid of tenants, it's outright intimidation," Mark grunted, getting dressed. "Makes us feel like we're infringing our own place! We pay rent for this!" Cora buried the comment that she paid the rent, while most of his money went to their savings. It was time to get moving now. Luckily the morning sickness had lessened and she was getting used to the heaviness that had crept up.

The world was designed by the discontented,

those unsatisfied with themselves. They dashed out of bed in the mornings, with an up-and-at-'em flurry to get out and be busy doing and getting things. They did not want to be alone with themselves any longer, nor to lie in bed in each other's arms, drowsy and relishing the warmth of skin against skin, and another chance of sex. No, the alarm was set, and just like the alarm clock, they sprang out of bed and away from themselves, throwing away any sense of self until after the evening rush hour, when they returned, emptied and discontented yet again. They were the ones who designed the world. Their identity was outside themselves, the world had it.

It grew worse week after week, going downstairs to pay the rent. Friendly Fred became more strident each time.

"You can't bring up a baby in that room up there. It's only fit for two adults. How are you getting on about finding a place? When's the wedding?" Mark received filtered versions of all this. Cora was astounded that Fred, who she thought of as a friend, a mix of landlord, father-figure and Dutch uncle, was able to treat them like this. But this was what power was like. Fred held both ends of the situation because now he produced the solution. He announced that he had just renovated a flat in Maida Vale that would suit them, and he would take them over to see it too.

7

Back in the cabin the captain addressed her personally from a panel set into the wall. It was like a communication from an employer or colleague. No, it was more like being in an authoritarian state which

Orwell would have recognised.

"Here is our progress report. We are now at Ushant, it is 11 a.m. Corner of France. We have entered the Bay of Biscay at seventeen knots per hour, which will be our average. We will disembark at 7 a.m. ship and English time, 8a.m. Spanish time. Misty and murky here round the Bay. You do get mists lurking round the Ushant. It is burning itself away now." He used a different vocabulary from landspeople. "Forecast – partly cloudy, 24 degrees centigrade.

It is a European immigration requirement that all passengers will need to disembark even if returning on the ship in the morning. The chief officer will speak to you re the disembarkation from the vessel in the morning. We look forward to seeing you all again in the future." Of course, they had not met – there were several hundreds of them – but it was a friendly gesture to make, nonetheless.

Within a second a Spanish female voice had repeated the entire speech in Spanish complete with noises from the café-bar nearby. Her accent was the sound of compressed sun and baking earth, sibilance and dryness combined.

Some time ago, in one of many previous bedsits, Sophie had dashed into Cora's place.

"I've met a poet guy, and he says he knows a publisher, well, someone who prints stuff at home. And I said that you were always writing poems. He's really interested, isn't that great? So, have you got anything that would be suitable?" Cora was hit by a thunderbolt.

"There's some in here, if you like," she said

doubtfully, opening a drawer stuffed with scraps of paper and a notebook. "They're just in handwriting, though, you know I haven't got a typewriter."

"Don't worry about that, he'll do it all. I'll bring him round and you can have a chat, Clive, that's his name. I met him at a poetry reading up the road." Pubs were beginning to lay on extra entertainment. They had discovered that poetry was far cheaper than bands and it brought in a better and quieter class of customer who tended to drink wine or spirits instead of beer.

While the affair with Mark started its rapid development, and with the shock of the pregnancy, Cora forgot things were being managed in other places. Clive and Sophie arranged the poems into a rough story shape, it was decided it would be called *Belsize*, and then it fell into the background and Cora forgot all about it.

The doctor handed Cora the programme of ante-natal exercises for her to attend. The leaflet showed the first one was on 1st January at Queen Elizabeth Hospital, Fathers' Class. The other appointments were on January 2, 9, 16 and 23rd at 10.50. It was as if pregnancy was a complete occupation in itself, quite apart from having to earn a living.

In early January before their wedding, Mark and Cora were taken across to Maida Vale by Fred to look at the new flat that he was planning on ejecting them to. Postcard notices in the shop windows round Hampstead of *Professional couple seek one bedroom flat nearby* and the rest of their desperate pleas had resulted in nothing. Jenny from the pub said she might be moving in with her boyfriend, but it would take some time yet. Fred was in no mood to see them stay any longer. The more Cora swelled, the greater his panic. Mark was trapped in the middle.

They had to agree. There was a large back room in this new flat that Fred said they could easily let and recoup some of their rent. A corner of the new ceiling was open still, like a permanently open hatch to an attic. He saw them staring at it.

"Oh, we did some work on the flat roof above, that's just left open to air it, get the sealant to dry out." A glimmer of something passed through Cora's mind but they were soon being shown into the large living room with its view of Warrington Crescent and they wandered into the small bedroom off it.

To move in, they would, *er*, have to pay an agent some £20 as an arrangement fee, they were to meet him here at the flat next week and then he would give them the keys and a rent book. One by one, the great savings they had made were being dispersed like Maundy Money to all the populace.

"There's a large area of private gardens that you can use too, very good for the baby, something extra like that," Fred added. They looked out of the narrow kitchen window at the back of the flat. There, spread below, was the marvellous devil-may-care dash of perennial weeds showing up through the snow and hidden lawns the size of football pitch. It stretched across to the backs of the opposite tall houses of Randolph Crescent, a private world.

In order to rent the flat and appear proper, they had already opened a joint bank account. This was more a necessity to cloak the fact that Mark, being under 21, could not take on a tenancy or sign anything official and Cora being 25 managed to paper over that. They sat in the bank manager's office on South End Green in an ersatz wedding ceremony as he congratulated them both. A chequebook in both names would be printed, they could call in and collect it in two days.

The next week they were married. Cora had nipped into Hampstead Town Hall registry office one lunchtime some weeks ago to have the banns put up in the foyer and pay the seven shillings and sixpence fee. It was amazing to see their names officially printed, and their status as spinster and bachelor, with her full name, Caroline Finch, now only used on documents like this and finding out Mark's middle name was James.

They stood on Hampstead Town Hall steps in the snow for the photos, taken by Mitch. Mrs Williams had warned Cora about wearing the leopard-print coat which was her favourite. It had been given to her by one of her cleaning employers as it was surplus and being thrown out.

"It'll ruin the wedding photos!" Cora obliged by wearing a plain black coat, the only alternative. Being seven months pregnant did not leave many possibilities; Cora had made a dress out of remnants of blue corduroy bought cheaply, with a collar of old lace from the Oxfam shop, and borrowed a handkerchief from Sophie to fulfil all the traditions.

The registry office ceremony was formal and quite moving, not a disappointment at all. Mr and Mrs Williams generously paid for drinks for all in The George opposite the Town Hall, and then they drove off home. Mr and Mrs Friedman left too at the same time. Mark and Cora stayed on and then suggested drinks for the few back at the bedsit. The small group walked back in the snow to their room. There they sat surrounded by assorted wedding presents, a heavy white enamelled iron frying pan, a set of cutlery, a Venus Fly Trap plant and most intriguingly, a brass tea caddy spoon with an elf curved on the handle. There was plenty of wine too, some of it also a wedding present.

The Jimi Hendrix *Axis Bold As Love* LP coloured the room with washes of music. There was a bottle of Matéus Rosé as a special treat and Cora was drinking it erratically now. Mark did not notice, he was fascinated by the Venus Fly Trap, a gift from Mitch.

"It's got a whiff of the jungle about it, but it's not going to have a good time here, is it? There's hardly any flies about in January."

"Perhaps the plant or pet shops sell dried flies to keep them going," Pete interrupted. He had given them the white enamelled omelette pan, which weighed a ton. "And see that you keep it white, too," he warned. A vicious plant and a heavy domestic implement, such an assortment to start off married life with.

Cora felt she was disappearing into the castle. *You've Got Me Floating*. It was where she secretly belonged as well as being here. It was easy to be in two places at once, especially after this much wine.

As the music finished at *Bold As Love,* one by one their friends left in various states of daytime drunkenness. As the last ones trailed off home, Mark suggested what about walking across the Heath for a celebration tea at Kenwood House. Gloria, the last guest, asked if they minded if she came along too? Or should she go off now? Cora and Mark both burst out laughing.

"That's it! The wonderful thing about living together before you get married is that we aren't rabidly dashing off after the marriage ceremony to bonk like crazy, because we've been living together for ages! No, you're welcome, we need to have a healthy walk after all this, and sober up, we can go and have a cup of tea at the café." Although it was a cold day, it was a crisp cold, not sleety and the red squirrels, used to people passing by, came down from the trees as they passed by, expecting food. Their red coats showed up brightly against the snow.

Sitting in the Kenwood tea rooms, it was an image of the life they were going to have later on. This coming summer they would be back for the outdoor concerts again, sitting on the grass. It was as much their place as anyone else's after all. The baby would be in a pram or left with a babysitter at home. It would all work out seamlessly. They were confident now and full of hope.

The snow had transformed the Heath into a wide piece of white paper. On the way back across the Heath towards South End Road, a few winter birds flew off as they approached.

"How sad," Mark said. "It's like the Garden of Eden never happened. The minute any bird sees a human being, they fly off. They've learnt to be afraid of us humans. Sad."

Later that week they went across to the flat to settle about the money that had to be given to the ugly beer-faced agent as a deposit or whatever it was for the flat. It was like a desecration of everything they were working toward. They had opened the bank account specially to deal with the rent and rates. It had to be a joint account as Mark was under twenty-one and could not sign official documents yet, so for once Cora being older was an advantage.

8 Right after the wedding they were living in two dimensions at once, moving into Maida Vale and leaving Hampstead. Mark's friends joined in enthusiastically. It was fun to them. From their windows Mark and Cora could see Mitch on the motorbike with the white-painted sideboard roped on the sidecar, driving up Nassington Road and off to Maida Vale. It looked like an ice cream van from this distance. When he got back,

"I could hear your *Purple Haze* all up the road, as far as the corner of Parliament Hill," he said, semi-disapprovingly. It was a last blaze of revolt and giddy hopefulness.

The Friedmans had given them a magnificent Cannon gas stove as a wedding present, luckily delivered by two strong men.

"It's built like a Sherman tank, this is, we don't see many of these," one of the men said, looking at the cream enamelled stove, "They don't make them like this anymore." It stood in the kitchen like a domestic pet elephant, waiting to be connected to the gas supply.

Cora cried when she saw all the furniture huddled on the landing of the flat, looking like embarrassed relatives at a funeral. There on the dirty brown lino stood a complete 1920s-bedroom suite, a coffee table, a large wooden radio. In a cardboard box was a collection of plates and bowls with assorted cutlery – old serving spoons, their nickel silver worn away in parts. Mark looked at them carefully, turning them over in his hand.

"She's spent ages polishing these, you know. I remember these serving trifle on Sundays as a child." Then he noticed Cora was crying and turned to put an arm round her.

"It's all right," he said. "You're part of a family now." Cora was weeping now, producing more water than sound.

"Just all this ... it's so touching. I didn't even know they were thinking of this." His parents were normal; they did normal things like think about furniture. Behind the gratitude was fear, the realisation that they had needed these furnishings and would not have been able to get them for a long time yet.

She dissolved, thinking how wonderful to be accepted, to be part of something safe at last. She could stop running.

They went around hardware shops that afternoon looking for bargain tins of paint and arrived home after the worst of the snow had stopped. As there was only one open fireplace and no other form of heating, they had also had to buy a paraffin stove and an oilcan for getting supplies. Gervaise, from the basement flat, had already told them that a van came round selling the stuff so they would not need to go off looking for supplies along Edgware Road or further away.

And there on the marble step was a huddle of kitchen chairs like stranded visitors.

"It's my Aunt Daisy, she was going to give us some chairs Mum said. They must have delivered them early – I didn't tell you; it was going to be a surprise."

"Well, it's a surprise right now. Lovely." Cora lifted one of the chairs over the threshold, liking the homely brown wood of the worn Victorian chairs.

"They're nothing special," Mark said. "They were made by the thousands, all the same design. You can see them everywhere. But they'll go with the table we ordered from that second-hand place. We should be getting that delivered any day now."

At the weekend, Mr and Mrs Williams appeared with a cast-iron mangle. Mark helped to carry it up all the stairs, Mrs Williams clucking frantically.

"It's a strain for George to be carrying things like this at his age, I don't want him coming down with something after all this." But it came to pieces and was reassembled easily. A husband was an advantage, and you did not want him damaged in any way.

9

It was like living inside a giant Hoover. They were like dust-mites, each in a minute cell off the maroon-carpeted corridors that went off into perspectives on all sides. Inside the cabins was like life in a capsule. It was easy to get used to it; someone had designed it with each human step in mind, however cramped.

Being alone had its compensations eventually as there was adequate room for two only if that twosome were of equal standard of height, width and tidiness. Two scoops on the sink-top for soap and so on –his and hers of sinks, toothbrushes, the hot and cold mixed waters. How all those massive suitcases and stacks of luggage sent aboard had managed to blend into these individual cabins was a neat puzzle. Being deeply in love would help too, casually brushing against each other a constant delight, sex coaxing in the small amount of space.

The proper welcome aboard began with a radio warning in all cabins. Beneath the mirror a dashboard-cum-console gave a message first in English then in Spanish, ending in tripulacíon which seemed as good a word of warning as any. A series of seven blasts followed ear-splittingly-direct right into the cabin.

"You were wrong about tripulacíon," a bluff Yorkshireman said. The ship was full of stock characters, innocent pastiches of themselves. "It means crew. It must come from tribe."

"And it's tribes that can give us tribulation," Cora retorted, ignoring the "p."

A long time ago back in her wandering days Louis and Diana had given Cora a Christmas present of two books, one by Iris Murdoch (An Unofficial Rose) and the other Evelyn Waugh's The Ordeal of Gilbert Pinfold, which took the reader through the writer's nervous breakdown on board ship. It had now transgressed from literature into reality. What he had written, apparently so exaggerated, was what the passengers now were experiencing, even if in a watered-down version. The idea of living in a small cell connected at all times (it was impossible to switch it off) to a central control room; to walk down corridors sprayed with an industrial perfume and scattered with unseen microphones urging to do this, warning about that, at every turn – all this became normal, as did sitting in fluorescent light indoors or mixing with strange people in an assembled floating town.

On Thursday evening, there was a sepulchral call echoing from along the street. It sounded like an angry man threatening a boy called 'Alfie.' He went on calling, again and again until they realised it was the man selling paraffin; it was seven o'clock. Fetching the can, they both went out into the dark street and followed a small crowd that grouped around a lorry with a man wrapped up against the cold who was pouring the paraffin into their cans. It was like something out of a Victorian engraving as all the group dispersed and struggled back with the heavy load of the dangerous stuff. It was a secret clue to the number of poor people who lived behind the ornate facades of the houses.

There were eighty-four steps up to the flat, eighty-seven if the front door ones were added although they did not really count as they were low, wide and of white marble. When they first moved in, early January, Cora had been shocked at the tatty state of the pure marble doorsteps – her mother would have been in ecstasy, along with all the scouring women of Liverpool, with anything like it. Those women knelt, scooping over the pavements, their doorways flat onto the street, scouring a semi-circle in front of their door. All along the streets, flagstones would have these soapstone-scoured imitation entrances. But here was the real thing.

Snow had gathered at the edges, but the centre was grubby with slush trodden into grime. People just ignored the possible beauty underneath their feet.

About to give birth, nest-building, Cora brought down the mop-bucket. It took two day's efforts to get the marble slab of the front steps back to its original look. She had to lug the bucket full of water all down the staircase to do it. Cream and white swirls ran across the massive marble slab, with flecks of blue here and there like later additions, extra thoughts running crossways aeons later, a tide trapped forever. She felt a real pride looking at the valuable marble, lugged here from God knows where and set for them to walk on.

The glamorous Frenchwoman who had the ground floor flat stepped out into the hall, exclaiming,

"You do not haf to do zat! Eet is not necessary, you know," she protested, waving her hands about. "Eet is not necessary in your state to be doing thees." People often wanted to pretend that dirt did not exist, especially when it was near to them, it was edited out.

"It was so snowy I thought it needed doing," Cora answered tactfully. "I wanted to make the place look good for the baby, as well as everyone else. And look!" She stepped back. "It's lovely now." The Frenchwoman agreed and was sensitive enough to feel ashamed, Cora thought. She felt awkward at putting the woman in such an embarrassing situation.

"Madame Perpignan, Lucille, that is my name." She put out her hand. "Do call in if you like. I am here at all times." And with that she swept back into her flat where a large chandelier was lit already in the January afternoon gloom.

Having started at the front door it was obvious that all the stairways needed doing too now. Some building work had been done, it looked like some time ago, and loose plaster and cement and broken tiles were scattered all up the building.

Cora started on the hall and stairs too, all eighty-four of them. Builder's rubble, cement dust, cigarette packets and ciggie ends, matchboxes, crisp packets, sweet wrappers all lay in corners of each landing. Here and there a mouse scampered off to a break in the skirting board. The stairs were only clean where footsteps had scoured them in passing – the trademark of neglect. The edges were scattered with industrial style debris with their added cigarette ends and scraps of old newspapers.

Cora decorated the flat bit by bit each day while Mark was at work and in between waiting for paint to dry Cora would clean a flight of steps each time. Like the front door marble steps, the stairs needed doing several times to clear smudges of dirt away. Luckily, they were all red tiles although one tile near the top was loose, dangerously, and she found some glue and fixed it that afternoon. But the next day it had worked loose again and it was probably better to leave the gap instead.

The next flight of steps up to their own flat was steep and wooden and had hardly any light at all. It was a different part of the building and she thought Mark was right when he said it was probably originally the nursery with the servants' quarters on the top floor above them.

"I do not want my child to be born into a slummy place like this. At least it can be clean," is what she wanted to say to the Frenchwoman, but of course that would have been an insult, so Cora had remained silent and just smiled as if she was silly.

"You've made them feel embarrassed," Mark said. "People get used to ignoring their surroundings and not taking any responsibility for them. They hide inside, that's the only place they feel power to control. And then you come along and blast all that careful pretending to pieces!"

Later, Cora was invited into Lucille's flat to find it was a smaller modern version of Versailles, with white walls pricked out with gold mouldings, thick carpets, occasional tables and Louis XVI chairs that looked as though they could skip away on their spindly golden legs. Luxury within, but Lucille could tolerate the squalid entrance without registering the difference. Public squalor and private affluence, it was right here. Lucille had a sort of servant, Gervaise, who lived in the basement. Those who had basement flats, and some of the ground floor ones too, had steps with access to the gardens at the back. But Gervaise was needed all the time by Madame Perpignan, and the entire building often echoed with her shouting "Gervaise! Gervaise!" often ignored from downstairs. Then Gevaise, grumbling, would appear up the back stairs and there would be a friendly row which all could hear before she went out on the messages or moved the rubbish.

They decorated wildly, trying to efface the drab misery of the previous tenant, turning a slum into something hopeful. But Mark was obviously unhappy. He sat in the captain's chair and looked at the large room, glumly,

"I don't want to live here," and started crying. Cora, trying not to show any emotion, stroked his shoulder, comforting him, saying how cheap it was, all considered and how they would soon be able to change it all, paint the place up, get it renewed in their own style.

"Don't worry, we'll make something good out of it – look how much improvement we've made already!" The orange ceiling glowed down at them, their outrageous achievement. "You can even see our ceiling from down in the street! We're changing the neighbourhood. Kirsty sad she could see our orange ceiling from across the road last week, the minute you finished it."

But at heart she was as unhappy as he was and felt just as abandoned. She thought all the time that it was her fault completely. If she had not become pregnant - and that had its own story, this would not have happened, this exile from Hampstead. It was Genesis being acted out. Written by one man or several men, it showed in allegory the change from a couple in love and ecstatically free, to a couple responsible for a child and a sensation of falling from that utter paradise of unfettered love and the feeling of complete power into a world of duty. Without pregnancy they had been free and with so many possibilities – now the future was a trap.

It brought the truth out behind the Bible story. There was an obvious part missing. After the so-called apple and snake event, there was no mention of Eve getting pregnant. Once that happened the woman became less capable of progress, especially in those days when a third (or more, if it was twins) person arrived who was totally helpless. No more sitting round the Garden of Eden waiting for the food to just drop off the boughs. No more being the equal-but-different mate of Adam.

And how had Adam known how to assist at a birth? It must have been a bit of a shock for him. And who did Cain and Abel and Seth marry, if not their unnamed sisters, because there was nobody else around? Cora's mother, a devout Catholic, had said that actually there were other people around at that time, they had evolved to a state where God just picked out this one couple as the representatives of the next stage of the human race. It was a potted race history.

The Bible story wrapped up neatly the reason why women were supposed to put up with everything without complaining. It embodied the resentment men had towards babies to ruin the rustic idyll. Without pregnancy, pleasurable sex could continue uninterrupted without any repercussions or responsibility; it was the penchant for women to become pregnant now and again, to become ungainly dependants that caused the difference. It also explained polygamy, which was certainly a way to cover all bases.

They had been cast out of Hampstead for making the same mistake. That pink and golden land was for the rich and free, not for people like them. As a young single woman, she would have been able to stay living there; so would Mark; but together they had dragged each other down to this. Banishment. Exile.

Yes, all the way to this slum and its smelly rooms. Later, Mark told her that he had been told the previous tenants had kept an Alsatian dog up here and that was why the back room had such a terrible smell. But for Cora, the slummiest thing was a sewing needle stuck into the wallpaper above the fireplace, some thread still in it, a close and personal shock as though the previous woman was still there, her presence in the middle of them both, a reproach.

The bathroom floor was unsteady, several of the floorboards were rotten and it was a tricky navigation each time they went to the toilet or had a bath. Mark went out and ordered planks and sundry screws to fit new flooring. He had phoned the agent, who did agree that the floor was precarious and was in a dangerous condition. Mark handled the situation perfectly and one week's rent was struck off and Mark set to work. Cora was amazed at his confidence and efficiency, how easily he handled the situation. He was such a wonderful mixture of the intellectual and the practical: nothing fazed him. With natural confidence and many cups of sugary tea he took on the messy task and made the bathroom new and safe. The offcuts gave a good supply of fuel for the living room fireplace, an addition to the smell of the oil stove, their only form of heat.

10

They went on being hopeful. Mark and Cora scoured and painted and created and changed. Orange ceiling. Purple walls either side of the fireplace. White furniture. They took the old respectable brown furniture from the Williams's back bedroom and hurled it into the sixties. The wardrobe was painted white and placed in the hall; the radio became sunshine yellow; the sideboard was white already. The dressing table, denuded of its suburban front-bedroom 1930s triple mirror, was painted Zircon blue. Their little huddle of kitchen chairs became three white and one zircon. They agreed on everything; their taste was impeccable and twinned perfectly.

At least the little bedroom off the living room was painted in their favourite Zircon, or as they called it, Hendrix Blue, although it was really a zingy turquoise. The bed took over most of the room, with a chair either side as a bedside table, a chest of drawers under the window, and just enough space for a cot at the end of the bed. The parents-in-law had bought them a new bed, complete with lilac candytuft bedcover. It looked slightly out of place here with its hint of nineteen thirties security, but the vivid walls overpowered it.

Months later, just before the baby began crawling, Cora had an inspiration and painted all the wood surrounding the carpet white too. The paraffin stove was moved to stand on the large table in the living room as a safety measure, out of the reach of the baby.

But Beryl had noticed that the living room had no curtains whatever. Being so far up, on the third floor, there was no one overlooking them. However, that did not make any difference to Beryl, who arrived on their next visit prepared with curtains and cord. George got on the ladder and screwed in hooks and a curtain cord and sprightly patterned cotton curtains were installed. Mark and Beryl and Cora looked up at the cheap yellow cotton as it barely met in the centre as George demonstrated how it looked. Cora had to be grateful and look happy. But the second Mr and Mrs Williams left, she burst into tears. The flat was really Beryl's, it held most of her furniture and household goods and now these appalling curtains. Mark laughed and took them down; he did not like them either and stuffed them into the sideboard drawer.

Before the wedding, when they had gone across to Ron Weldon's antique shop in England's Lane to get some chairs, they had also ordered a kitchen table. He phoned that a couple of men would be delivering it, gypsies, genuinely good furniture dealers, calling that afternoon, was that all right? Cora was pleased that all the pieces in the jigsaw were joining up so well.

Two swarthy men arrived, small-built, with darting black-deep brown eyes, like dark animals. Beneath their drab work-jackets one wore a yellow waistcoat, and both had a gold chain, gold watch, and gold earrings.

The wiry men manoeuvred the table up the flights of stairs and slid it into the white kitchen.

"It's come from a massive kitchen in Maida Vale, that's sure. Good bit of wood too, you've made a sensible choice here." Cora paid them the £2..10..0 and they both shook hands with her as if it was an important ceremony, a handclasp.

She went to the front room window and looked down, watching their pony and trap going off towards Randolph Avenue and was amazed when they both turned and waved from the end of the Crescent because they intuited she would be watching. Their shabby outer clothes hid the rich glow of the gold jewellery they wore. She could see even from here the brightness of the younger man's yellow waistcoat and the flash of his smile.

And for that second, a wire strung between them, like birds calling to each other across a space.

Linked by thinking the same. Valuable. Then the cart faded into the distance with the trotting pony and she would never see them again. Link cut. Their intangible gift taken away with them.

She turned to the table and began to rip off the scarred white American cloth that covered its surface, thinking of all the servants who had worked upon it, perhaps through two world wars, a small domestic history lesson.

The kitchen was now a totally whitewashed room, but the dirt round the stove was hard to get rid of. Grime was embedded behind the pipes and the stove itself; the white paint had to give in to the grunge. The original Victorian iron range had been removed and there was a large space for the stove to be put into.

There was a small dead mouse snaked around the gas burner on the stove top.

"It's gone there after any boiled-over food and got gassed," Mark said helpfully.

"But I keep it absolutely clean and there's nothing for a mouse to eat here. We finish everything off ourselves, you know that." Cora looked at the pathetic little grey body but was glad it was dead. Mark had a word with his Dad who brought round some brand-new shiny mousetraps when he came round that weekend. Sure enough, a few evenings later the loud snap of the mousetrap carried clearly into the living room, making them both jump. The body was put in the rubbish and taken down to the communal bins in the basement outside the large window of Gervaise's living room.

"But we can't go on like this. I'd rather do without," Cora said, and Mark agreed with her.

The flight of steps up to their own flat and the one above was steep and wooden and had hardly any light at all. It was a different part of the building; Mark said he thought it was probably originally the nursery.

"This floor would have been for the children and the nursemaid and then the governess. They wouldn't have wasted space on the servants, not this floor, not given them that big front room or the one with the view of the gardens. No, they would all have been sleeping upstairs and they'd have had their meals in the basement. There's less floor-space upstairs anyway, it would have all been bedrooms." Cora thought of the lives that had been here, the thwarted ambitions and the obedient skivvies and cooks.

The kitchen's open shelves looked perfect once the glass storage jars were placed strategically. Lentils shone a merry orange next to the white of rice and the bright tins of tomatoes and baked beans. They had been so proud of those storage jars, three small and three larger, with their ground-glass stoppers. Cora used to buy one jar a week on the way back from cleaning at the Reitzmans' and always meant to go back and get about twenty more shining storage jars at least, a full kitchen's worth. But it never happened. It was soon the end of luxury, as their savings depleted daily. And Mark now had so many foods that he did not like, it was getting difficult to know what to do at mealtimes.

"I've run out of possibilities" she laughingly chided Mark. "What else do you eat? What about you make me a list?" He produced the official list of items that evening, and Cora stuck the list on the back of the door of their newly whitewashed kitchen. All the things Mark would eat and a permanent shopping list:

corned beef	5lb potatoes
baked beans	1lb carrots
beefburgers	1lb onions
½ lb bacon	cauliflower
braising steak	tomatoes
eggs	oranges
peanut butter	apples
bananas	cheese

That was the basis of what Mark would eat, the mix repeated week after week. Then there was all the rest which had to be considered essential too: bread flour butter rice sugar curry powder mixed herbs ½ lb tea tomato sauce tomato soup tin coffee marmalade

Cornflakes Shredded Wheat Shreddies
toilet rolls bleach Surf soap shampoo
and the constant background essentials:
Gas electric launderette paraffin

And then, when the baby was born, the list added extra foodstuff: Ostermilk, Farlene, rosehip syrup and 14 Heinz baby foods, for a week's dinners and teatimes. The seven-day tins of baby foods became the Holy Grail, the first things to buy every week as money got tighter and tighter. Those main baby meals had to be ring-fenced as nothing became certain anymore. The line of merry little tins stood on the shelf, each day with its own identity of main meal and afters. Gerber did a different range of flavours, but they cost a penny more for their shiny glass jars and so were not a possibility. She lusted after them in the window of the chemists in Clifton Road. Eleven pence each and completely out of reach. As it got worse and worse later that year, some of the items on the kitchen list grew scarce or were never bought again, but the weekly fourteen Heinz baby food tins remained.

11

For people who did not gamble or drink, there was the so-called observation deck, a thickly carpeted galley with the ubiquitous club chairs. About twenty-five people sat in total silence, some reading books or newspapers, others siting as if awaiting death. As if commercial life would not let go, occasionally a raised voice or a gust of music came through the sound cladding from the cinema next door.

Occasionally a mildly drunk man would amble through finding his way through to the general part of the ship. It was preposterous that only a wall separated them and only another couple of walls away was the casino where numbers and results were being barked out, and the Stargazers' nightclub, not in action at present.

The readers went on reading, with one brave couple conducting a conversation in whispers, listened to by the militantly silent and alone. From a corner came a sound very like a snore or a coffee machine working up to a climax and then stopping abruptly. Along the deck, a curtain opened at the window of the deluxe cabins and a haughty woman looked out, an original POSH, left over from Empire surveying these trippers.

Out on the decks, lifeboats were affixed to metal girders. Pylons, winches, ropes and strange parts of machinery all massed along beyond the rail. Here and there rust showed its merry orange against the glossy white paint. Tight metal wires, plaited with tension emanating from them were quite rusty too, but obviously important. Perhaps someone oiled them now and again.

Of course, there was another bar on deck. Like locusts or lemmings' people had congregated here, table after table, leaving all the seats along the decks (covers for lifejackets, boarded over) empty for the odd puritan couple to breathe pure ozone. There was a separate café-bar for the truckers, strategically placed next to the gambling tables. The temptation was so neatly presented for them to fall into.

In early February Mitch and Mark decided to start up a decorating business together. The job at the Friedman's was obviously coming to an end; Mark had virtually rebuilt and then decorated the entire house. He had to think of another job this year as this one petered out.

The two of them wrote an official founding agreement in a special notebook, starting their accounts with the cost of the notebook itself at 1/6d.

"From each amount incoming to the partnership A&B we both agree to reserve 25% of the sum, putting this excess into an account under our joint names, and to split the rest on a basis agreed by us both, this to be discussed & fixed with concern to each single sum, usually to be, our both working equal time, 50% to each, A&B. The joint account of this partnership is to be under scrutiny of us both & none other, as is each withdrawal by one partner from this account. We agree both to be equally liable for any debts which we may jointly, through this undertaking incur, & too as aforesaid be responsible to each other, within the partnership for the joint account of it."

"On this day 10th February the joint account

contains £15 from which £4 has been taken & spent on advertising literature. Account now stands @ £11 black." Cora was impressed at the legalese he had managed to construct. He was so full of surprises and able to cope with any difficulty with ease, a natural confidence.

It was a success at first, a friend of a friend of Mitch's father needed his offices redecorating throughout. They worked at the weekend as Mark was still at the Friedman's. But as that job was petering to an end, it was obvious there was nothing else coming up. Their poster promised every possible outcome would easily be coped with:

Mark & Mitch,
Interior & Exterior Decorating,
Fencing, Floor laying,
Plumbing
Carpentry & All Building Work Undertaken
Estimates free.

"I didn't know you could do all this!" Cora exclaimed, amused and puzzled.

"Well, we can't really, but as long as we can waffle our way into a contract, my old man will know some retired tradesmen we could bring in. It's just getting our toe in the door, that's all." Mark's usual confidence papered over the cracks. Cora, vastly pregnant, went round all the Post Offices nearby distributing posters from the fifty he had ordered. She had even gone as far as Edgware Road, giving their poster to be put in the windows for a couple of weeks; nothing happened.

He had already discussed with his parents that Cora should go out to work instead of himself.

"The Civil Service pays according to age, you

know that, and you said you used to be a civil servant in one of your jobs, so you would be paid more than me. I could stay at home and look after the baby and you could work in an office instead." Cora was uncertain about this. A part of her mistrusted him being at home, he would not keep to the real routine with the baby and he would be off visiting friends all day. She would come home to a heap of housework waiting to be done.

And marriage, pregnancy and childbirth, they would have no meaning if she found herself back sitting at the same job at the same desk as some years ago. This was Mark's chance to establish some career – he could not disappear from employment forever, evading any routine or responsibility. It would never change, once he got used to it, he could bounce into a better post elsewhere. It was a chance he might not get again.

Mark said this Saturday they were going to go and see the two girls in their new place.

"It's not far from Portobello, and it'll be a change to see them at home." Rhona and Kirsty had moved to some rooms in Cornwall Terrace. Up the worn stone steps, the big doorway was festooned with rusty drawing pins left over from torn-away messages. About ten doorbells were at the right, cards with various names or squiggles in each name-slot.

"We don't have their room number. Which one would it be?" Mark and Cora stood there, choosing.

"I think they're at the top, remember?" Cora said brightly. With that, the front door opened and a wildly- haired West Indian loped out, graceful and uncaring, giving hardly a glance at them, though he left the door open behind him. They wandered into the dimly lit mustard-coloured hall. A plain, drab young woman came out of the big room at the right.

"Looking for me? I'll be ready in a minute." She beckoned them further into the room. It was an awkward misunderstanding. This was a prostitute, looking for indoor trade. A slight figure with dark curls, no make-up, just in sweater and jeans; probably not dear. She sat down in a shabby easy chair with a mottled maroon pattern, and semi-smiled at them both. In front of them she inspected her bare feet idly, as though it was a matter of life and death, which it was.

"I'm running out of veins now, got to use between my toes," she made it sound as ordinary as shopping. She went on with this unnecessary disclosure. "I keep something special for him, keep something back from them," she said about her boyfriend, the man just gone. How could a body be so controlled, Cora wondered, surely it went off on its own at that point. Mark, beginning to be embarrassed, said they were looking for the new tenants.

"There's two new girls on the top floor. You can just go up, nobody's stopping you, you're welcome to go and see if it's them." She went on searching between her toes. Cora nudged him and turned to the door.

"I didn't want to stay and see the full works, thank you. What a place to live!"

"Well, it's not all Hampstead for everyone, you know," Mark countered, inwardly ashamed and slightly worried for his friends. Fancy living here all the time and trying to keep looking respectable.

They went up the narrowing stairs to the room

that Rhona and Kirsty had at the top. It was merely one room with a double bed squashed into one corner, with their clothes hanging up from the picture rail because there was no space for any wardrobe. A chest of drawers was covered with cosmetics, shampoos, and other personal clutter. Over in a corner was a small sink and a gas ring for the least amount of cooking physically possible. It was a Victorian bedroom trying to provide for a twentieth century life for two young adults with all their expectations crammed into this small space.

Right in the centre of the room was an ironing board and incongruously, Rhona was leaning down, bent over it with her long black hair spread out under some brown paper, while Kirsty stood ironing her hair to its usual flat sheen. The work that ordinary girls got up to just to be that one bit more different from the crowd was amazing. As they both stood there, there was little space left for Mark and Cora, no more room to move and only one chair. A row of high heel shoes and knee-high boots scattered along the skirting board next to some empty milk bottles. It was a triumph how bandbox the girls could look, emerging from such a slummy cramped room. No one would have guessed.

"It's nearly done now, don't you think?" Kirsty asked. "We want to get out before the weather changes." Rhona stood up and the long black hair fell past her shoulders like a sleek curtain.

The four of them descended out into the square and went along Portobello to The Duke of Wellington pub for a Saturday afternoon drink. Cora saw these surroundings differently now, both with the new security of Mark beside her and very conscious of being pregnant. The pub was mainly West Indian, and they could feel the sense of being here on sufferance, it was a challenging mix of types. Men kept going outside and coming back in again. Cora suspected it was about drug deals, but could not be certain, she was unsettled enough to keep noticing the door constantly opening and closing. It was a setting that Kirsty and Rhona found exciting, which she could not understand. If they were gold-diggers, there was no gold to find here. It could so easily become dangerous for them, country girls in the big city, looking for kicks and all the razzmatazz they had never got back at home. Kirsty told her that they had both worked at a local hotel up on the Scottish coast with clear views of the sea and a golf course.

"We were both wondering what to do next, there wasn't anything interesting to do there, just a little village all focussed on the golf course in the season. Rhona's parents had a croft and she certainly didn't want to stay there! So we transferred to being chambermaids in London and the chance of living out." Rhona said the place was empty in the wintertime and the job would never be enough to live on.

"We decided to move here, we met Mark and then we three decided immediately that we were going to save up to go travelling round the world. Everyone else is!" But Cora had spoiled that plan; they did not seem to mind though, and easily accepted her into their circle. They never mentioned it again, there seemed to be no resentment. How they were ever going to save money, to go round the world, with the rent they now had to pay, did not make sense.

Already Cora was learning about this entire new underworld of ante-natal services, midwives, hospital appointments, baby-gear, layettes, nappies and the ultimate dependence on doctors, midwives and how near the nearest hospital actually was. She was also learning how ignorant most young women were about all this sub-structure that most of them would ultimately need. It showed the flimsy reality that all the women's magazines promoted of unceasing glamour and a flighty selfishness. Pregnancy changed all that immediately.

It had been one of Mark's prime factors in getting a phone in earlier than the normal service arrangement, where it could take some weeks.

"My wife's pregnant, she's alone while I'm out at work, left three floors up in a large house in Maida Vale." The telephone installer was amazed to see that she really was expecting a baby.

"Oh, people, they say anything to get a phone put in early, they do. It's a two month wait otherwise, and they try to swing the lead something wild, they do, so I was surprised to see your hubby had said the actual truth!" It ended up with the phone being installed in the bedroom as that was the nearest place to the stairs and the best place to connect the wires. In an ironic move they now had the ult in luxury – a phone in their bedroom. It was at the side of the bed, attached to the wall on a little bracket of its own. Cora eyed it thinking of desperate birth-pangs and having to ring up for ambulances. The ante-natal classes increased, as if women had nothing else to do all day. There was usually at least a dozen of them, probably women who did not need to work. Relaxation on the floor (and... *breathe*...,) lying on mattresses after such a tough rush to get there was a luxury for Cora. She would then have to hurry off afterwards to go cleaning in the afternoon.

They were being trained to control the forthcoming birth pangs by using their own breathing pattern. The nurse walked up and down the rows of recumbent women, talking,

"You breathe in now, a real lungful, in for the count of three; hold it for a count of three and then let it out for the count of three. Then you spread your hands wide and let the pain disappear from the ends of your fingers into the air." They discovered how most of the time they had been shallow breathing. "You put your hands on your diaphragm and feel yourself fill up with air. And when the pain strikes regularly every minute, at the pinnacle of taking it in, you then release both the breath and the hit of the pain. You become in control and almost in tune with the spasms as they occur. They'll start at every three minutes and then increase to once a minute." She then gave them a try of the mask for using gas-and-air. Cora found it an intriguing mix of a couple of glasses of gin and upsetting memories of childhood pink gas masks and their smell of rancid rubber.

The medical authorities had allowed her to keep the original centre up at Queen Mary's Maternity Home by the Vale of Health; she should have gone to Harrow Road; their new flat was in that catchment area. Luckily the 187 bus route would join the two ends of the thread. It was a last stubborn link with Hampstead.

At the special evening ante-natal classes (so badly named, it sounded like anti) Cora was happily surprised to see that Mark was the best-looking man in the room. Most of the couples seemed to have been lucky to have teamed up; they were dull and worthy-looking. Middle age would see them disappear into oblivion. Everyone here was at the edge of a precipice that they would all soon have to jump over; at least they had that in common.

Various other classes were held mid-mornings, 'Gas and Air,' 'Baby Care,' 'Feeding Times.' It showed how far women had been in ignorance of anything to do with rearing babies as there were two entire sessions devoted to learning what to do. Women's magazines only showed how to trap your man; be glamorous; buy this; they never gave a hint on what to do about any pregnancy or the resulting baby afterwards. They never mentioned maternity wards closing down as a move to centralisation of so many services into bigger hospitals.

As usual, Cora was out of step with the accepted rules. The nurse was explaining to them about making up several bottles of milk and putting them into the fridge.

"And then, when the baby wakes for a feed, you just put the ready-made bottle into a pan of water and heat it up gently, then testing it on the back of your hand for the right temperature." All well and good. Cora's hand went up, like at infants' school.

"But what if you don't have a fridge? We don't have one." A silent tut-tut of disapproval spread through the room. The nurse looked shocked and, for an instant, at a loss. Then she recouped herself.

"You would have to make up the bottle from scratch, then, boiling up the water and waiting for it to cool down before adding the milk powder, it's quite easy."

"But by that time the baby would be purple in the face and think no one was coming to help," Cora persisted. "Anyway, I'm going to breastfeed." This was a contested area. Breasts were promoted as a totally sexual feature, one of the main ways to allure a man - now, suddenly, they were changed into a feeding station, the property of a small guzzling infant. Bottle feeding avoided the border contest here and kept the breasts sexy.

The nurse had pointed out that there was an advantage with this, as any bottle-fed baby could be left with anyone and a father could then easily feed his child.

"And grandparents could join in too," she added helpfully. "Bottle-fed children are just as contented as those who are breastfed." This did not seem true. Rolling over in bed at the first sound of the baby waking, latching onto each other immediately, the breast-fed baby would not experience any crisis, no feeling of being abandoned or any mounting hysteria.

"But what about the gas or the electricity? There could be a power cut, or they could run out of money for the meter." The world of the official baby-rearing was all roses and honeysuckle, constant hot water, heat, fridges, boundless or gas.

By this time the nurse was running out of patience and said it was up to parents to make adequate preparations. The war between the two types of mothering was not encouraged to continue. The rich and lucky and the poor and unlucky, their babies were already classified. It was not worth discussing.

Crossing the Crescent, or trying to, one afternoon Cora was left stranded in the middle of the road, unable to go further and so, tried beyond patience, pulled her tongue at the passing cars in disgust. Rush hour here was often filled with Rolls Royces and other expensive chauffeur-driven limousines as businessmen returned home to North London.

"There I was, stranded, right in the middle of the road, obviously massively pregnant and not one of them would pause to let me cross." When she told Mark, he found this extremely funny and so did Cora, now she explained it to him.

"So there you were, a pregnant woman standing there in the middle of the road, putting your tongue out at passing cars! Priceless! They don't even notice you. The only thing a car relates to is another car! A pregnant woman means nothing to them. You didn't stand a chance. Pedestrians are screened out."

13

A surprise from the near past; Clive, a poet friend of Sophie phoned up.

"Sophie gave me your number and you'll be interested to know about this development. Your poems have been accepted and are going to be published soon." Clive suggested that he would come round to fetch them both to go off to a small-press publisher's house in South London. Her poems had found a home.

This was a house dedicated to hand-printing small runs of poetry booklets. A printing press took up the entire front room of a small terrace house in Stockwell. Shelves and boxes of paper and printing accessories showed it was now a workshop. Mr Marr was enthusiastic about Cora's *Belsize* collection.

When he learned that she could also draw, he said she should send him drawings to accompany the writing.

"Nice thick lines, now, so that it's easy to reproduce. Back biro would be perfect. Do you think you could do that?"

Cora agreed, cautiously as thick black lines was not her style, preferring mists of colour, but this was obviously a chance that would not come again, not a time to be quibbling about details of style. The drawings could be posted to Mr Marr and he would do the rest. It was magic. Clive was enthusiastic too, a tall sharp-featured man, his smile took up all his face. He motored them back through the dark streets. Mark was pleased at this show of progress and could see a bright future for them both, with their own publisher, once he got his own history saga to the finishing line.

As the few days left before the birth crowded around, Cora drew quick images that fitted with the poems and sent off eight drawings, plus one for the cover of a woman sitting beside a coffee pot. After that she forgot all about it as real life crashed around her.

They lay in bed discussing names for the baby.

"We need a name that's long enough to be special but can be shortened, and still be snazzy enough," Mark pointed out.

"Like Jonathan?"

"No, because that gets changed to Jon and sounds like John. No good."

"Or girls' names, Jessica changes to Jess, Francesca to Fran, Constance to Connie! I mean, I started out as a Caroline and ended up as Cora. You have to be careful."

"Like Ignatius turns into Iggy or Piggy in the

playground, you have to look into the future for them."

They ended up agreeing that Samuel, with all its variations would be a good choice or Rebecca for a girl.

"Sam or Becky would be lovely and easy to spell too." Then they moved on to what they would do if the baby was disabled. Blind or deaf would be O.K. but anything worse would be a case for smothering. A couple in Holland were being prosecuted for smothering a disabled baby that very week. They would smile and dissemble and, once home with the baby, work out a way of getting it dead as painlessly and as soon as possible before even more problems set in. They were agreed on this; probably smothering it overnight would do.

Pregnancy was this real seesaw. Apart from the physical stuff, you could produce a Jesus or a Hitler without meaning to. Average would be the best. They continued to have rollicking sex until the last few weeks, when her stomach grew like Mount Everest, according to Mark.

"I'll have to leave it for now, it might squash something!" he joked. One of the doctors at the health centre had let Cora listen to the second heart within her, thinking it would be an encouragement. Instead, it had made her feel extremely squeamish, walking back to the bus with two hearts beating inside her.

In the week before the baby was due, Mark's friend Sarah arrived at the flat, post a suicide attempt. Mark did not explain exactly how they knew each other, she was definitely not an educated girl, perhaps she lived near his parents, or perhaps she had gone to his original elementary school before he was whisked off via a scholarship to Haberdasher's Askes. He kept producing more and more friends, just as Cora daily lost more and more of them. As they had both a double bed and a single bed acting as sofas in the gigantic living room, it was impossible to refuse to put someone up. Sarah went off to the Labour Exchange to get her address changed for her dole. At least she could pay for her own food, Mark said, not leaving any room for disagreement. They joked and giggled together, leaving Cora out of the conversation.

On a whim, Mark and Sarah decided to clean the windows together, he inside, she standing outside on the balcony, a tall giggling, giddy blonde, while Cora, mountainous, had to stand on the floor, rooted like a sack of potatoes, watching this mimicry of sexual activity. She felt out of place but had to be kind because of Sarah's emotional state. The mass of healing cuts on her wrists showed the attempt and its aftermath. Apparently, it was about a boy leaving her, but how that made her homeless too was not explained or any clue as to where she belonged. Any questioning was regarded as being mean.

They were left together when Mark went to work, and Sarah joined in the painting of the doors and skirting boards. The flat was as ready as it would ever be. Cora was now ten days overdue and was called in by the doctor. They had made arrangements; she was to go over to Hampstead's Queen Mary's Nursing Home on Tuesday morning. Mark took her in the sidecar of the Norton. The motorbike swooped into the courtyard and as Cora blithely stepped out of the little door of the sidecar they were met by a surprised nurse waiting on the steps.

She had got a special dispensation to continue with Hampstead as the destination for the birth. One visit to Harrow Road maternity dept was enough to change her mind. Really, their new flat was in the

Paddington catchment area of St Marys Harrow Road, where the nurses managed to keep totally flat headdresses on, like a starched handkerchief affixed outlandishly at the back of their head. It seemed to have nothing to do with medicine at all. Here, the nurses wore a smaller and far more sensible white cap.

They were shown into the labour ward of over a dozen beds and Mark put her belongings in the bedside locker, kissing her and wishing her good luck. And at that second, their worlds separated. He went back to work leaving her in the ward of a dozen or so other women.

Left alone, with Mark gone off to Finchley and the never-ending decorating, she was stranded here. It must feel like this for children left at boarding school, this break with any link from home. It also cut across anything to do with marriage if she was to be left here to face this particular music on her own. But they had both agreed that birth at home was a repulsive idea, enough to put any one-off sex for life.

Across from her bed the six beds dotted along the ward held various women with problem pregnancies. A woman told her that after six months' pregnancy she was in for 'bedrest' as she was in danger of losing the baby.

"I've got to stay here until the birth, or I might lose it completely. My waters broke prematurely." Another separation. At the end of the ward was a television and they all watched it avidly, pretending to be at home. Cora, used to a television-less life found it a form of indoctrination, control, as all conversation stopped, sleep was impossible and quiz programmes, pop music and newscasts took over until 10p.m.

Morning brought blood pressure monitoring,

blood tests plus breakfast followed by iron pills, an enema and a nurse shaving off pubic hairs. By now there was so much happening that Cora did not have time to be lonely. Screams, however, were coming from a private room near the door of the labour ward. Blood-curdling screams, so bad that several of the women were getting upset. They asked one of the nurses what was going on, would it be like that for them too?

"It's a foreign woman, she's very distressed, but no, don't worry, she is not going through any more pain than is natural. It is her country's normal state for a woman, it's different for them. Don't worry, it won't be like that for any of you," the helpful nurse told them. It would take many years before female genital mutilation and the pain it caused in childbirth was ever mentioned.

After lunchtime – salad followed by lemon meringue – all those who were overdue, who were going to be inducted, were given an injection in their buttock. Quick, easy, and soon over. By half-past one several of the women were wandering about complaining, clutching their stomach, and moaning about their pains. Cora had a bit of indigestion, probably from the excitement and the increasing panic around her and perhaps the lemon meringue pie. She went off to the toilet block, where her pee exploded black mud all up the white-tiled walls. It was like several bottles of Indian ink splashed in wild protest. Along the corridor she found a mop and bucket in the sluice room and hurrying back before anyone found out, spent the next quarter of an hour mopping down the walls and the black-flooded floor. Saying nothing about it (there were still faint black traces left on the grouting) she ambled back to the labour ward. A nurse pounced on her – so it meant her innocent look had not fooled anyone. Another vaginal examination. It was getting like Piccadilly Circus down there, any trace of squeamishness had gone, Cora had lost any sense of privacy.

"You are in the first stages of labour! Why on earth didn't you say anything?" Cora was puzzled, the pain was negligible. The rest of the ward-full of women stared at her resentfully, grasping their hurting stomachs. She looked perfectly calm and unpregnant. She was immediately put in a wheelchair and taken off to a private room as they gazed on indignantly. It was a special isolation room almost unconnected to the outside world.

A single bed, a chair, bedside table with a jug of water; isolation. But there was also an intriguing distraction. The entire right-hand wall held a painting of an Enid Blyton type of village, complete with people going about their daily life. Village shops, school, Post Office, library, bus stop, village pond, church – little people wandered round from one place to another. She could lie there and make up stories about them following the inhabitants from greengrocers to garage to grocer's and wonder what they were doing, while the pelvic pains grew deeper and wider. It was unsigned; she would ask who the artist was and write to thank them.

By visiting time, Cora was scarcely on this planet. She whirled off in red clouds of pain that shuddered through her entire body and consciousness. Mark was shown into the room by a smiling nurse who told him the process was well on the way. He sat by the bed, sometimes clear, sometimes a red blur as Cora tried to focus on him and try to be coherent. But he faltered almost immediately.

"I can't stand this, Cora, I'll have to go off. I can't see you in pain like this. I've got to go!" He dashed out. The next visitor was the nurse and a doctor, who Cora could faintly see at the end of the bed. He looked concerned. She felt sorry for him; something must be going wrong.

"Some pethidine" she could hear him say in a serious voice and the nurse sped off. Now the pains shot through every three minutes. A gap, enough to ring the bell and ask for a bedpan; wait for the next wave of pain to go; get on the bedpan; wave of pain; pee; wait for the next wave of pain to go; get off the bedpan; wave of pain. She teetered between pain that spread as wide as the universe and then an instant's return down to normality. All personality had gone. All the exams, the work, friends, placed lived in, clothes, marriage – all gone. The only thing left was her name. Everything important was inside this red whirling un-merry-go-round. She was somewhere out in space, a part of the universe where names and identity did not matter. Her mother had talked admiringly about Odette, caught in the French Resistance, who had her fingernails ripped off in torture by the occupying Germans.

"A person blacks out eventually if pain is too much, the body just shuts itself down." But Cora thought about the baby - she was not alone in this agony; the baby was also under pressure; they were knitted together in this pain.

At ten o'clock Cora was wheeled into the delivery room, where intense lighting made it like a filmset. The pains had lessened, a mixture of the painkiller and the fact she was getting used to it. You stopped fighting it eventually and there was a kind of easing once you gave in and let the pain do what it wanted.

Actual birthing was easy, the midwife had given her a gas and air mask, but it brought back ghastly memory of visits to the school dentist's and Cora threw it aside immediately, ready to face the final hurdle alone. After all the straining and effort, they asked her to do little dog-panting breaths to slow down the contractions and at last the baby – "It's a boy" – slid out.

The atmosphere changed as the midwife and her assistant cleaned the baby and wrapped him in a shawl, giving him to his new mother. It was a couple of minutes past midnight, so it had become the spring equinox.

The baby boy looked shocked at being out in this world. He sat there alongside Cora, a compact lump, bright blue eyes, startled, that had seen nothing yet. No one had mentioned that, how all babies had blue eyes, whatever the eventual outcome. Schools should have told them that, it was an important item of human information, far more important than algebra.

He sat there, perfect, shot out into the world waiting for him. She leant across and put (or tried to) her tube-strapped hand round him, encouraging him in these new surroundings. It was almost worth telling him that she felt a stranger here too. The two midwives had gone; still at their half-past midnight lunchtime. Just before they left, the dark-haired midwife had turned back at the door, looked at the spattered blood on the floor, hesitated for a second and then said,

"Oh dear, there *is* blood on the floor" But the other one said,

"Ah we'll see to that and mop it up when we get back." Cora, sympathising with their problem and still feeling as strong and omnipotent and as wide as the world had said,

"Don't worry, I'll clean it up for you" from her high trolley bed forgetting the drip still attached to the back of her hand and the newly landed baby. She felt strong enough to clean the universe.

14

The next thing Cora experienced was morning and a nurse was wheeling a crying baby to her to be fed. She never asked – or was told - what the baby had been fed on during the night, or had he crashed into a post-birth after-shock sleep. Cora herself had fallen into a depth of sleep she had never experienced before, backing out of the world into a luxurious deep well.

The baby had been sent off to the nursery overnight and was brought to her bedside at five in the morning. All that superhuman strength had gone; she had fallen into a black velvet sleep and here was the tiny child as a proof of what had happened. He latched onto her breast and they joined again out here in the tangible world. He was the expert; she merely followed his lead. The first feed produced a dark molasses-like oily flow. It was quite repulsive, like a leak of engine oil. She asked the nurse, worried something had gone wrong,

"Is there anything wrong with me? This doesn't look like milk!" A couple of brown drops fell from one of her nipples.

"That's absolutely O.K. It's colostrum, or you could call it beestings. It's nature's way of giving a baby the best start in life, full of protein and antibodies. It's specially concentrated too, easy for a tiny baby to digest." Cora looked again at the repulsive dark goo oozing from her nipples, full of essential vitamins. "It sets your baby up for life," the nurse went on. The real white milk kicked in soon after as the baby obediently guzzled with its devotion to the only food it knew.

She was told it was time for a bath. A large pot of salt was placed on the side of the bath to help clear the bleeding. Instructions, framed above the bath, told how much to use and a wooden ladle was lying alongside the pot. As Cora was sitting in the bath with this new empty body, a cleaning woman in the domestics' uniform of green apron and cap came in and washed her back. It was completely unnecessary and the sort of thing the rich paid for at posh hydros and health spas out in the country. Cora wondered if the woman got some pleasure out of it and as no one ever reported it, the mild intrusion was overlooked by all. The authorities probably did not know it happened and the new mothers, in their altered states did not care. Or perhaps her function was to report any extra blood loss or bits of placenta still emerging.

Mark arrived at visitors' time, direct from work. He smelt of the outside air and seemed larger than she remembered. He took the baby into his arms and looked at the contented little round face.

"My parents will be delighted with him. He looks perfect." They talked in between the crying of other babies and the chat of other visitors. Apparently, Sarah was still at the flat but would be moving out before Cora and baby Sam were coming back. They all had ten days in hospital, a chance to adjust all round to the new routine.

But a day later the same nurse came by, quite worried.

"We have noticed your baby is always the first to wake in the nursery, and his cries set all the others off crying. We are worried that he might not be getting enough milk, so we are going to weigh him before and after his feeds today and find out what might be the problem." Only a day or so old and already a social problem. They found out he was getting the genuine four ounces of milk and they were relieved.

"He must just be an excessively lusty and thriving baby, that's all," the nurse smiled. "Congratulations."

Sophie arrived in the afternoon with the one red rose that Cora had asked for. She looked a bit embarrassed.

"What would you like me to bring?" she had asked, thinking of baby clothes or toiletries. And Cora had asked merely for this red rose, which represented everything instead. For months she had been gathering baby-stuff from the Oxfam shop and wanted something glamorous instead. She kept the dried rose for months before being able to throw it out, meaning all that time to do a drawing of it but never having the time to concentrate. By that time it had become a deep almost black colour and had dried out, becoming like tracing paper.

After the births, women were told to lie on

their stomachs after dinnertime. Cora saw the skin puddle into shape again. The elastic of skin was magical.

The weather improved, it was a sunny day at last and the new mothers were encouraged to sit in the hospital's gardens with their babies. As soon as lunches for mothers and babies all round had been finished, the nurses set about sending all the women and their easily-wheeled babies into the gardens. They had these ten days of being looked after as if staying in a health spa. Sitting in the spring sun, babies drifting off to sleep in the heady mix of sunshine and fresh air, the new mothers sat in deckchairs like aristocrats. They all had about another week left of their allotted ten-day stay. It was like being in a small stately home with the nurses as staff.

Sitting on the terrace looking across the lawn, there were banks of daffodils and brilliant early tulips and now Cora was sitting reading about them, even more red in words. She fished out the copy of Sylvia Plath's *Ariel,* looking at the hospital grounds, red tulips brilliant in the sunlight. And here too, the nurses flitted round smoothing and gliding from bed to bed just as in the poem. She had brought the book with her, Billy had been talking about it and said he would lend her his copy, no, she could keep it after all, it was a woman's book. He said she ought to read it and here was a suitable time. There had been a lot of fuss when this came out, and she had missed the boat. It was as starkly vivid as the tulips. Each line was stripped to the bone. The poems showed how far a few words could be stretched and yet how much emotion they could carry. It was legions away from the whimsy of other current and usually male writers.

That was the last time Cora read it or any other book for several months as housekeeping, homemaking, mothering took over. There was no room for anything else. It disappeared for those months, buried somewhere. Her only book was the battered second-hand copy of Good Housekeeping's Baby Book, which gave a heavily edited version of what to expect. The next day, however, was the baby blues day. It was devastating. Swoops of tears came in like tides. As fast as one set of tears subsided another flood would come in. There was no way of controlling them, the entire body was taken over. Women avoided each other at times as the miseries grew, or they went off into the toilets or bathrooms to cry in private.

"Can you get me a new nappy from the cupboard?" a woman asked. Cora wondered why the young round-faced woman could not manage to walk along to the corridor where there was the cupboard full of clean nappies. Then she noticed the slow tears coursing down; baby blues had struck.

"Ah, of course, I understand! It's your third day, the baby blues! I'm over the worst, will get you two, right?"

A few days later there was a cold snap after that glorious afternoon on the lawn with the groups of tulips in the hospital grounds and they did not go out again. Surprise flurries of snow showed that winter was not going to give up yet.

At visiting time an irritated Mark came in, saying he was worn out coming here, didn't she realise it took two buses to get here after work and he started quarrelling at the bedside. He left in a huff, watched by the single parent Maureen from her bed across the ward, who thought they were a perfect couple. Sarah was apparently still living at the flat. There was nothing to be negotiated when someone was as desperate as that, Cora must understand, he said, and not be so selfish about other people's difficulties. Luckily the problem was solved because Mark arrived with his father and mother in the car to take them home. That meant Sarah would definitely have to disappear as Cora returned to the flat from hospital at the end of March after the ten days.

The mothers were given a bag of baby-stuff, with samples of various foods and milk mixtures. It included some condoms to use before the six-week appointment. They were told, however, to refrain from vaginal sex before those six weeks were out as blood would still be issuing at (as it turned out) an alarming rate. It was the first time Cora saw a new condom apart from the discarded ones at Fred's cleaning up after New Year's Day. That was so long ago, yet only three months away.

Mark explained why he was so tense about the scene in the labour room and why he had walked out.

" I never really told you about being adopted, did I? Why they chose me? Just seeing you there in so much pain, I had to get away. I was scared stiff. It brought to life my father's story – adoptive father, you know, - but he's really a good guy, a real good guy. Well, once upon a time there was a man and his wife, and they were in love and they were expecting a baby and they went to hospital just like we did.

Except that the woman died in childbirth and the baby died too. Both dead at once. And the man's hair all fell out overnight. And he was only thirty. And that's Dad's story. He's stayed bald as a tennis ball all these years. The thing you see now is a toupee, it's his new grey one after the brown one looked wrong. After ten years alone he married Beryl, she worked in a local tobacconist's, so he saw her nearly every day when he bought his cigarettes and the Daily Mirror. She said she had kept herself properly all those years. I think she was a virgin and probably still is.

Anyway, she said she wanted a baby and he said no, that was impossible. Then they went off to an orphanage in Camden Town and there I was. And she said that as George would never let her have a baby otherwise, I was their only way out. So you can see why I got panicky when you were passing out with pain like that. Perhaps history was going to repeat itself."

"So you saved them from the tragedy."

" Only sort of. They wanted a little teddy bear and they got me instead. I was a little intellectual and we were, on both sides, quite disappointed with each other. And that's all my story re babies and deaths."

16

While they had been involved in their domestic drama, out in the world there had been anti-Vietnam rallies protesting, going from Trafalgar Square to the American Embassy in Grosvenor Square. On Sunday, the 17th of March there was the Battle of Grosvenor Square and there was another demo on 28th of March.

"The police told people later that if they had got into the embassy the Americans would have shot them," Mark told her from the news. Sarah had magically disappeared, and Cora did not feel like enquiring about what she had done about getting somewhere else to stay. They moved the oil stove to heat the little bedroom as a chilly spring changed suddenly.

At last, it was time for the sixth week appointment – they'd dwindled to having no more sex, and Cora was still bleeding. Sex hurt, using the condoms given by the hospital. It was the first time Cora had ever seen new packets of these balloon-like items close up; no man had ever used one with her. In fact, they had always mentioned them with amused distaste, something to be avoided. And any woman, is she had produced one, would have immediately labelled herself as complete trash. The gossip would have sped round the pubs like wildfire. But Mark had been waiting. He tried getting into her, but it was not a success. She cried him to stop, and it ended up an embarrassing mess, with Mark dejected and disgruntled. Recognising some of the new mothers at the clinic, the Irishwoman said she did not obey the six-week rule, no one could.

"You have to go with your man, or there's trouble, it's what they want after all, you can't wait the full six weeks." They were given appointments at the Family Planning clinic for further contraceptive advice, but in the meantime, here was another packet of free condoms to help them. They were told the cheering news that breastfeeding was no guarantee against getting pregnant right away, contraception of any kind was necessary now or they would be starting the entire process all over again, too soon.

A month later it was Mark's nineteenth birthday She pasted roses from a 1967 calendar onto six boxes of matches as his only present. There was nothing left in her Post Office savings account book from South End Green that had been kept as a memento. It was a situation like *The Gift of the Magi*, but her hair was too short to sell and copy the girl in that story. There was nothing valuable to sell right now.

17 Mark's job of house decorating, and his company formed with Mitch was faltering now. Cora had enthusiastically gone round pushing baby Sam in the pram and dispersing more leaflets round Maida Vale but with no success. Mark then gave in and went to the Labour Exchange and found he was to become a civil servant.

He said he needed his tobacco-coloured corduroy jacket to be cleaned. It was so he would look smart for his interview for any proper job. He left the instructions written on the flyleaf of her copy of Iris Murdoch's *An Unofficial Rose*, a present that had managed to move, as if by levitation, across all the bedsits in London. The book was now ruined, his writing digging into the front page. It had been the other book along with *Ariel* that Cora had taken to hospital to have the baby. All she could remember now was that it began with a funeral and could not remember how it ended.

Mark looked smart in the rejuvenated outfit. He had to ask at the Employment Exchange for a B1 form to begin regular employment. The clerk was delighted that someone from the margins, as he put it, was deciding to join the usual National Insurance scheme.

"No, we are pleased when people join in the system with a proper National Insurance job," the clerk said at the Labour Exchange. "This is a good decision. We find that you can only hold on so long outside the general employment pattern. You can start right from the beginning now and build up your stamps towards your old age pension." This was the last thing Mark needed to hear right now, but at least an indoors office job with a regular assured wage was an improvement, of sorts. Freedom to be independent meant only being permanently on edge, as anything could happen to upset the applecart. They had not realised how near the brink they had been; it was a chancy life plan.

"Well, you've certainly started off well in life here with Haberdasher's Askes, very impressive. Then I see you've roved about a bit, drifting in various occupations well beneath your qualifications. Luckily there's no harm done so far!" he joked. "We can offer you something far more suitable. In fact, as you have two references here already, and with your educational background, with three A Levels, you could be accepted as an established officer without having to go through the usual entrance examinations yourself." They immediately produced a place; he was being sent to the Ministry of Education Examination department. And as this was at 1 Chepstow Place it was easily walkable from home, Mark realised.

That was the only point in its favour. It was a boring office job, but it was a quick toehold into security. Mitch, living at home did not have the same problems and was considering what to do next from an almost luxurious situation; his father was a consultant at Whitlingham hospital and his mother was a lecturer at a training college.

This new civil service job would pay £15.10.0 a week. It was the going rate, but it would be permanent and was guaranteed to gradually improve over time. Their rent and rates still ate up most of the money. Dashing home, he told Cora about their new status.

"It's all settled, and I need £2 a week for myself, it's really important because I need cigarettes or tobacco, you know that. And if I don't have that I can get mean, really mean." It seemed a sensible arrangement at the time as he had the responsibility for going to work and paying the rent; but she noticed the threat behind the words and later, looking back, saw the worm in the apple, alive and secretly consuming from the inside.

Now that was all settled, Mark was going back to concentrate on writing his great book.

"Rather like that John Fowles thing, remember, but it's on a mediaeval theme. I took Sir Gawain and the Green Man as the basic but adding in weaves of the King Arthur legends. Have you ever read T.H. White's *The Once and Future King*?" She had not. It was one more thing on an invisible list. In the evenings he waded through sheaves of papers and a couple of centuries, trying to create a creditable world out of it all. When he was on a writing spree the outside world completely disappeared unless it was one of those evenings when he was playing the guitar. His song-playing had never been mentioned, in fact it had not featured in their room in Hampstead. Cora had not noticed the guitar much before; it moved into their flat like a pet dog.

Mark strummed away and made up songs as he

went along. They were all slightly off-key, meandering on and on, never reaching a real tune or a real conclusion. It was unsettling and there was something creepy about the sounds. It was upsetting, and after a few evenings she asked him could he keep it in the kitchen, as it was a kind of moaning and upset her in a way she could not explain. It was as if he was having an argument with himself endlessly. Going round to Mal's he borrowed LP's and went over *The Incredible String Band* with the same intensity that he used to give to the Beatles' *Sergeant Pepper*.

Luckily, she was producing enough milk for the baby and Sam was thriving. But of course, if they went out on a Saturday afternoon to Portobello market – a way of buying cheap vegetables as the stalls closed down after six-ish, there was another problem. The world did not have any provision for breast-feeding mothers with their infants. It made sense now, the normal process of nursing, but it was driven underground, cities designed by men and women who did not breastfeed. They slipped into a nearby church which was open and empty and while the baby fed, Mark walked round inspecting the stained-glass windows and the altar candlesticks.

"It doesn't matter so much, it's only a Church of England place," Cora said. "There's no consecrated host in a Tabernacle or anything sacred, you can see the altar is empty, they have just a big cross with figure of Christ on it." The baby, coming to a stop in his guzzling, was soon winded and burped and they were back into the late spring afternoon. A few months later they noticed the doors of the church were stoutly padlocked. A notice said that because of vandalism and theft the church was to be open for service times only in the future. The soft places, one by one were getting closed as they did not make money and only businesses were being left to thrive.

18

The ship had everything any town would need – shops, newsagent, cafés, jewellers ,clothes shops, a medical centre, library and even a gambling casino. Cora wandered around staring at it all, fascinated by its compact design and the various people. Some were tourists, ready to dash off into the sun and explore. Others were disabled, here to have a break from their housebound monotony. Those in wheelchairs were pushed by spouses who were always much smaller in height and girth. It was as if they had spun a coin to choose from the nursery rhyme which one was to be Jack Spratt who could eat no fat, and the wife who could eat no lean. It was an easy terrain to navigate, all accessible via the lifts and sloped gangways. Being on board for all this time ad wanting something extra to do led to Cora going up to the eighth deck where a wildlife officer hosted the daily dolphin watch. There were diagrams set out along a noticeboard and spare binoculars and one gigantic telescope. So far there was nothing to see except the clear horizon of nothingness.

"We saw something last year," a woman with a broad Lancashire accent said, in wonder. "It's as if they want to talk to us each time."

"There's a spot there where there's no wind at all – it's absolutely flat," her husband pointed out, putting his binoculars down. All these people were married; they were elderly; they were stiff when they

got up to walk and made jokes about it. But the dolphins were important to them, they were here in some form of assignation. They had paid for the cruise so that they could be here again, at exactly the same spot, with the same devotion, a secular pilgrimage.

And then out of the ultramarine water, first one nose and then another appeared as the dolphins grouped alongside the ship. It was as if they had been secretly waiting for this entertainment to turn up and they sported in and out of the water. It was easy to imagine, however, hundreds of years ago that sailors stranded on long journeys, given their constant tots of rum and perhaps sparse rations, should mistake these beings for mermaids.

Cora saw them more as parts of the subconscious trying to reach daylight, with the effort to attain another element, always being beaten back, having to return to the sea and submerge again. Fleeting ideas that could not be fully grasped, no matter how often they surfaced.

And Shakespeare had thought of it centuries before:

> *Full fathom five thy father lies;*
> *Of his bones are coral made;*
> *Those are pearls that were his eyes:*
> *Nothing of him that doth fade*
> *But doth suffer a sea-change*
> *Into something rich and strange.*

"I saw a pod of about fifty dolphins one sunset last year," the wildlife officer said as if describing a vision. "It's something you remember forever." The dark blue shapes followed the ship for a while and then decided to draw back as though they had

remembered somewhere else to go to. It was like friends leaving, a benevolence withdrawn. The passengers and crew would go back to land and might never encounter each other again while the dolphins went back to their secret life and waited.

Climbing down the iron steps from the eight deck with the ocean alongside, just the other side of the white handrail was the steep drop into the neutral I-will-drown-you-ocean, which was surprisingly black right now, changed from ultramarine, a black and white liner surrounded by black sea.

Late afternoon, still in April, the carpet started to rise. It ruffled and furled like a tide coming in. Cora watched it, fascinated and scared. Mr Williams had brought round the large carpet from one of the in-laws. It was multi-coloured, luckily a classic pattern, and managed to cover most of the centre of the living room floor. Now it was like the illustrations to Ali Babar, *A Thousand and One Nights*. Or perhaps Scheherazade. It flowed, floated, fluttered. The intricate pattern rumpled, changing in the April light. After a while it flopped down flat again, and she risked walking across it to reach the kitchen.

Cora knew what this was. Post Natal Depression. From one of the library's books she knew that one in ten women suffered from depression postnatally. It said, 'they are extremely distressed, hallucinating and suicidal.' That explained the moving carpet. She had never liked it, but Grandpa had brought it round and of course, it was a covering for most of the floor. But now she could not trust it or herself, there was no solidity. You did not need to take drugs. Drug effects came towards you these days.

It was only a couple of days later, at the weekend, that Mark was in the room too and witnessed the same phenomenon. He reacted matter-of-factly,

"It just shows you how draughty this place is, that's a real draught coming up through the floorboards. You can see it stops when there's no wind." No hallucination at all, no madness. She looked at the carpet suspiciously. How could it behave madly when she was alone here, but have a logical explanation when Mark was around? The baby, as usual, was a neutral observer.

Mark told her then that there had been a threat of bailiffs coming because of the previous tenants' debts, but he had managed to head them off.

"I wrote to them that we were brand-new tenants, and we had a proper tenancy agreement, we had no link with the previous ones. And, for good luck, I gave them Fred's contact number. Serves him right."

He also told her, at this late time, that he knew all about his previous girlfriend's mother and his mum being in cahoots about her, phoning each other in fright as soon as he had told them about being with Cora and that she was pregnant.

"Oh, Mrs Carter said it was the oldest trick in the book, how could we all fall for it? And further, how did I even know that the baby was really mine? She was disappointed with it all. It had all been expected, sort of planned, that Amy and I were going to go off to university together and marry sometime after that, two academics together. My mum was upset then, and I had to persuade her that it was all OK and it wasn't like that at all, but she worried that you were older than me and you'd been around a bit and it was unfair on me to go and get pregnant like that."

Cora was astounded at the dirty minds of the respectable middle or lower classes, or however they wanted to label themselves. They had minds like sewers to think such devious things about her. No thought of her being thrown out of the Marie Stopes Clinic when she went there for any help in contraception methods and being sent away until 'she got a proper fiancé and a settled relationship.' Then they would be most willing to help her, the medical assistant said. And, with a smile, she had added that Cora did not look twenty-five at all, which was totally surplus to the situation. She knew what she was being condemned to by their sanctimonious twaddle.

"Oh, you didn't tell them the truth, did you?" Sophie was shocked, back at the bedsit house. "I told them I had a boyfriend in the RAF and his leave time together was precious to both of us while we saved up for our wedding. They gave me a cap right away, there and then, most helpful. You shouldn't have told them all that." The medical lady had mentioned that the cap would have cost two pounds ten shillings, which was nearly half a week's wage and only ten shillings less than her rent. It was already something well over the horizon.

But here was Mark, like a century later, telling her of even more mudflats she had managed to struggle through.

The previous year's blissful hippy summer was breaking down on all sides. Peacefulness was over. On

7th May 1968, the headlines were: "At least 10,000 students riot in Paris on a scale unequalled in post-war years."

19
A phone call from Billy, the poet entrepreneur and dedicated writer - could she come and do a reading at the Lamb and Flag? Paul had another engagement and Charles was unavailable. People would be interested in her new *Belsize* poetry collection; it was selling well. Anyway, a young woman would make a change from all the men, probably. She was at once insulted and overjoyed.

"Two lots of ten minutes, that'll be enough. You'll need to be here at a quarter past seven and you'll probably get a few quid, hope that's fine by you." It was wonderful, the baby needed new clothes, and this was better than nothing. Mark would babysit for the evening.

She got the underground from Warwick Avenue to Oxford Circus and decided not to change from the Bakerloo line but get out and to walk along Oxford Street towards the Lamb and Flag. It was amazing to be going back to the same pub where Mark had taken her to an Anarchists meeting a lifetime ago.

Spring evening, nearly 7 p.m. Even here there was a feeling of cherry-blossom on the shopfront air. She walked along, exhilarated in the post-rush hour space, a slackening in the traffic. All shops were shut and the busy working and shopping crowds had gone home to eat their dinners in peace. But she noticed several men, dispersed amongst the shop entrances, loitering, window-shopping. It was difficult to explain why they were there, each one alone. But now she noticed that as she approached, each man stepped forward onto the pavement, a slow shuffle. One after another they jingled coins in their pockets. It grew worse and worse, until she had to weave a zigzag pattern as she tried to avoid them by walking on the roadside edge of the pavement. This made the men venture further out from their burrows. Other uninvolved people, couples, or other women walking towards her also caused hazards, sometimes she almost bumped into them, becoming clumsy out of embarrassment.

Part of her wanted to stop the approaching men and say sarcastically,

"Look, it takes more than a pocket of coins, you know. I know the rustle of pound notes won't sound very loud out here, but a couple of coins! It's demeaning!" Sparrows chirped from the unseen rooftops above Selfridge's and Marks and Spencer's. Spring was there, behind all those buildings, a benevolent warmth, pink skies of almost-sunset above the grubby manoeuvring of these loitering men.

By the time she reached Leicester Square and the corner of Rose Street she was worn out with this exhausting minuet, having to avoid the approaching men, where it was herself to blame for being a woman out alone on a spring evening. Her first time out alone in the evening after the birth too, it was a disgusting start.

On duty, already beginning to be on stage, at the corner of Rose Street, she smiled as if nothing had happened. The pub was crowded and Billy was relieved she had turned up.

"I'll never forgive Paul for letting us down like this. It's a good job you could step in. Ready now? No time to have a drink, get one later on, I'll bring it upstairs afterwards, just get upstairs and find a seat." He went outside to look for more punters turning up before meandering up to the long wooden-floored room upstairs. It was the same room Mark had taken her to an anarchist meeting when they were first together last year, impressed by Mark's knowledge and contacts. All men, all old shabby men, pleasantly surprised at Cora being there. This was more or less the same, with a surface veneer of entertainment.

Cora began to be used as more than a stand-in. Another poetry reading, this time back in Hampstead, had been crowded. The hall was full of happy people only too ready to soak up whatever the poets had to offer them. Luckily, it was still at the beginning of the surge of popularity and audiences' patience was not yet stretched to their limits, the poems still made sense or were exceptionally entertaining. There was often a guitarist playing between the readings and give a pleasant background in the interval.

This time Cora followed a famous journalist, who successfully contrived to mix a political stance with his witty but heartfelt diatribes against injustices. He managed to make the listeners feel worthy and justified, safely rebellious. Protest was fashionable. It was Cora's job to add a spice of ginger and sugar, to give contrast and so emphasise his worth and message. They made a good duo, a fact he acknowledged, coming across to her at the end, with,

"I must say, of all the supporting poets I've been with, you've been the best, thanks a lot for your input." It was only several hours later at home that Cora realised that good or not, Edward had not managed to give her his phone number or any way of getting in touch with him and realised that congratulations or not, their paths would not cross except by accident. She was too shy to ask Billy about him.

Billy was too busy having a tearful row with Jason, who was refusing to go off home with him in a taxi. The crowd dribbled past the heartfelt wheedling as Billy and Jason went through another part of their painful relationship in public. Billy turned in defeat at last, as Jason waltzed off to a conveniently offered lift in a well-heeled couple's car and a probable night in their centrally heated Hampstead home, drinking their whisky, insulting them and then crashing out on their Heal's sofa and vomiting on their cat. They had cleverly bought the complete poet experience along with their entrance ticket.

Billy, disgruntled, pulled Cora towards him and said they could share a taxi.

"It looks like I'm going your way anyhow now," he said crossly. They sped through the streets towards Maida Vale as Billy gave her the long story again, though mostly it was a disgruntled moan about why didn't Jason love him. From Cora's wide experience of that state, she knew there was no answer, just months and months of distraction until it faded away from lack of encouragement. Billy should have known that by now, he was older than she was and must have been through this Slough of Despondency before.

Billy of course, had little money on him as usual and Cora had to dip into her night's pay to fund the trip, as Billy got out earlier, leaving her in an empty cab as if the evening had never happened.

Traipsing up the dark stairs from one failing

minutière to another, with mice running out of her way here and there, Cora could hear someone talking when she reached the flat.

When she got in, Mark was sitting on the divan with Emma, a name like a mumble, the room light off and only the small lamp that she had made from a cider bottle, a wire frame and a remnant of a coat lining giving a subtle warm glow. It looked very intimate and she felt like an intruder in her own home, as though she ought to back out, go elsewhere and come back later when it was more convenient and less embarrassing for them both.

Mark and Emma looked at her as though she was a stranger walking into the wrong room. Then Emma smiled.

Of course, Mark then had to walk Emma along to Warwick Avenue station and of course Cora had to stay with the baby. No way out of this cat's cradle. Escort Emma herself? They hardly knew each other. Get the baby out of his cot, carry him downstairs to the cold pram and walk round the streets with him? Leave him alone in the flat while all three of them went off to the station together? She had to smile as though nothing was going on. If Kirsty or Rhona could not babysit, Cora had to risk the appearance of various of Mark's friends while she was out. The poetry was beginning to pay a useful amount; they both got new shoes out of it one week. When they were lucky and he was able to accompany her on the bus for the evening's performance, he spent the time mixing with strangers in the audience, being charming and friendly.

The nappies began to rule their life. Poor

Mark came home from work to a flat seething with gales of pee as the nappies were boiled to clean them out. Mrs Williams, emergency planning as usual, had produced a gigantic saucepan, large enough to manage a day's supply. The nappies gurgled and swirled in the kitchen, spreading the killing aroma of pee as far as the stairs. The pan was stamped with a sign that said, 'Made in Germany,' and that it held 12 quarts. It was like something out of the Middle Ages, bustling country life and home preserving or brewing. It was only when the day's lot was done that Cora could move on to the ordinary washing of the baby's clothes, and then on to their own stuff. That took most of the morning. There seemed to be no gaps between the breast-feeding, winding, nappy changing, and responding to the child's crying now and then. She just had to get through it.

The helpful Williams's had previously brought round a mangle, which had been left in their garden as a remnant of the war years. As it was cast-iron, poor Mr Williams and Mark had difficulty bringing it all the way up the many stairs. Mrs Williams fluttered around,

"Oh, do take care here, I don't want my George to have a heart attack. He's not strong now, he's not a young man at all, and this is putting a strain on his heart. I don't want to be left a widow like this." Cora felt guilty as if she had put Mr Williams through such a danger on purpose.

The nappies often did not dry in the bathroom, staying damp and then going rancid, needing to be boiled up yet again, adding to the current day's heap. Reaching up to the indoors clothesline slung over the bath, Cora noticed some small black dots on the corner of the bath. Perhaps worry was giving her hallucinations now, it was more than likely. She could see the minute intensely black dots clearly but was not sure that she was really seeing them. Reality was getting worse by the day. She told Mark about the dots.

"They're small as grains of Nescafé" she said. Mark looked, bent down to the windowsill and the edge of the bath and said there was nothing there, nothing at all, she was imagining it. But she was worried enough, and Cora stood her ground enough for him to mention it to his father. When Mr Williams next came round, he was taken into the bathroom and shown the bath like a forensic exhibit.

"I can't see anything here, it's really puzzling. You've probably seen some young Mayflies, that's it, small midges, they've long flown out of the window by now, there's nothing here, you won't find anything here." Cora was definitely scared now; she could see about fourteen of them minutely circling round each other in their miniscule kingdom. She must be really mad by now. How long should she hide this strange vision and what was going to be the next stage, when would it get truly frightening and interfere with real life? She smiled and suggested they had a cup of tea, but Mr Williams said he had just called round with some veg from his allotment and a magazine on motorcycling for Mark and wouldn't be staying and they were invited round for Sunday dinner tomorrow.

A few days later, as she was putting the clean nappies onto the shelves in the bedroom Cora saw the black dots clearly walking over the white squares. It was clearer here. It was definite.

They had an appointment at the Baby Clinic

for an injection that afternoon and Cora mentioned the dots to Mrs Murgatroyd, who said that anything walking round a baby's nappy was an infestation and the Public Health had to be informed.

"In fact, I'll ring them up right now," she said. "You can't bring up a baby in a flat that has an outbreak of insects in it." Mrs Murgatroyd redeemed herself from her previous neglect, although Cora was worried that her new obsession would be found out to be totally imaginary by the Public Health services of the City of Westminster and things were getting out of hand. But best to find out how mad she really was before it got any worse. She did not tell Mark about the council pest control man coming round.

He did remark, tellingly, when she told him about the baby's afternoon's appointment for the injection,

"Just think, it is the first time his skin has been broken." The world was gathering them in, bit by bit. "It's the beginning of him belonging to the state, not to us, as a being you created in your body. They are going to track him now; it all starts here."

A few days later, a bluff Londoner vermin exterminator arrived with sets of pipes and a canister of spray. He stepped into a brown overall and put on a head-covering, with attached goggles.

"Killer stuff this is, works in up to twelve hours." He bristled with energy and enthusiasm. Cora hesitantly led him into the bathroom and pointed to the side of the bath. Perhaps he too would be unable to see the tiny flecks moving about on the white enamel edge. She must be going mental. Here would be the proof at last.

He would get terribly angry with her and there

might even be a fine for the misuse of public services. He stood still and bent down to the side of the bath.

"Yes. Seen a lot of these. Do you keep pigeons by any chance?" It was getting worse. Bizarre added to bizarre. Then she remembered the ones out on the drainpipe.

"No, but there were some pigeons that did nest in the side of the gully just overhead, or in the corner, sort of. I haven't noticed them recently."

"That's it then. These are pigeon fleas. They live in the nest and wait for the pigeons to return, but by now the youngsters are fledglings and spend more time out of the nest. And mum and dad might be off somewhere else too. So, the fleas go out looking for some sustenance." He saw her face. "Oh, you're all right, they don't go for human blood, ours is probably too rich for them to digest or something. Now, you'll have to go out of the flat with the baby while I spray it all." He started on the living room first, going all round the skirting board and all over the floor. "You can come back in an hour; it's not too bad unless you suffer from asthma."

Cora collected the baby and some belongings and went out for a walk along the Crescent, staring at all the insect-proof houses. When they came back the flat smelt of a mix of disinfectant and petrol. The next day there was not a trace of the minuscule fleas. She told Mark about the man spraying the flat and how she had been right all along, but he swept it aside as though it was irrelevant and the man from the Public Health Dept had not existed either.

That weekend, however, Mr Williams arrived with another present, a black and white television set.

"We've moved on to a colour set, thought you

might be interested in this, you can follow the news and films, it'll save you money instead of going out." He had kindly paid a year's TV licence to start them off. Cora thought how much of a debt she already owed to the Williams's and how some way in the future she would go about repaying them. There was a scheme where people could buy weekly TV licence stamps to save for the licence and Cora got a card from the Post Office, wondering how they would manage to pay it at all.

A lovely May evening, at last, it was her appointment at the North Kensington Marriage Welfare Clinic somewhere along Portobello Road. The timing was so Mark could look after the baby while she went off at seven o'clock. Further and further westwards, the roofs grew lower and lower, the peach sky lit up with a wide sunset and there was even the sound of birds signalling sunset. The fresh air gave her a new bout of strength, being out in the street alone was enjoyable, a forgotten luxury. After the inspection she was given a packet of the latest pills and contraception was now all sure and certain with no more worries from now on. Cora wandered along Ladbroke Grove and over the little metal bridge back into Formosa Street and home.

The flat was eerily silent. Mark was huddled over the baby lying in his arms, as he was sitting on the couch, both of them asleep. There was a large hole in the wall, plaster broken right down to the laths, like a parallel secret flat looking in at them.

"Punching a wall is often implicitly about saying 'You could be next.'" Where had she read that? Was it from an article in the Observer? This was slummy and weird. She stood there feeling old, responsible for two

children now, one of them likely to be dangerous. The thoughts were not as clear as that, it was a shadow of fear, something to be filed away, 'B' for beware. After she gently untwined Sam from Mark's arms and placed the sleeping baby in his cot, as usual a cup of tea broke the tension. Mark was upset, apologetic,

"It was the crying, it wouldn't stop, he just went on and on crying and I didn't want to hit him, I couldn't ever do that of course, and so that was how I managed to get over it, just hitting the wall."

It looked like the new pills promised a Shangri-la of sexual possibilities. They were to be started right away, no need to wait for the menstrual cycle to find a suitable day. But loss of libido was not mentioned. Not in the small print. No clues. The word did not exist. The days became like living underwater. It was intriguing at first, as if it were going to end. But as it dawned on Cora that this was forever, it was frightening. Drowning, day after day, with this invisible water all around her. Talking to people as though they were in this underwater world as well, but knowing they could move on, away, out of this wreck-explorers' depth. She felt like a goldfish in a tank, swimming through green fronds of seaweed. It became normal because it had to be.

Quotes from Mark, which were no help right now.

"The nuns must have taught you something, given you a centre to hold onto."

"Children, animals and Cora are permanently high."

"You have no subconscious, it's all available on the surface for you."

"You are one of the few persons actually able

to have original thoughts."

"You are a subtle blend of Teuton and Celt."

"You have an almost mediaeval thought system. All that stuff about blue skies being Our Lady's cloak – and all the rest downwards."

19

A surprise phone call came from Maura, one of the poetry crowd, who, it was rumoured was starting up a new magazine.

"I got your number from Billy; know you wouldn't mind. Well, how's everything going? You're making waves, you know."

Cora did not know. The nappies were the most important thing on her horizon, plus constant budgeting. She waffled carefully. But Maura continued happily,

"Liam said he wants to see you. He's entranced by your poetry and he wants you to sign his copy of Belsize. Can you come round for a chat?" Liam was yet another writer, doing various dead-end jobs while filling notebooks and sending pages of writing off to magazines and publishers. He had got as far as getting a typewriter which was a distinct advantage. This was strange, the thought that the stuff in her book was spreading out further and further, like petrol on water, rainbows connecting.

They arranged that Sunday afternoon would be best, about two o'clock. The baby would be having his afternoon nap then and would not be any trouble for Mark. Off on the 187 bus and then a walk along the roads alongside the Heath, old stomping grounds. Cora saw it with different eyes now; not a place for children, it never had been, never would have been. The flat was the ground floor, high ceilings and large rooms. Maura was also a writer; she was always going to start this magazine that never emerged but was always exciting. It was rumoured that her father supported her, she did not need to work.

Cora was led into the gigantic front room facing Willoughby Road. The room was so big that a girl lying spread out on a double bed in the corner did not look superfluous. One glance at her showed expensive rich-hippy clothes, velvet skirt and suede boots. On closer inspection she was not merely sleeping, more completely passed out. Cora stood there, feeling medically pure, breast milk still emerging, still clean. She was also puzzled. Where was Liam?

"I'll just go and tell him you're here," Maura said, going upstairs. She came back soon, alone.

"He'll be down soon. You're really honoured, he's had a really bad trip last night, you see." That explained the strange atmosphere, although Maura was floating happily above all the problems, always confident and cheerful. Her father probably paid the rent for all of them. Liam all-but staggered into the room. He looked pale and drawn. He smiled ruefully.

"Feel a bit rough, like the flu. Good to see you." He wanted to know how she wrote the poems, what happened, how were they constructed, what was the process? She looked at him in horror. Didn't he know how it happened? He was a writer too, wasn't he? It was not a recipe that they could swap. Each poet was out there on their own, unless they followed the old-fashioned strict metrical forms and even then, you didn't always know what was going to happen next.

He surely knew all this. He produced a copy of her book and asked her to sign it. Then he got a bit sentimental,

"I shall never forget you, because we have the same name, Corcoran." The silent girl on the bed moved a little and Maura and Liam giggled.

"She's been well out for the count since yesterday," Maura smiled. Cora felt so far away from them and wanted to run back to the baby and normal life. But that was another extreme; there was nowhere she really belonged to now, although sitting on the 187 bus again was a relief, it signified safety again.

As Cora pushed the pram along the Crescent, on the way to Formosa Street a large fat lady with flyaway hair stuffed under a maroon felt hat drew up alongside the pram. Taking no notice of her, the woman looked closely at the baby. Sam smiled up at her. She smiled, first at the baby, then at Cora. And that was how they met the Baroness.

"I always have a way with babies. What a little beauty! How old?"

"He's four months, just." Each day was another identifying marker; only adults counted in years.

"You're new here, aren't you? I haven't seen you before. I know most of the young mothers round here, you see, I'm babysitting for some of them. You can ask me if you need to. I live just along the Crescent."

"That's strange! We live there too!" They were a couple of doors away from each other. As the houses were so large with their railings and pillared entrances, 'a few doors along' was quite a feasible distance away. Neighbours were only new to each other in a street of terrace houses; these London mansions were separate worlds. You could hide from the police here easily. "But we don't really have enough money to pay for babysitters, so I don't think we'll be asking you even so," Cora being honest and pessimistic, said the worst.

"Oh, that doesn't matter," the Baroness said. "Just give me something to eat and it counts as a night out, as far as I am concerned. Call round or put a note through the door when you want me to turn up. There's no phone." She gave the address, only a few doors away. "My name's on a card by the bells." She smiled, friendly, encouraging. Just like someone from a fairy story, Cora thought. She is going to give me the fatal red and white apple or run off with the baby. Kindness in disguise. She held out her hand now to properly introduce herself. "My real name is Lulu, from Louise, but it's got changed to 'The Baroness' round here," she said with a blithe smile.

The Baroness turned out to be a treasure, a find, a tattered Fairy Godmother. It was obviously her technique to pick up women with prams, make friends and offer to babysit, as she had done right there on the pavement. Cora was delighted for the friendly face as much as for the offer to babysit.

She told Cora that one family were angry because the first word their baby ever said was 'Baroness.'

And sure enough, when Cora went round, there it was, a small card in the display of room-names beside the raft of bells, 'Lady Banks.' So, it was settled there and then that the Baroness would come round to tea and meet Sam at home and of course be introduced to Mark. Luckily, they hit it off really well, he found her a cheerful character and the Baroness in her turn found him an interesting and intelligent young man. Sam took to her as if they were related, grandson and grandmother.

"Or batty aunt," as Mark said after she left.

The Baroness turned up promptly at six o'clock and shared their usual meal of bacon, eggs, and beans on toast.

"Scrumptious!" she said. "You can't beat good plain English cooking!"

"Perhaps that's why her husband left her," Mark said afterwards, "if she served him that in their stately hall. I hope she's all right with the baby. She's absolutely and totally *mad* – you do realise that?" He added, "I didn't think they made people like that anymore. She looks as sane as a herring in a privet bush. She's right out of P.G.Wodehouse. I bet her stately home was an absolute hoot."

"But she's warm mad, not cold mad, that's the difference," Cora said.

Cora imagined tiled, marble and parquet floors, lumpy chintz sofas scattered around, dusty chandeliers and several cats, semi wild, and dogs, probably spaniels, wandering around. Books and newspapers (always The Times) littering every surface, clothes carelessly strewn across chairs, washing left drying on a stand before the drawing room fire, a kitchen stacked with unwashed pots and pans, staff unable to keep the place decent and a constant stream of visitors. Happy chaos, shoes and discarded wellington boots cast liberally around, with a vaguely loopy husband wandering in and out and two beautiful children, golden-haired sunburnt boys, who were either running round having adventures right out of Enid Blyton or Arthur Ransome or packed off to boarding school.

At the library, looking up Debrett's in the Reference Department, Cora found there was indeed a Lady Louise Banks, born 1908. 'The wife of a Baron is known as a Lady' so she really was a genuine baroness. She was a gleam of happiness, their very own Margaret Rutherford.

The latest baby book from the library nailed it,
"Fed up with no sleep for about a year, a body that has been shocked out of shape, being at home alone with a baby and not at work with other adults can cause depression."

They read in the paper that a young mother had jumped from a high-rise flat near St Pancras, holding her baby. They had both crashed to their death. Mark understood immediately.

"You can't go and isolate people like that, floors and floors up in the sky. She must have felt awful. I can even see it as a William Blake engraving, you know, those floaty people he does, she'd be going past people's windows and they wouldn't realise what they saw at first, and then there'd be the awful crash landing."

When Mark left for work Cora even talked to him for a bit more via the intercom down at the front door. He could be the only adult she would speak to all day except for shop assistants.

Now and again in the afternoons she lifted the hallway phone and listened to snatches of conversations as people passed by in the street three storeys below. It would have made a wonderful Avant Garde recording, critics would go mad about it, so much potential wasted in what was available in the everyday, the here-and-now.

Behind her back, Mark had been phoning up her friends, starting with Sophie.

"If you're any kind of friend of Cora's, why don't you ever visit her? She's on her own over here with the baby and I'm at work all day. Why don't you hop on a bus? She'd be really glad to see you." He was trying his best to help, being tactful by hiding it from her. They had not met since the nursing home visit. The dried red rose remained in a jam-jar in the kitchen, already a souvenir of a happier time.

Sophie duly came around after a phoned appointment on her own, for once. A sunny afternoon, they walked round with the pram to the semi-secret entrance to the communal grounds at the back. They sat on a bench on the warm side of the grass. The grounds stretched as wide as the entire Crescent and looked even longer down here at eye level. It was like a country estate. They almost had it to themselves, few people were about. Sophie was telling her of all the latest goings-on in Hampstead, everything she was missing out on. But Cora, who thought this was what she needed, was shocked to see toads, frogs, newts, lizards and small snakes issuing out of Sophie's mouth and falling, grey and shapeless, onto the grass at their feet.

Cora watched, struck by the truth in all the fairy stories from childhood – is this what they disclosed? That reporting bad happenings affected the person who carries it on and tells it, even if they are unaware of how it is affecting them. She thought she should tell Sophie what was happening, but it would have been no use, they were on different planes. She was also too polite (from the same proper upbringing) to point out to Sophie that she was speaking in frogs' tongues.

The slimy animals kept falling out onto the grass while Sophie went merrily on, reporting one disaster after another. Their old lodgings were being cleared of tenants, room by room. She had been looking for a new place. She had gone after a new flat and had called round to a place in Willoughby Road, which turned out to be a heroin commune.

"It's all the rage, apparently there's a few of them locally, and the main guy was really good-looking, what a waste, really gorgeous in fact. But I said I didn't take drugs – the flat was beautiful, by the way – and so it was not suitable. He said they could take me on and sort of train me. It would be a marvellous chance for me to reach a new level of reality. It was hilarious." Cora thought it sounded as if it was near to Maura's place in Willoughby Road.

Jake had a fight with Nora right outside the pub on Sunday night, Pete got drunk and threw his wallet at the Mag and had to be restrained by old Michael, one of the teachers at that strange boarding school in Scotland who was had up for … She continued with the outpourings of discordant goings-on:

X had attempted suicide yet again, it was a real mess, X had run off with Z, X had stolen from Z's flat, Z was pregnant but didn't know by whom, X was back at being an alcoholic, scenes everywhere, Z had been attacked on the Heath at night, X had an abortion but blamed Y for it, X was homeless again and sheltering in someone's garden shed, X had showed blue films at a party, Z's children were neglected, everyone knew that, X and Z were having an affair while Y was in hospital, Z kept taking all his clothes off at parties, X and Z were homeless and sleeping out on the Heath... Cora heard it all as if it was in a foreign language or a report from a traveller from a distant land. Everyone was falling. So were the slimy snakes and toads, but Cora could not point that out to Sophie, or she would never be seen again. Loneliness led to a lowering of standards and here was the proof.

Summer evening and Mark went off to visit his parents over in Liddell Gardens. He walked back home through Kensal Green and West Kilburn. He arrived back edgy, upset.

"Oh, it's nothing to do with my parents, they're the same as usual. It was the way back, as I walked along past the houses it was frightening, even for me, and I've lived there all my life. Black men standing at the ends of streets or at their front gates. Just staring at me, really hostile. It was stark, scary. It was as if they didn't want me walking through there, it was their own district."

"Yet we go and criticise your parents for being prejudiced and wanting to move out," Cora pointed out.

"They heard about one of the old men nearby getting mugged for drug money on his way to the British Legion's place one evening. They're more worried about drug addicts."

A few days later Mrs Williams brought round an old-fashioned mincer, which could be clamped onto the edge of the big kitchen table.

"I thought you'll be needing this. Our Mark likes his beef burgers, and you'll be able to make the ones he really likes with this, proper home-made burgers. You can get cheap stewing beef and make your own, it's the healthy kind of stuff you like." The mincer, a Universal Food Chopper, L F& Co, New Britain, Conn, USA, was a sturdy contraption of interlocked bits of iron. Engraved on it were various dates of patents – October 12, 1897, Apr 18, 1899, Sept 5, 1899, Canada12 Oct 1897 Great Britain 15 May 1900. Obviously, it was a strongly defended item all over the world. In fact, it looked like an item of torture and that is what it turned out to be.

Seeing Mrs Williams out, Cora then went across with the baby to the butcher's and, triumphantly bringing home a half pound of stewing beef, began to make that evening's meal, the proper home-made beefburgers. Clamping the mincer at the corner of the kitchen table, she fed the bits of meat in gradually. The blood ran all down the leg of the table, as if she was killing the animal all over again. Cutting up the onions brought suitable tears. So much of cooking was like this, a hidden drama of killing and creating. Mark, however, genuinely appreciated the home-made burgers and so it was another item on the to-eat list though she dreaded making them again.

Another time, a few weeks later, Mark's mother phoned up to check an arrangement about coming round.

"I just wanted to make sure it's Tuesday I'm coming round to lunch. Don't worry about food now, I'll bring round some boiled ham and we can have it as a salad or in sandwiches. How's the little one?"

"He's getting another tooth. Ten pounds already, it's surprising how it's all piling on, he's growing by the second." Baby Sam smiled up at her, giving encouragement. Mrs Williams arrived laden with bags.

"Oh, it's stiff getting here, I can tell you. The bus was crowded. Now, I've got some fresh bread here, and butter, the ham and some lettuce and tomatoes. There's a homemade cake for after. And I've got some new baby clothes for him, there's a sale at Ashworth's." Like a summertime Mother Christmas, Mrs Williams spread her gifts all across the single bed that did as a couch in the living room. The food was taken to the kitchen where Cora had at least been able to provide the plates, knives and forks.

Sam's little chair stood waiting for when he would be big enough to manage how to sit in it easily. It had started off in life as a high chair, but someone had sensibly sawn off most of the long legs and now it stood set-square near the floor. This was something Cora had learnt the hard way. Everything to do with babies was far better done on the floor. She had started off changing Sam's nappies on middle of the double bed, wide and a convenient height. But going across to get the talcum powder was the very instant that the baby had learnt how to roll over and with a loud thump, Sam had fallen onto the floor. Even worse, that was right on the corner of the boarded-up fireplace with its marble slab surround. She had hurried Sam across to the doctor's then, to have his head seen to. He had not cried very much, which worried her more.

"You have to look and see if any blood comes out of his ears," was the advice. "But he seems to be

OK. Come back if you see any changes." She did not tell Mark, waiting to see how it turned out and she certainly was not going to mention anything like this to Beryl. They sat in the kitchen at the big table that the gypsies had delivered.

"Oh, don't you live rough," were Mrs Williams's first words here. "You don't use a tablecloth!" No, but I do know how to talk using adverbs correctly, Cora thought, humiliated enough already by the descent of so many gifts. There were only so many times you could say Thank You in one conversation. One had to get up from a crouching position eventually. They had nothing to talk about apart from the baby, who played his part as well as anyone could. Then even he ran out of amusing things to perform and it was time for an afternoon nap, worn out trying to entertain two disparate people at once. Cora decided Sam could have his rest in the pram while they both walked to the bus stop.

"It's good to see a bit of sunshine like this," Beryl said. "But if this weather gets any hotter, remember, you can keep your drains sweet by putting soda down them regularly. Stops them smelling. That's what my mother always did." Responsibility for the public drains; a new duty. And with that, the bus to Kensal Rise appeared and Cora was free.

21

"Don't be so stupid!" Mark was cross with her for questioning why and how he was wanting to piss all over her.

"But it would ruin the mattress," she objected

like any logically-thinking child.

"You do it in the bath, easy."

"I don't like the idea of that. Do animals do it? Or is it just human men?"

"It's not just men, silly. But they do go to prostitutes for it to be done to them, it's called Golden Rain. They pay extra for it to be done, specially." He had this authority, this extra world-knowledge, wherever it came from.

"It all sounds absolutely bonkers to me, ludicrous!" she said dismissively. "To think there are men like that walking about – or driving posh cars!"

He was cross at her making fun of the idea and not taking him seriously and said,

"The trouble with you is you've been on your own too long." He shook her shoulders, threw her aside and got out of bed to roll a cigarette instead in the living room. She thought this new idea was at the borders of insanity and could be blamed on the concept of free will, as given by God, being stretched further than intended, into these perverse areas where the Devil started to govern. She did not imagine rich women would go anywhere to have men piss all over them. It was more a male idea. She hoped he would not force her to take part in it and wondered what few bargaining chips she had.

It looked like none whatsoever. Marriage was private, here, three floors up and isolated, at two o'clock in the morning with no clothes on and a baby asleep in a cot at the end of the bed. And it was raining as well, not a time to be walking out – and to where? No advocacy advantages in the here and now, just play for time. How different things were in the daytime, with all your clothes on and everyone in the street up and about. Night-time sealed you in, especially if things were going badly. Women had to be cleverer than men just in order to survive.

They used to have baths together last year, but it was difficult to feel anything romantic or sexy now, sitting in a bath in a cold bathroom with a clothesline of drying nappies hanging overhead. When they lived in Fred's place, Cora would go down to the bathroom with the radio and a bit later Mark would join her and they would sit like the painting of Mars and Venus and enjoy smoothing and lathering each other with soap and bubbles. It was a delightful mix of sexy and childish and they had to keep quiet which added to the excitement. Then they had to leave separately and dash upstairs and have unrestrained sex, laughing in each other's arms on the large bed.

But this was long gone. Mark got beyond putting up with the awkward and the embarrassing and insisted they should go to the doctors. The complaint really being 'My wife doesn't fuck. This toy is broken. I got it for Christmas. Its battery doesn't work anymore, and the shop doesn't sell this size battery either. Do something about it, you know how, you're a doctor, it's your job. Can you give her something for it? Here she is.'

Cora sat there, ashamed, cornered and secretly quite frightened, wanting to do the right thing but knew she had lost track of her own body. Even if the doctor could change it all, take away the drowned feeling, she was not sure she wanted to leap out and feel the same rampant joy she used to have about sex. It was a lost language now, like those faint traces on Egyptian stones that no one could decipher. She was lost to herself, not available anymore.

Dr Shanahan was at first puzzled at seeing two patients.

"If you both want to see a doctor, you have to make separate appointments, you know."

"It concerns both of us," Mark answered, "We need help."

Cora felt worse, being responsible for Mark being defrauded and upset so often. A non-wife after all this time. The purple walls and orange ceiling were no use, that first blast of confidence, their proclamation to all the world. You could see the orange ceiling from the street, when the light was on it blazed cross the road. Dr Shanahan sat like a plump Buddha and dispensed mild marriage therapy from behind his mahogany desk. It turned out that the contraceptive pill was to blame. The choice was a new prescription, new pills or a cap and cream. Cora, apprehensive about anything chemical entering her body again, opted for the external objects, a cap that could be taken out in the daytime, no interference in her own bloodstream or playing round with her mind. Humouring Mark, well there was no medical way to get round that. The cap and cream denied to her some years ago at the Marie Stopes clinic was now prescribed, exactly when it was too late. (*We cannot give you any contraceptive as you don't have a proper boyfriend. Come back to us when you have established a proper relationship.*)

A few days later, a great gloop of silver-white discharge came out of her vagina as if it were waste being disposed of.

She looked it up in a library book on innards, in the reference section. The library served as a neutral friend, just giving endless information for the reader to choose what to do next.

"The consistency of vaginal discharge has a reproductive function. When it is white and lumpy, generally right before and after a period, it blocks the semen or at least does not facilitate its travel. At ovulation it gets clear and stringy, often compared to egg-white. That is the good gloopy stuff that helps the semen reach the egg."

Off to Telford Road Marriage Welfare again, with a note from Dr Shanahan, this time in the daytime with the baby in the pram. At last the pill was going to be officially stopped. It was going to be cap-and-cream from now on. The diaphragm came in a white container like a face-powder compact. Inside was a circular shaped notelet which had instructions and diagrams. The side view of the rectum, vagina, uterus, and bladder looked like a map of rivers and lakes surrounded by mountains. It could easily have been adapted into a map like the Underground's abstract lines.

It was accompanied with a tube of spermicidal cream. If you were totally profligate and decided to have rampant sex in the morning as well, a suppository had to be inserted beforehand too. A drunken or drowsy woman or one in the throes of real lust would not be able to manage all this conundrum and kerfuffle.

"You can keep it under the pillow if necessary," the advisor added helpfully. "And you have to keep the diaphragm in for several hours afterwards before you can take it out. Wash it in warm, not hot, water and leave it to dry in the open air. Don't put it near heat." It was all like running a scientific experiment. All that was missing was a

Bunsen burner and a petri dish or two. The advisor already wore a scientific-looking white coat. Love had to take on all this riff-raff burden and still seem spontaneous. For the man however, there was no difference, he went soldiering on as usual.

Cora walked home with six month's supply of creams and suppositories, with their phone number if anything went wrong. Apparently, each woman was different in size and one had to be careful. There were about twenty various sizes of caps. It all depended on the spring of the rubber edging. It was clear why so many women had rushed into using the contraceptive pill if this was the only alternative.

But the experience of being permanently underwater disappeared. After a couple of days she came up for air, transformed from drowning, to human, from fish to person, a mermaid who had survived the change. There was no one to tell about it though.

As a complete surprise, Gloria called round one Saturday afternoon, while Emma, one of Mark's wide stock of friends, had also called round. It grew very strange; Mark and Emma were always in another room, it was like some slow adult party game. From kitchen to living room and then just as adroitly, from living room to kitchen, the two moved easily like dancers. Gloria noticed a look that passed like a baton-torch between them, leaving Cora out.

"Am I imagining all this?" Cora asked, as she and Gloria were suddenly left alone in the kitchen, as Mark and Emma swiftly moved off into the living room. But when Gloria and Cora went into the living room soon after with their cups of tea, Mark and

Emma got up and moved back into the kitchen.

"No, you're not imagining things, Cora," Gloria whispered. "This is being done on purpose." When they had both gone and Cora mentioned how odd it was, Mark said it was done out of tact, to let her and Gloria talk together, and really, she was imagining things a lot lately.

Mark was definitely becoming jealous of the growing popular response to Cora's poetry although he never said anything about it. It looked as though he was acting it out by being like this with Emma. You go off to do readings and this is what you can expect.

Back in the poetry world, Clive had arranged for an overnight trip to Ramsgate on a June weekend to a poetry festival with a stay in a poetry couples' house. He could give Cora a lift, but only one way. They would pay the return fare to London as part of the invitation, plus the fee for the reading. While the festival included their own local poets, it was an enjoyable evening; they accepted Cora into their midst. The couple organising the festival took her home and she slept a sound sleep on their sofa.

But in the morning a rapid change of plan had to be made as there was a rail strike and Cora could not get back to the baby quickly enough. Her breasts overfilled with a weird pain that only the baby could heal. Any erotic responsiveness of her breasts had disappeared now that they were overloaded with fresh milk. She had to get the local bus to the coach stop for London. Going by coach instead took longer, plus then having to get back via bus from Victoria Coach Station. As she staggered up the stairs early that evening Mark had just given the baby a bottle and she tried to force the baby to drink from her, but it was impossible. That night she asked Mark to take some milk from her to relieve the prolonged aching.

"Strange taste, it's even slightly sugary too" was his verdict.

22

Summer evenings Mark would go into the deserted damp back room and watch the neighbours through his binoculars. It became a regular part of his day, like an alternative life, his own clandestine film. He could see through into peoples' flats (not many drew their curtains) and enter their private lives. It was like parts of an unwritten novel or a survey.

It was as if he was ruler of a tiny kingdom and had to review the subjects' daily lives. Cora was completely uninterested in this, but it became an obsession that he could not resist.

"I finish up voyeuring almost every night this week. Cora thinks (I think I agree) that I am going mad," he wrote in his journal.

She avoided the back room at all times and never let the baby into it, darting in to empty and change the buckets around and strew more newspapers on the floorboards. They had left a note downstairs asking for any old newspapers from the other tenants as they could not have afforded a daily one. The Observer was their only treat for each Sunday.

Lifting a yellowing newspaper, Cora saw a shocking report on a couple in Maida Vale torturing their baby with cigarette burns. There was such evil in the world, and probably all these newspapers covering their floor were full of evidence of evildoing and destruction done not far from here. You had to keep apart from it all, somehow.

Doug and Kirsty had come round about half seven and Mal turned up later. No one had any money and visiting each other was the only way of having a cost-free night out. Occasionally Mal – or almost always Mal – would bring round his latest new record and they would listen, discuss and then if Mark was lucky, he could borrow it and search out patterns of chords night by night in the kitchen. Tonight, was without records though. Doug and Kirsty had managed a new job with an office-cleaning agency.

"We're going to set up our own agency in the future, you see," Doug announced.

"So, we wanted to see how it was done properly, from the inside, like," Kirsty chipped in.

"And what's it like?" Mal asked. "How many offices do you do?

"One," Doug smiled. "But it's an entire building, all advertising, floors and floors and just us. We're locked in, and they let us out in the morning." Seeing their disbelief, Kirsty explained

"Oh, there's tea and coffee and a meal ready in a special fridge. We just have to cook it. Spiced chicken at one in the morning."

"Sounds like a jazz title."

"We can cook anything else we want if we need to. There's a selection." Mark thought this arrangement very strange.

"Bizarre. Let me get this right- you go in at nine in the evening and come out at five in the morning."

"Yes." Doug smiled brightly again. He had found the perfect job and here was an unbeliever.

Smiling brightly had become his modus vivendi. Like the lacquer that kept his long hair neatly in place on the inside of his collar, the never-ending smile signalled all was well. "We do the same hours as everyone else in the outside daytime world, but we're other way round."

"Doesn't it get spooky, though?" Sam was also an unbeliever.

"Well ..." Kirsty trailed off. "You tell them, Doug, you can."

"No, it's not spooky – there's a guard with a Doberman who trails round semi-with us. But it's disturbing sometimes, what we see." He looked round at all of them, like a stage conspirator. "All the filing cabinets are locked of course and so are the desk drawers and any of the office machines. But then we see papers on desks and bits in wastepaper-baskets. And there was this one room left open once by mistake, where they had reports and examples all around, of different flavours – bacon, onion, chicken – all foodie flavours. And sweet tastes like peppermint or strawberry."

"That's not weird, "said Mark, being superior, a man of the world. "It's an advertising agency, you said, after all. They go in for things like that, get samples and so on."

But Doug did not smile any more. His all-purpose idiot smile was off.

"It *is* weird. It said that these flavours would go on anything, anything, mind you and would be so effective that people would eat them. They could be sprayed on paper or cardboard and people wouldn't know. You see?"

They saw. The ramifications were tremendous.

Mark backed down.

"So that saying about the cereal packet having as much nutrition as its contents might be getting true soon. Hmm." Doug and Kirsty did not tell them about the other hints in the laboratory-like department, reports about LSD and other drugs being placed in various commercial foods as social experiments. Other offices held examples of all type of printed forms lying about carelessly – driving licence applications, empty birth certificates, and official personal papers. They were too frightened and wanted to get out of the situation as soon as possible. Saving up for their own agency was the problem though, fear versus finances. Kirsty felt they had already said too much. But who else could they let off steam to, otherwise? Mark was an old friend from school, and Cora was just a quiet person, she would not betray them, and Mal was trustable too.

Cora had bathed Sam and put him into his cot, brushed his hair, had put two nappies on him for the night and had given him a bottle and then spent a good ten minutes winding him, waiting for those definitive burps, rubbing his back. Tucking him in, stroking the downy head, stooping over for a last kiss and then, freedom as she tiptoed out into the bright living room and back into the adult conversation she was missing.

But within half an hour the room would be going red all over, Mark's friends' voices appearing and disappearing like bad radio wavelengths. She would struggle against this like a bad swimmer struggling against drowning. Mark did not help; Cora began to be sealed out of the conversation, unable to contribute anything relevant or amusing. A woman who could once entertain almost an entire pub could hardly speak at all now. Second by second, she would begin to drift away from them, grappling to come back. But by nine o'clock she knew a voice not really her own would be saying, she could hear it,

"I'm really tired now, I really must go off to bed, so, goodnight everybody." And they would always seem surprised as though Cora was betraying them with something better to do. And then she would stumble into the darkened bedroom and crash into a deep black sleep. Mark would give her a glance as she left the room, a questioning look as if trying to find out if she was play-acting, betraying or up to something else, with another important place to go to.

For once, this time it was different. As Cora went towards the bedroom, where the phone was, it rang, and so she was the one to answer it. They were all surprised to see her stagger back into the living room crying. But before any of them could speak, she said,

"It's happened again. You're all witnesses now. That was another of the silent phone calls. There is someone at the end of the line, I can always hear them breathing." Cora sat down heavily on the couch and Mark came across and patted her on the shoulder. It was obvious he was ashamed of this hysterical wife he had, showing him up in front of Doug, Kirsty and Mal.

"There's a lot of phone numbers in London, Cora, and people do make mistakes. Then they get too embarrassed to talk."

"Yes," Kirsty leapt in kindly. "They just hang up because they don't know what to say. It's not personal." But Cora had seen the second of tension cross between them all and at that second, she had known she was the accuser, and they all knew what was going on. Mark had already suggested another cup of tea. Cora sniffed into a handkerchief. Involuntary sobs kept coming.

"I don't want tea. I want these phone calls to stop." She realised this was her only chance, as if this were a casual jury sitting round their living room. "It's strange, you see it's only when I go and answer the phone. Only me. Whenever Mark answers it, whatever the time, it's always Mal or May or Mr Friedman or one of you. It's only the times I answer it that it's silent."

"A puzzle, all right," said Doug.

"Have a good cup of tea," said Kirsty, having made it after all, while Mal said,

"Cheer up. Don't answer it at all. Just leave it to ring."

"What?" Cora gave a shocked look. Her only link with the outside world shut down? Ignore it?

"No," Mal said. "Next time – whoever – just lift the phone and don't you say anything. Wait for the other person to speak. Fight silence with silence. See what happens then." Mark, Doug and Kirsty gave him a puzzled look and then Mark led her off to the bedroom with a comforting arm round her shoulder. The baby, of course, had slept through it all. His sleeping body oozed safety and content as Cora took off the day's clothes and climbed into bed in the remains of the once glamorous black nylon nightgown that Mark had shortened. Now it looked like a badly fitting gymslip.

Mark would come to bed after midnight as usual and would try a fumble at her. But these nights mercifully he left her alone. Or so she thought, unable to remember any morning whether they had made love the night before or not; or had sex. There was no other way to name it. Either way, it was lost in a fog. One night he fingered her "to see if you're wet down there" and said he was inspecting her to see if she had been playing with herself secretly. When Cora asked why, he said it was the only explanation for her lack of libido. She had no privacy now either outside or inside her body. There was nowhere to go. He raged outside like a mediaeval foeman.

She felt sorry for him as well and tried her best. Once after a session of sex he thanked her.

"Thank you. That was just like going to a prostitute." Did that mean he did? She had just tried to give of her best, really sacrificing herself, forgetting self and giving whatever remnants of herself to him and it had not been enough. It was like a desert giving up its last teaspoon of water. Something not noticed in a land of plenty.

She was being discarded and could do nothing about it, exhausted every day. To walk across the room meant a slight stagger, tripping over things that were not there. A day lasted a week; crossing the road could take a fortnight. Cora wondered if he had had a session with the pathetic girl in the downstairs flat where Rhona and Kirsty used to live. Possible. She would have been cheap enough.

23

By 2.30 there were many comatose men, their spouses keeping watch in the various groups of seats near windows. Bits of rust showed round the iron window frames. It was like a sea-borne old folks' home. Three young men wandered round, clutching bottles of coke or cans of orange drink, looking lost.

"I've been drunk twice and sobered up twice already," the leading one confided loudly. They had continued, changing outfits, to chase girls with temporary success -it was Saturday afternoon now and the big one was in sight. The cover of the brochure, after all had a white-clad Elvis impersonator heralding an evening of real entertainment.

Trailing behind, the youngest teenager looked more and more lost, especially without the silver ghetto-blaster that even he realised was over the top here. The ship had its own music when necessary, already provided. In the middle, or to be more exact, hovering, the third lad was perhaps wearing the same grey jumper as yesterday. He looked like someone let out from an institution. He laughed dutifully whenever the loud one made ribald statements, like that girls, after him, had to be taken off to hospital, so excessive was his rogering of them. The other boy sniggered. If only it was true. They were desperate, their leader kept hoisting this flag but nothing happened. There were no available girls on board.

The roll of the floor became addictive as if some skill could be achieved, some Olympic training done to achieve the perfect cross of levitation and gliding. It was like being drunk with none of the other sensations. Emotions were untouched; no crying in the toilets or the urge to be the heart that beats for all the world. No, all the threatening by-products of drunkenness were edited out here; just the delicious unsteady walk, that sliding of reality, that being able to surrender control.

Here and there in side alleys, gambling machines waited aglitter, dancing pockets of light enticing money out of random pockets. It was obvious there were two worlds – the nightclub end and the reading room end. Cora found an entire sitting room, with sofas, framed paintings and potted plants (plastic, it turned out) and deep grey carpet. Of course, everyone in here was playing at being at home. On board, all could make their own time; it was unconnected with anyone's life. Almost amoral. The cafés and restaurants opened and provided food, bars produced drink, attendants crept out of the lower deck and brought fresh sheets and towels; an entire community of servants functioned, parallel but unseen.

Mark went out most evenings, going round to the flat in Shirland Road that his group of friends, Kirsty, Doug and Mal, had recently moved into. It was really convenient for him. He also went round to Steve's place a until the early hours, discussing all types of legends, history and conspiracy theories.

Cora woke up one night, a sudden crashing out of sleep. The bed beside her was empty, Mark still out somewhere, as usual these nights. But what had really wakened her so abruptly was the crowd of black birds which were wheeling round the ceiling, whirling above her head. Crows, rooks, ravens, it was not clear, there were about ten of them, the sound of beating feathers distinct in the silence. She was scared, horrified and needed to get out of here as quickly as possible. The baby continued to sleep peacefully and she knew the birds would not attack him, but she was too terrified to stay and wait. Slipping on her shoes and grabbing her coat on over her nightdress, Cora ran out into the empty street and dashed round to Doug and Kirsty's flat. Even if Mark was not there, it would be a place where she could get help and one of them would come back with her to see things back to normal.

She knew she was doing something unforgivable; no mother would leave her baby in the middle of the night; this was really taking a risk, but she could not stop the panic and return to the room on her own. Running down Shirland Road, she found the right house and luckily the front door was not locked. Pushing open the door and stepping into the hall, Cora saw there was a crowd of people, as if it was the end of a party. And there, leaning against the wall, deep in conversation with a small girl with short red hair, was Mark. He looked across at Cora with a type of distaste.

"It's Mark's wife!" someone called out, shocked. They walked towards each other.

"What are you doing here?" he asked, totally nonplussed. She spluttered about being upset, waking in an empty flat. No way was she going to tell all these people about strange black birds flying around the ceiling. She could still see them and was still scared. Mark said a stilted goodbye to everyone and walked round the corner with her.

"I don't know what you're up to now, but what on earth do you think you've achieved by doing that? I was just coming home now anyway." He was now in a really bad mood with her as they reached the empty flat and the contentedly sleeping baby. "You're not supposed to leave the baby like that, you were taking a real risk. Anything could have happened, you're supposed to take care of him. You can't go running off in the night whenever you feel like it!" He grew angrier. "And you really want to keep tabs on me at all times? I need some freedom; you can't stop that." She kept quiet. Telling him about the birds would only make things worse than ever.

When they got in, the bedroom was as normal as ever, the baby asleep and the ceiling its usual white grey in the dark, the curtains drawn, a slight shaft of light from a streetlamp showing through a gap between them.

During the week Cora had a bout of diarrhoea and was exhausted. She kept having to go into the bathroom and closing the door behind her. Mark was cross that the bathroom door was closed like this – he rattled the door. What was she up to in there?

"I've got diarrhoea, that's what."

"Well, why have you locked the door?"

"Because I don't want to be seen like this, even by Sam." But Mark objected to this and said they should have no need for this sort of privacy, it was not necessary, she was being too fastidious. Any embarrassment was in her mind, not his. Cora came out to the kitchen sheepishly, hoping the worst was over. It was not worth having any further discussion about, she hoped.

Mid-afternoon. Although it was a summer day it was too cold to go out to the park and anyway, they had been out already to the Health Clinic along Harrow Road. Mrs Murgatroyd – despite her name a hefty Ella Fitzgerald look-alike – had been pleased with the baby's weight gain. Cora did not quite trust

Mrs Murgatroyd, never having forgiven her for not visiting the flat at all. Health visitors were supposed to see a baby's home setting, but she had claimed to have rung the front-door bell some months ago and receiving no answer had never returned.

This non-event had broken some thread of trust between them; Cora was convinced Mrs Murgatroyd had never bothered to visit in the first place. There had been no proof, no visiting card stuck through the door downstairs.

The phone rang. By now it was only by counting up to five that Cora could manage to lift the receiver, but she remembered Sam's advice and kept silent.

"Maarke? Maarke? Is that you?" It was the accented voice of Ines, the Friedman's au pair. Cora, already puzzled, answered,

"Mark isn't here; he's supposed to be at work at your place, isn't he?" Ines thought this over.

"I haf been out, so haf not seen him."

"What do you want him about?"

"He ees *getting something* for me." There was a note of triumph in her voice.

"Oh," said Cora as everything fell into place neatly. She felt sick. "I'll tell him you called."

"Yes. Goodbye." Ines smiled off the phone. The baby looked up from the cot, awakened from his afternoon nap.

There was only one meaning when a man was "getting something" for a woman. Abortion pills. How Cora had picked this up from two innocuous words she could not have explained. Perhaps the memory of Dorothea's abortion connected somewhere here. Her own weirdness now had a slight break of real daylight in it; she knew she was right. Settling the baby on the rug with a rusk so that he could play at eating, she tried to get back to normal. Getting out the sewing box again she started to cut out more of the doll shapes, hoping to have eight dressed cloth dolls finished by the end of the week. If Mal could pass them on to his friend with the stall at Portobello market it would be a wonderful start. After the rent and rates there was still only a fiver a week left over for the three of them to live on.

When Mark came home at five-thirty the fried tomatoes, sausages and mash were ready, with beans on toast squashed in at the side. Cold days were easier to cater for than hot days. A new quarter of tea meant they could have as much tea as the milk would allow. She had trained herself not to protest if he drank up the milk and she would go and drink water from the tap instead. How a body could transform tap water into breast milk was a miracle which someone must have researched in a lab somewhere. It was obviously why the tiredness grew; her body was too busy working away inside itself, a twenty-four-hour factory making milk.

"I've got something to tell you and to ask you," Cora said after the plates were cleared away. This was like jumping off a diving board, disturbing everything. But as everything was already disturbed wasn't it better to bring it all out into the light?

"Oh, yeah? What's that?" Mark fiddled with his cigarette lighter and the hand-rolled cigarette barely thicker than a straw.

"I had a phone call from Ines this afternoon."

"Yes, so -?" He looked a cross between impatient and bored.

"What are you getting for her? Why are you getting her *things* ?"

"What are you going on about?" He tried being superior.

"When a man is asked to get things for a woman, it usually means something to do with pregnancy."

"Oh, well you'd obviously know all about that, wouldn't you, with all your *bohemian* past or whatever you want to call it." He was right; she remembered Dorothea's secret abortion and having to call for the ambulance, but it was better to keep that secret.

"She's the one who's been calling all this time, isn't she? What's going on? It's been her all along!"

Mark kicked back the chair, standing up in a rage.

"So, what if that's it! She's actually interested in me; we get on together really well. It's different with her. I was giving you time, time to get back to normal but no, you've gone and disturbed it all, and now it looks like you've gone and upset her as well!" He pulled his jacket off the coat-hooks and charged out of the flat, banging the door. The baby started to cry and in comforting him, Cora's tears began and then would not stop. She managed to give the child his bath and an evening feed from herself, feeling as if the two of them were stranded.

"We really belong somewhere else, but I don't know where it is," she told the top of his head where the whirl of hair began. He went on sucking, safe in his baby world while her tears landed on his hair, sliding down the light golden hair shafts.

After tidying up the two rooms through

gulping tears, Cora went off to bed too. The child's sleepy breathing was no comfort tonight. Waking, sleeping, crying, she passed several hours in bed until Mark returned at some time in the small hours. He dug her in the ribs, waking her.

"You'll be happy now, won't you? It's been absolute hell, after you interfered like you did. And you might as well know, yes, she's pregnant. She's going back to France; she's getting rid of it, if you want to know that too. Happy now? And now, you can please just leave me alone." He turned on his side and Cora spent the night stifling her sobs into the pillow. Mark left for work in the morning without speaking. They circled round each other in the kitchen, the baby the only one acting normally. Only looking in the bathroom mirror after he had gone, Cora realised why the day looked so dark and why Mark had looked at her with such distaste.

Crying all night had made her eyelids puff up and all the flesh surrounding had swollen up too. Her eyes were looking out at the world through two slits set in the midst of blue-tinged flesh. It was impossible bring the swelling down, as she sponged her eyes with cold water.

"It's as bad as if he's hit me," she said to the ugly stranger who peered out from the bathroom mirror. Only the hair was the same. The smashed-up mirror woman watched her wearily. "There is no relationship. We are together alone. It's a shamble of an existence," it advised. It was hardly even a real female now.

She did not know precisely where Mark had worked or what Ines looked like. She had never gone out to East Finchley, never having the money or opportunity once the baby was born. Mark told her a bit more later in the week, after a few days and nights of controlled distance.

"You've only got to know about it now it's over. I told Ines that we two had to stay together here because of the baby and being married and all that. She's got the chance to start again, she's gone back to her family in France now. I hope that satisfies you." Although he said this starkly, Cora could see he had made a sacrifice and it was up to her to mend their relationship too. They had to reconstruct whatever dream they had had at the beginning. But there were bits still whirling around.

Ines would have obviously known Mark was married, as Mrs Friedman had attended their wedding in January and must have left her in charge of the two children at the time. And with Mark working up at the house daily, the birth of Sam would have been another bit of excitement – Mark would have been leaving to dash to the hospital that day at visiting time or earlier. Ines would have known all that, but still went ahead betraying a wife and child just as much as Mark had done, partners in betrayal. It was all so long ago, it seemed now. Cora would have to make more of an effort now and start from the beginning.

But each time as she reached a sexual climax it was like reaching a black wall, a sense of loss that did not fade however much she tried to be a new person in a new place. It was all a performance, a pretence that might lead to a new reality. She tried to make her body behave in the expected way and leave her feelings in a box somewhere. But underneath, the fracture was there, a chasm that perhaps enough ivy, overgrowth or small rockfalls might fill in and heal eventually.

24

Every morning at a quarter to eight, whatever the baby was up to about waking them, the alarm went. Except, this evening it was missing. It was her duty to wind it up every evening.

"I can't find the clock!" Cora turned to the bedroom chair on her side of the bed; on Mark's chair on the other side he had his pocket watch, tobacco, cigarette papers, and the cigarette-making machine with its little hammock in the middle, cigarette-lighter and usually a notebook and biro.

"You've probably knocked it onto the floor. It'll be under the bed. We'll hear the alarm all right when it rings. And anyway, the baby will wake us up, it's his job after all. Don't worry." He put his arm round her and drew Cora to him, pretending to be a pantomime villain, "It's a long time to the morning, dearie!"

As usual, Sam surfaced at dawn and so Cora got up and meandered into the living room leaving Mark sleeping until the time for his tea in bed. She got the right time from the radio and woke him and started looking under the bed for the silver clock.

"It's not silver at all, just some shiny metal, but I like the shape, it's sort of Art Deco, curved and simple." She had not told him that it had been left behind by a boyfriend one Christmas.

"Oh, it's not that important," Geoff had said, "You keep it. Late present and all that." She never brought up any stories about previous boyfriends as it would upset Mark and only fester and grow in significance in his imagination. No use in adding fuel to future fires.

But the clock was not under the bed. When he had gone to work Cora moved the bed and the chest of drawers, finding nothing - there was no other furniture for it to slide underneath. It was way past any sensible solution. The wardrobe was kept out in the large hall. The clock was always on that chair; the baby had not moved it. She had been with Sam all yesterday, he had not been in the bedroom except for his afternoon nap, put right into the cot, then his nappy changed on the middle of the bed. The clock had been there then, surely. Even if Sam had played with it, he would have left it on the floor. She would have noticed it or heard it fall as it tipped off the bedside chair.

They had both gone out after that to the library in the afternoon for yet more novels and cookery books. It was one of their two free afternoons, Tuesdays and Wednesdays. Mark had stopped level-pegging each book she read; it was a relief to be able to read what she wanted at any speed and not have to share it all with him in parallel, though she did miss the discussions they used to have before, like on *The Group* of Mary McCarthy or *Cider with Rosie*. Perhaps the influx of cookery books had caused this lack of interest, plus Mark had his own line of study, his T.H White and other sagas he was rapidly consuming as part of his own research. He had embarked on writing a complicated saga that held so many myths and fables that he often lost his way and had to go back and retrace his steps again and again, all the time adding even more names and quotations to the mix. Weekly he wrote down even more books for Cora to collect from the library.

"It's the only free resource that we have access to. The powers that be will start restricting it if they can. So, did you leave the flat door open when you went out? You do sometimes, when you pop down for the milk and the oil, you don't lock it. And when you go across to Mrs Mac's for shopping, do you leave it unlocked then, too? You must have left the Yale on the snick?"

"No, I wouldn't do that. Anyway, the front door is always automatically locked downstairs, you know that. The only people in this building would be the ones in the next flat down, Mr Osram and his wife. Their little boy would be at school, Mr Osram, he'd be at work, Mrs Osram would be the only one perhaps still at home. But how would she or whoever know the door might be open and the clock was there?"

"It's small enough to shove in a pocket. There's not much else to take, not in our flat!"

"The couple upstairs, the Palmers, are out all day at work– then I can hear them come in and sometimes hear their footsteps above. She runs up the stairs after four o'clock. And I can hear downstairs radio from the Osram's if they are in. I can't see the elderly music-hall couple from flat two coming all this way up to steal a small clock – and they seem such a nice couple and not in need of any money. And as for Madame Perpignan – well, she's too plump to traipse up all these stairs and I doubt whether a little clock would mean anything to her and it's the same for Gervaise in the basement."

There it remained, a mystery, with the family below in flat three left as the only possible suspects, and that was only possible if Cora had left their door unlocked, which she denied. Did she, didn't she? End of story, apart from unease and her doubting herself, expecting the clock to reappear by the bedside or be found crunched against the skirting board or mixed in with Sam's toys.

It was only some weeks or so later, rummaging about in the sideboard drawer, Mark was impatiently looking for his binoculars, usually kept in the left-side drawer of the white-painted sideboard. They were both proud of rescuing the neglected piece of Victorian furniture with its intricately carved doors from Fred's garden, discarded in the rain. It had been counted as one of their wedding presents from Fred along with the lumpy double bed and the narrow single bed they now used as a sofa.

"Have you moved the binoculars?" he wondered.

"Aren't they in the drawer, that one?" Mark gave her an unbelieving glance. "I've just looked there, silly." They were not in the other drawer, nor had they fallen into the cupboard below. Not in the kitchen either, not on the bookcase, not on the windowsill of the unlit and deserted back room. Not behind or underneath any of the three beds, not in the dirty linen basket, not in the bottom of the wardrobe, not in the baby's basket of toys or under his cot.

"They're in a plastic-y imitation leather case, they're far too heavy for Sam to lift. And he'd need a chair to reach that far up. Are you sure you haven't left them in the back room?" The water-infested back room was his favourite place for spying across the wide recreation grounds in the evenings. Mark strode into the back room and was back in an instant.

"No. And I'd never have left them there on the windowsill, too damp." As the back room was liable to flood at any time a collection of buckets, bowls and even yellowing newspapers covered most of the floor. It was left to stew. There was no furniture. They had to be careful to keep the buckets and any containers right underneath any potential leaks from the ceiling.

Fred had been here with his building firm and had mended the ceiling and roof, which was how they had been inveigled into moving here.

"This back room - wonderful view – will be perfect for you to have a lodger in, that will bring down your rent easily," he pointed out. At the time, Cora looked up at the corner where the plasterboard was left with a completely open corner. She did not have to say anything.

"Oh, that's so we can see if there's any complications as it all dries out," he cheerfully added. They had got away with it so far. But after Mark and Cora had moved in, a mixture of thawing snow and a winter deluge broke through. Rainwater streamed down, seeping through their floorboards to the flat below. Mr Osman had come banging on their door, not a happy man as water was falling onto his sofa in the flat beneath theirs.

"My wife and son were watching television and suddenly all this drip, drip started on us all. We wondered what was going on. What is happening up here?" They showed him the deserted room, unaware, that first time, how bad the situation was. Promising to get more buckets and bowls they apologised for something that had not been their fault.

Fred was brought back by the landlord to re-seal the tarred flat roof belonging to the Palmers' above. Mrs Palmer loved her roof garden apparently and it was her darting about watering and fiddling with plant pots that had broken up the seal of the tar. But the landlord over in Brighton was not going to retar the roof garden every month or so and Mrs Palmer certainly was not going to stop enjoying bounding across her beloved garden in the sky. The Osmans had every right to sit on their sofa and not be spattered with water from the ceiling. Mark and Cora were trapped between two warring factions but getting all the blame. But one evening Mark had come into the living room almost ashen faced.

"I was just in the back room looking at the gardens and everything and all, and... well, there was someone with binoculars staring right back at me from a window over the other side. Really scary. A real shock, I wasn't expecting anything like that, it was really intimidating."

That was the last time he had used them. And now Mark was accusing Cora of stealing, or, well, selling the binoculars.

"It's all right Cora," he said sympathetically, "I know how things are. We're in a tight fix. If you want to tell me all about it, I'll understand." He sat beside her and gently put his arm round her. "Did you sell it, or did you go to a pawn shop? We might be able to get the binoculars back, then, if we're quick enough." Cora looked at him, puzzled.

"But I don't know of any pawnbrokers near here at all. There might be one, way down Edgware Road but that's too far to go with the pram. Anyway, where would I hide the pawn ticket? And if I'd had any extra money it would really show immediately, we'd have had more milk and cakes and real beef and even real salted butter."

"Hmm. You know how the bedside clock

disappeared? Well, Mr Osman could easily have nipped up here and pinched the binoculars as well. What do you think of that?" Mark suggested. "He could have heard you go out that time too."

"You mean in revenge for the leak? But that was months ago and anyway he would have been at work."

"Hold on, there's also Mrs Osman, she's at home and their boys about ten isn't he and he might have been home ill or a half-day or something. They could easily have nipped up while you were at the library that day." Cora insisted again that she had closed the door properly when she had gone off with Sam to the library those weeks ago, the Yale lock clicking behind her.

"Look, even if that Yale lock was on the snick, no one passing by – and why should they – would have guessed the door was not totally locked. You mean to say that each and every time I went out, any of the Osmans dashed up to check the door to pinch something? No, I can't believe that." But by now she was doubting her own version of events and could not remember how she got back in. Just pushed the doorhandle or had to use the key? She could not say for definite. The details whirred around, and it did not make sense. Sam, sensible as ever sat on the carpet with his new toy from his grandparents, a small circus roundabout with little plastic figures sitting on multicoloured horses.

She began to cry, not because of the accusations but because of the madness of it all. None of it made sense. Things were disappearing and she was somehow responsible, but she had no memory of handling these two items. Clincher – if she *had*, where was the money? What had she done with it? She had none. It remained an unsettling mystery.

The next week, Mark had an idea.

"There's something I've remembered. Should have thought of it before, it all makes sense. They mentioned it in the office when I told them where I lived. Apparently, there's a lot of burglaries committed round here by people climbing along the roofs and balconies and entering flats through the windows. That's probably what's happened. They watch places – they'd have seen you going out with the pram, they could hardly miss you with that and so they know the place is empty. So, a whistle up to their accomplice then, and they could be in and out in a few minutes and you none the wiser. That's what probably happened." Then he thought of something else. "Remember when the nappies flew down into the street?"

One day of good weather, and Cora had put the drying rack out onto the little balcony outside the living room with the nappies hung out to dry in the sun. But a gust of wind meant that several floated off and landed on the pavement, as she did not have any clothes-pegs. Kind passers-by began to stuff the dry nappies through the letterbox downstairs, a startling instance of collective good-naturedness. So, people would have known which flat the baby came from.

Cora was both comforted and disheartened by this. How would the person in the street remember exactly which flat she was coming from? Was her every movement being watched and did they know now there was nothing else to steal? What if she came back too early and the burglar was still in the flat? In the middle of the afternoon? They would be easily visible from the street below, doing all this aerial breaking in at the front of the houses. Their flat was not at the top floor, they would have needed a rope to abseil down from the rooftop in full view of the street.

Or the burglar would have climbed into the Palmers' flat above, through a sash window, assuming the Palmers were both out at work, and then let themselves through their place, not stealing anything at all. They would have come downstairs and tried the door into their own flat, found the binoculars and disappeared down all the flights of stairs not being noticed. After all that they let themselves out of the front door downstairs, with amazing good luck. It did not make sense. It was the pigeon fleas all over again, only far worse.

The seven-day baby foods became the Holy Grail, the first things to buy every week as money got tighter and tighter. Those main baby meals had to be ring-fenced as nothing became certain anymore. The line of merry little tins stood on the shelf, each day with its own identity of main meal and afters.

Gerber did a different range of flavours, but they cost a penny more for their shiny glass jars and so were not a possibility. She lusted after them in the window of the chemists in Clifton Road. Eleven pence each and completely out of reach.

As it got worse and worse later that year, many of the items on the kitchen list grew scarce or were never bought again, but the weekly fourteen Heinz baby food tins remained. Gradually the braising steak turned into stewing beef and then into whatever scraps were left on the butcher's trays. The gorgeous young assistant with his dark eyes seemed to know how bad things were for them as he followed their choices of cheaper and cheaper meat. And then she had the bright idea of buying something on the butcher's tray of bones, stacked next to the offal – a bone that would have appealed to any dog. The young assistant managed to exude sympathy, guessing they had no dog, it was for human consumption. He wrapped it in greaseproof paper as though it was a special present.

It was only when she got back to the kitchen, having carried Sam all the way up the stairs after bringing up the shopping that Cora looked at what she had bought. It was a full working knee joint of some large animal. A bull or a cow, or a mammoth. It still worked.

Any medical student would have been delighted - a complete working knee, like an anatomical model. But she felt like a murderer and quickly put it into the large saucepan and started peeling carrots and potatoes to normalise it. After boiling it for what seemed ages, a few bits of meat detached themselves from the bone. That made the details of bone even worse and she decided to never get something like this again.

Bits of sustenance from it would steep into the stew with any luck. Mark quite liked the thick stew even if it was not his favourite beef concoction. With plenty of bread it filled enough corners for the time being. No wonder they were tetchy, with days hung between one scanty mealtime and another. Scraps of end-of-slice bacon would be the only way out now. The butcher's assistant followed their gradual change of orders, taking items from the scraps tray, mixed ends of meats really meant for dogfood. There was a genuine glimmer of sympathy from his eyes – even Mark said he noticed it when he had fetched whatever scraps of stewing beef they could get. And later Cora often wanted to tell him everything when times got bad. But the next day, the bones having been stripped of any disguise showed the workings of the muscles and ligaments and how silkily and smoothly the hub rotated in its socket. She wrapped it up and took it separately down to the bins in the basement area like a killer disposing of evidence.

On some summer Sundays they were taken to visit Grandpa's allotment. He drove them all in the car to this backwoods assortment of thriving and messy plots. It was a strange mixture of indoors and outdoors, as Beryl produced fold-up chairs and a thermos of tea and mugs and cake. They sat and admired his rows of vegetables, but his real pride was the dahlias, which he entered into various competitions each year. Now and again he won first prize as the blooms grew more perfect and resplendent during the season.

They sat in a group, as if at home on a carpet in a front room. Mr. Williams took photos to share with his relatives. When Cora saw the photos a few weeks later she was amazed that there was no trace of the sadness behind her laughter in photo. They looked like a normal family on an afternoon's outing. Back at their house, Beryl loaded up a box of food for them to take home and a few of her cast-off dresses. It was a clear label of kindness and their need.

"It's not much help, now, really is it," Mark mused when they got home, "to see you wearing my mother's old clothes."

"They'll do for the time being, until I make some new ones." The few tops and skirts left over from Hampstead days were shabby now and the overpretty dresses were of no use at all, so daytime clothes were needed like this, she was not in a position to refuse.

Mark decided he wanted to move to the country. It was definitely the best thing to do right now.

"Beware all enterprises that require new clothes," That's definitely the civil service summed up, all right." He quoted Thoreau's *Walden: A Life in the Woods* and listened to *The Incredible String Band* and Cecil Sharp's collected folk songs – all of them led away from here. He was influenced by whatever he was currently reading too. It did not matter that Henry Thoreau had lived in a cabin for a mere two years, without any wife and child, claiming he had lived on fruit, vegetables and rows of beans. It did sound impracticable, Cora pointed out W.B. Yeats's nine rows of beans, in the Innisfree poem, which was surely excessive for just one person? Mark said that packets of seeds or beans always came in excessive numbers, his Dad was always complaining about that, the allotment couldn't always have yards of rows of any vegetable. The Incredible String Band whirled on and on. It ate into Cora's mind day after day but Mark could not get enough of it. For him it was a modern folk song, countryside dragged into Carnaby Street and Portobello Road.

This week his driving interest was *Back to Nature,* Thor Heyerdahl's account of living with his bride on an island in the Pacific, isolated from any civilisation and how revealing it was, starting with constructing a hut out of plaited bamboo. The couple had left Fatu-Hiva to visit a larger island for supplies. When they returned after a few months, they found the jungle had begun to recapture the clearing and nature had taken over. Thor Heyerdahl's wish to live a life being at one with nature was certainly tested to its uttermost here.

While they had been away, the main four bamboo poles rammed into the ground had sprouted greenery and leaves covered the roof, with branches spreading across. The cabin door was plaited with creepers and they had to shake the whole frame loose. This was their jungle home. Mark was inspired. He wanted the same experience, more or less. It escaped him that the account was from a stay on a Pacific island in the nineteen thirties, when even London would have been more countrified.

"We're going to live in the country, we can do without electricity, we can go back to the land and grow our own food. It's obviously a far better existence than living here in an urban centre like London." They already had the oil-lamp with its golden glow, from their last time of having any surplus money, an early Christmas present they'd paid for together. Cora obediently dismantled the electric foot-pedal from the sewing machine and threw it in the rubbish, another decisive step into that free future of greenery. They were already living in a form of nineteenth century living, as a way of coping with lack of money; country living was an obvious next step, growing their own potatoes, tomatoes and even keeping hens; it would all work out better. Probably somewhere in Wales would be the best place.

"We could even save up and buy some land, that would be massive, there must be cheap places hidden here and there," Mark added.

To take it further, the next time she went to the library she got out books on wartime cooking and rationing and was fascinated by the idea of haybox cookery. They still had a tea chest in the back room, left over from moving in, but where could they get hold of hay? Mark suggested a pet shop, they would sell that sort of thing as bedding for rabbits and so on. A thick blanket was also necessary, placed on top to retain the warmth. But reading the full instructions it seemed something more suited for an apocalyptic crisis. The haybox had to be near the stove in the kitchen: the cooking saucepan had to avoid any temperature loss. The photos showed a large iron saucepan, a genuine example of luxury.

"You'd never be able to lift that, it's really heavy, once you've got it filled up with meat and veg," Mark pointed out. "But as a scientific experiment it would be interesting if we could try it one day. Preferably when we won't care if it all goes wrong," he added. Cora was entirely mistrustful of the method.

"It says you put a bacon joint in and surround it with vegetables, cook on the stove and bring it all to a rapid boil, simmer for 15 minutes, then dash off to the haybox, cover it all over and leave it for *ten whole hours!* But how would it cook properly? I'd be worried about undercooking and poisoning everyone. It must be one of the riskiest ways of cooking ever." She could still see the Christmas pudding proudly made in their bedsit last year, and how it had remained pale and floury right up to the end, taking over five hours to change into its proper brown richness. It had taken an entire day, with her not being able to leave, constantly topping up the pan as the boiling water clouded their room with steam. The haybox looked like another version of the same thing, with added possibility of botulism.

25

Europe was growing restive and after the March 17th Demo against the Vietnam War, the determination to make a difference grew among more than the original 25,000 who had marched from Trafalgar Square to Grosvenor Square. The disruptive and confident opposition whirled around them all summer.

By October, a bigger demo had been planned, for the 27th, with rumours of a sit-in at the London School of Economics. There were other stoppages planned, with universities and colleges all over the country joining in. The real focus, of course, was the American Embassy in Grosvenor Square although everyone knew that would be heavily defended. The Government could not afford to lose face with its American overlords, so as usual the demo would be diverted to Hyde Park where no one would see it.

Mark and Cora could look down like lighthouse-keepers and watch a group of young people coming out of a front door opposite to join a larger group waiting at the end of the Crescent. Standing on the wide steps, a boy and girl unfurled a sheet-made banner, *"Stop the War."* Giggling as the other lad stood on the pavement – the first time it had been seen in the open air - they wound it back round one of its poles, probably a broom handle and went off down the

Crescent along to Warwick Avenue and into town with the others.

Other lively groups of protesters went by, also on their way to Grosvenor Square. There was an air of excitement. Something big was brewing. Mark leant over their balcony watching them.

"We can't go. We can't get involved," Mark said, like a child not invited to a party. But Cora understood perfectly. She too, felt jealous of the enthusiasm and confidence of the chattering groups along the road.

"What about we could go and watch, stand at the edge? We'd be safe there. Just watching."

"You don't know. The police do swoops and catch up whoever's in reach. They have mounted police too, it can get dangerous, we've seen it on telly after all. Plus, we could get separated. Fights break out – you'd be unmoveable with the pram; you'd get trapped in the thick of it." Cora watched the group with the banner turn the corner out of sight to Warwick Avenue Station The baby gurgled and pointed like a tiny king from his balcony.

"If you got taken, though, it would be just as bad. Even if you got home tonight, there'd be a court case. And we can't afford a fine, or even if you had to have a day off work to go to court. If they really arrested you and you got into prison...or lost your job..." She tailed off into annihilation. Only the glass in the window separated them from all that disaster.

" But if you got arrested I'd have to stay at home with the baby or give him to my Mum and Dad. All our life would be knackered. Normal families like us can't take part. Only people who can risk it, are people with nothing to lose. No children, no risky jobs. Only students and the unemployed. Then they criticise them and say they're irresponsible. We can't win."

But then Mark turned round,

"Oh, what the hell, let's go, anyway. If we keep to the absolute edge, we look respectable enough, taking a baby for an afternoon walk. We might see the TV vans and all that."

"The mounted police? Sam 'd really like to see them."

"Too dangerous. The horses could get startled and rear up."

"But we're going?" Their eyes met and they grinned.

"Yep." Their youth was paramount. They had to join in. To stay away was to be old before your time. Cora agreed, packing extra nappies, orange juice, biscuits and toys. Her shoes needed mending, but it did not look like it was going to rain. This excitement was more important than worrying about shoes.

Mark and Cora stood with the pram at the edge of the crowd, deciding not to go on to the rest of the march to Hyde Park. She watched from the corner of Lees Place at the demo fermenting round the embassy where so many of the secretaries and maintenance workers had come from the past to the little sandwich shop where she worked. Demonstrators outside, the ghosts of those English workers inside, the world at crossroads and Vietnam separating them all. She remembered how the London-born typists with snazzy Victor Sassoon haircuts ordering lunchtime sandwiches used to say *tomayto* and mayo, in homage to their employers. They would also have said

*Add*ress, if asked, becoming more and more fake Americans by the day.

They sped back home with the pram to see whatever the TV news could tell them about what they had just seen and taken part in. With the baby fed and cups of tea on the little coffee table they moved from BBC to ITV in constant flux. The six o'clock BBC news led with scenes of Grosvenor Square outside the American Embassy and the mounted police. Switching rapidly from the BBC to ITV they watched how news was made. The BBC said it was only 20,000 on the march whereas ITV upped it to 40,000. They watched the lie unfold. 4,000 were actually in Grosvenor Square itself. It was inevitable that the American Embassy was the centre for the real clash between police and demonstrators, not the wilds of Hyde Park. The establishment did not want this demo to appear out of control for any transmission to American TV networks.

"They always want to shunt people off to the middle of nowhere in Hyde Park, where no one can see them. They're stopping demos in Trafalgar Square too, because there, well, you are obvious, and you can snarl up the traffic. They want dissent to be hidden and not discommode people on buses or driving through London," Mark said, worldly-wise, "We've just been educated," as he rolled another skimpy cigarette. The exhilaration had worn off and both felt defeated. The bottom of the bucket had been reached.

"We couldn't go in any further, you know that. If I got arrested I might even get the sack, as a civil servant, we are supposed to be neutral."

26

Beyond the Sea - that was from the Charles Trenet song, banned by Desert Island Discs. Although the pretend castaways were surrounded by apparent water, too many of them wanted a song about the sea being the cradle of their heart.

Perhaps the irony of this, repeated, had frightened the producers. Here on board, the sea was both reassuring and threatening. Its absorbing strength gave her vertigo, so that she was attracted to it, to throw herself into it, yet at the same time was repulsed by the threat of its depth, of annihilation. The lifeboat would have to be quick. It was so like marriage, that beautiful surface and the enthralling depths beneath. "In thrall" - no one mentioned that being possible since Shakespeare and Midsummer Night's Dream.

The couples on the covers of Hello magazine navigated these treacherous waters constantly, changing partners, divorcing, re-marrying and all the time managing to remain photogenic.

No trace was ever given of their bad times or how they got through them.

Cora started to make notes about their poverty. She had some idea of doing a book called 'Make a Success of Being Poor,' after the brash American style of articles in Writers' Digest:

'*I Became a Corporation President – after leaving school at 14*'

'*Blindness, Deafness and Malaria did not hold me back from mountain-climbing*'.

'Just three words a day – and now I speak ten languages.'
'Now I earn thousands after taking just one lesson.'

Such messianic glee in spreading their getting-up-from-nowhere zealotry could surely be applied to straitened housekeeping. By chance, that weekend The Observer had a question for its readers, as a professor had written in saying his family could not make ends meet on his wage of £2,000 a year. Advice was asked for. Cora sat down and began. They were experts on this, easily.

A polite official letter from The Observer arrived on good-quality paper and in an excellent envelope. Her letter was going to be used in the follow-up article. Mark was delighted. Their life had become technicolour and was going to be splashed all over the colour supplements. On Sunday morning he went across to Mrs Mac's early and returned home with their weekly luxury, the Sunday paper. It held all the new records, films, plays, concerts and books that they would never see, plus political alarms and other social hazards and trends to look out for. Katharine Whitehorn's column reassured and piqued interest like a wise aunt, the prefect distant relative. This week's column was even entitled 'Mums with the weeps' dispelling the idea that it was terrible for a mother to not feel delighted at all times with her new baby. As usual, the advice faded out after its title had done its work.

The article they were looking for, advice for the lecturer and his family who could not manage living on £2,000 a year, was buried in the ordinary columns of newsprint. No coloured photo layouts but some of their snippets were there, mixed with other contributors:

If you have radio and TV, do you need a daily paper?

How much hot water do you waste? Remember that wartime red line round the inside of baths – are yours two feet deep?

As you have an appearance to keep up, it is far more difficult for you than us near-hippies. Try shopping at Oxfam for clothes and books.

Start brewing your own beer (at about twelve shillings for four and a half gallons.)

Write articles for magazines, write a book, play, TV series. Sell your own clothing.

Two hot-water bottles and a pair of bed-socks equal one electric blanket.

Write out a weekly shopping list and keep to it.

Get a sewing machine and make your own clothes and curtains.

Other people chipped in –

My wife shops at the Co-op and our half-yearly dividend has provided most of our savings in the past.

Cut down the number of cheques drawn – draw one big cash cheque to cover small local payments. Elimination of 10 cheques per month will save about £10 p.a.

Cut off the phone, cut out subscriptions and stop running a car, at least for a while, and send your wife out to work.

Cost the car use carefully. We discovered that over a period of a year the price of repairs and increased petrol and oil consumption was almost equal to hire purchase on a new car (small) which was at least guaranteed repair-free for one year.

The consensus was, though, that the wife should be

sent out to work and any teenagers should do paper rounds, gardening or babysitting.
Best of all, though, was one ironic comment:
Acquire an education of some kind, so that the resources of the mind may be trained to compensate for the lack of other entertainment and the scarcity of possessions.
To add to the confusion, the column alongside had an article about window blinds, at a price of eight and sixpence a square foot and eleven and sixpence for laminated material. The contrast between the two articles was between amusing and tactless.

As some home money-making, Cora had already gone back to making soft toys out of scraps of material bought from a stall on Portobello market, sewing dressed rag dolls and rabbits. Mark's friend Mal knew someone on another of the stalls and so he would take the finished dolls and leave them for sale, at a half-and-half discount. It was a great amount of time, stolen when the baby was having his naps, but the end product was quite pleasing, Mal agreed.

The Baroness continued to help out now and again doing their babysitting and so Cora suggested that, as a form of repayment she would do a cleaning session of her flat. It was about the only thing she could offer and the Baroness was absolutely pleased.

"Yes, dear, that's lovely, you can come round with little Sam and I can take him out to the gardens while you do the necessary." And necessary it certainly was. The tiny room was stuffed with belongings. It was not really dirty, but absolutely cluttered with clothes of all sorts scattered over bed and chair. It was as if the Baroness changed outfits regularly but never put anything away. There was no trace of a wardrobe, just a chest of drawers, almost crushed under towers of books, newspapers and pamphlets, leaflets and correspondence. In the corner was a two-ring gas cooker and a sink. Saucepans and a crumpled tube of toothpaste competed for space. The whole room was a total happy chaos that most people would run out of, screaming wildly. Cora had brought their own hoover and started on the part of floor that was visible although all the space under the bed was crammed with plastic bags full of bulging oddments. Toys fell out of one of them and the Baroness happily gave Sam a handful of brightly coloured cars, soldiers and stuffed rabbits.

"The families I babysit for give them to me as their little kiddies grow out of them, to pass on to other families. Sam's really welcome to whatever takes his fancy." She went off with him into the gardens through the French windows that were her own entrance to the wide-open space of the gardens, the only advantage of her room.

When Cora had done her best, the Baroness was delighted and rooting among the muddled stash under the bed, produced a present. It was a shopping bag full of stockings of all shades from dark brown to almost white.

"You'll be able to make use of these no doubt, no worry about ladders after this!" But Cora discovered later that the stockings were all different types, sizes and colours and only a few made up matching pairs. She dreaded to think that these were, as she suspected, a lifetime's worth of the baroness's discarded underclothes but there was no other logical explanation for how such a mass of them could have accumulated.

Thinking over what to do with them, she plaited the stockings into a long rope and, sewing it together, produced a passable fireside rug. However, putting a few offcuts on the fire afterwards showed that the nylons spewed a vicious swirling black smoke spurting various lights and fumes, so the rug was moved to the other side of the living room.

As they went to Portobello on a Saturday afternoon, they had to lift the pram up the steps of the little metal bridge over the Grand Union Canal. At the side of the road was a single dwelling that was due for demolition, a piece of Victoriana being obliterated, the corrugated-iron curtains already shuttering the front door and all its windows. And there, on the wide windowsill of the bay window, was a Della Robbia Bowl. At least, that was what Cora thought it might be.

"I don't know where that name came from, it's just a guess." It stood there, a remnant of some safe respectability that had been abandoned and was now going to be destroyed. They could imagine the torn net curtains behind the covered windows and the patterned wallpaper stained by damp. As they could not take it all the way to Portobello in the pram, Mark went up the steps, lifted it off the cill and hid it under the straggling privet hedge.

"It's almost as if it's been left here as a sign for us, asking us to save it," he said, wiping his hands. They went off to the market for the mix of people-watching and cheap groceries and vegetables. By the end of the day, prices could fall dramatically.

"And it's a way of making shopping exciting," Mark said. "It's entertainment and a sort of day out for all of us, cosmopolitan and fresh air too." They came back with bananas and potatoes, red onions, cauliflower and fruit. "We're saving it all from going bad - look at it that way," he laughed. The bowl was there when they got back. Not proper Della Robbia, it said Leeds Art Pottery on the bottom and had been badly mended, though it still looked impressive. Intertwined white flowers floated round an ultramarine base, twirling round the edges. To put real flowers in it would have been overkill.

"You have to admit it, the only thing that would suit it would be an aspidistra, that's what it's designed for and now it's an orphan." They put it up on the wide kitchen shelf over the broken range in the kitchen like a museum exhibit. A home was made of so many random things like this.

27

It was such a hot day that Cora let Sam lie naked on a nappy in the all-encompassing pram. He was over six months now and the books said to let them have sunbaths if possible. So, packing a bottle of rosehip syrup as a treat and with extra clothes and nappies, they went off to the park, where, being undressed, his arc of piss hit his own face, startling him. She wiped him and laid a clean nappy across instead. Sitting on the grass, she joined a mixture of locals and passers-by. It was crowded; surely some of these people should be at work? Perhaps it was their late lunch-hour, but it was, really, mid-afternoon now. A young man in a business suit was sitting on the grass nearby and they got into conversation. He asked did she live nearby and, well, what about going back there together now?

"But I'm a married woman."

"And I'm a married man." Everyone was deceiving each other these days. The whirl of sixties freedom was affecting everyone, they all wanted to follow rainbows in all directions and ignore the results. She wondered what his occupation must be, the black office suit making him look slightly ridiculous among the sunbathing groups set here and there on the grass.

Cora could not believe it – here, walking along the Crescent, was Steve, one of Sophie's ex-boyfriends. She stared, stopping the pram and then they both smiled in surprise.

"I can't believe it's really you!" His blue-grey eyes stared at her, unbelieving. "What on earth are you doing here?" He looked smarter these days, his light hair cut a bit shorter, with a more settled air about him. Perhaps it was the suit and his not being in jeans as usual. She grabbed his arm and said, semi-jokingly,

"You've got to come back for tea! I can't let you just disappear! We live right here."

"That's fine. What a coincidence – I live not far round the corner, Clifton Gardens, top floor." She brought him back in the house right then and up the stairs for tea at five o'clock. Mark was intrigued to meet Steve when he got back from work and they chatted happily in the kitchen as if they had known each other for years. He became a friend of them both, though Mark rapidly took him over completely. They discussed folk song, ancient history, motorbikes - Cora was soon edged out of any conversation, reduced to silent tea-maker.

But Steve called round one afternoon to say he could see what was going on – Mark's obsessive need – and he wanted to be friends with them both.

" That's really reassuring of you, thanks. I feel like a sack of potatoes most of the time," Cora told him.

"But you don't look like one!" he said. "You let yourself down, thinking like that."

Steve was a probationary teacher in Islington and told her that he had become incredibly involved in the problems of his pupils.

"It's worrying, what some of them are going through at home. We're not supposed to visit their home address, but I do call round secretly and see where I can help, if the family is missing out on help they're due and don't know about. Or sometimes they need someone to help them through a complicated set of forms to apply for allowances. There can be hosts of problems that no one is doing anything about and sometimes the parents are just short of being totally illiterate, that sort of thing."

Cora's favourite book had always been *Miss Lonelyhearts,* and she knew that any concerned person getting secretly involved with his circle's problems would only lead to disaster. That book followed a Christ-like journalist who became an agony aunt and started to visit his letter-writers, with a fatal result. And here was Steve replicating the same difficulties.

Added to that responsibility, Steve also worked as a telephone operator for the GPO on Friday nights until midnight.

"Oh, ten per cent of phone-calls, we listen in, the Irish lads weekly phoning home on Friday nights, that sort of thing. We are told what to look out for." It was amazing, the random yet mildly efficient control the authorities had, unseen, unknown except when people like Steve let it be known, just one corner of the blackout curtain lifted for a second. A different kind of Wizard of Oz at work behind the scenes. Cora said nothing but remembered it forever.

The baby was beginning to crawl which meant the floor had to be kept as clean as possible. To save his knees from being rubbed raw, she cut off the sleeves of an old cardigan and drew them over his baby-grows as cushioning. He soon picked up speed and could cover the distance between the rooms with amazing swiftness. Cora had to keep aware of whereabouts he was in the flat and judge by any sound to guess what he was doing. Silence was the worst.

Basil became the smell of poverty. From being something exciting, one of the set of six little herb and spice jars, its sharp smell became a stink added to their stews, as the beef carbonnade degenerated further and further. All that remained was the rough oak-like crunchy strands of cheap beef.

Late autumn was Cora's birthday. Her mother-in-law gave her two tea towels with the words *It Doesn't Take Much to Make Me Happy* printed above next year's calendar. She burst into tears the second Mrs Williams left.

Mentioning needing some extra money, a friend from the pub, Rita, had suggested that Cora could do some cleaning.

"Our place would be empty and so you could

do it with the baby, it would be easy all round." It was a chance that had to be taken although it was quite a walk to Swiss Cottage, but the advantage would be over ten shillings extra. After an afternoon cleaning at Rita's, it was an effort pushing the pram through rush-hour gloom back home. As the weather changed in winter, walking through fog, rain, sleet, snow and traffic dangers, Cora kept focussing on that little head, snub nose and happy eyes looking at her over the edge of the piled-up blankets. Then, overcome by the cold air, Sam would nod off to sleep. The baby was safe, with a thick woolly hat and cuddled up in his large pram with its hood sheltering him from the worst of the cold weather. By the time she got home the rain had seeped into her shoes and they had to be dried out before tomorrow. Screwing up newspapers and leaving them overnight was the only way out.

13th November 1968 They watched, fascinated and appalled, the BBC's *Cathy Come Home* on the little black and white TV. It was already on its third showing; they had missed the earlier broadcasts and it was already notable. The Shelter organisation had already been set up as a safety blanket after the outcry all over the country from the first showing on TV in 1966. It was too near their own story, more or less, being reflected through the screen. They were both too embarrassed to admit how near the same precipice they were. You started off with two people earning wages and living in two places. Then, it's two people, two wages and only one rent as they move in together, almost luxury. Then one has a baby and it's one person's wages, with three people to support. It had a mathematical formula that would show where the fractures would begin, the move to a cheaper place, the second pregnancy, the implacable slide downwards.

28

As a special Christmas Day exception and a sort of present to each other, they bought a pack of disposable nappies to give one day off from washing and drying. They were invited to Christmas dinner at Mark's parents in Liddell Gardens. It was reassuring to be part of a genuine old-fashioned ritual like this. Only one year ago Cora had been here on probation and now she was accepted as part of their family. The living room was thick with the encouraging smell of roast chicken drifting in from the kitchen, with the sharp tang of Brussels sprouts blending in. It was wonderful to be able to eat to excess and enjoy being greedy while calling it a celebration.

Sam had Christmas presents to open, a mechanical rabbit that jumped across the room and a clown on a bicycle. He was fascinated with the movements that were so random, with its tinkling bell that made him giggle. Beryl kindly gave them extra cake and slices of chicken to take home and George gave them a lift back through the quiet after-dinner streets, so it was a day of approximate luxury.

As preparation for the New Year, on ITV there was an entrancing new advert for a P&O cruise, with a slim long ship carving its way across a sequin-spattered black and white sea. Even as Cora staggered across the room it caught her attention, she fell into the dream it promised. In sharp black and white, it bit into her memory.

They had a row on the first weekend in January. Mark had been edgy all over Christmas and it spiralled into Cora telling him to stop being so precious and 'grow up.' That was fatal. He grabbed his coat and charged out of the flat and did not reappear. She did not know where he would be staying that night, it was useless to go round to Kirsty and John's flat if he was not there; it would expose too much. He rang up at 9a.m. on the Sunday morning and came back. No questions asked and no information given, best option all round. They had another deep talk and decided to start again. Mitch appeared with a Fairport Convention LP and that mended the atmosphere, while Cora stayed in the kitchen tired and unable to work out what to do next. Tomorrow was back-to-work day and she knew Mark hated his job. Perhaps he could see that she might be able to sell some paintings in the summer show in Hampstead, like before they met? Or was all that gone, evaporated like pure turpentine.

Later in January a deep-seated winter's cough brought Mark down and he went at last to the doctors after work. But by the time they had enough spare money to pay for his prescription, Mark had spluttered and coughed, almost gouging out his chest, for a fortnight.

"It's no use to go now, it's not fair to take this out of the housekeeping, I'll just keep on with Fisherman's Friend instead." The prescription went into the fireplace as usual. It was obvious that money was crucial. She had to earn some money, proper money right now. The stuffed rag dolls were no good; to sell to shops they would have needed proper hygienic stuffing, not just cut nylons and rags. She had run out of any scraps of material and wool for the dresses and underclothes. Even remnants of gingham and Broderie Anglaise cost money that they did not have, and Mark was in as bad a mood as ever. This week's three rag dolls loped together across the sideboard, unsellable and growing daily more unattractive with their lost promise of a small toy-making business. Mal's friend had not sold any last week from his stall on Portobello.

"It takes a while to start a new line, these are beautifully made but really these should go into a toy shop, sorry."

Mark had stopped her painting long ago, coming home from work one day and finding her in the midst of painting a landscape, a piece of hardboard leant against the mantelpiece.

"What are you doing? I want to see the flat cleaned properly," he said, running a finger along the skirting board. "This needs hoovering first before you start any artwork. There're things to clean, you ought to hoover every day because of the baby. And why should you be painting like this anyway, while I have to do a rotten job all day? The office was absolutely stuffy this afternoon, you don't know how lucky you are here! You can do the housework in the daytime, that sort of thing is for the evening!" He knew she had no energy after seven p.m. So, it was an edict against painting. She backed down. It was then that she decided to concentrate on the poetry, it was easier to hide, it never looked much and could be attended to and shoved aside easily. It was only bits of paper after all. Later, later, there would be a chance. This housekeeping, homemaking was all she could do now.

"I was thinking of how to get money, but of course, a painting takes time and it doesn't always get sold." The silly idea of painting and selling them at summer's Hampstead Artists' Council's open-air art show fell into nothingness. Tubes of oil paints cost money anyway and good frames that were essential for making a sale cost even more. All the paintings from before their wedding had been left behind. Stacked under the stairs back in Hampstead, they had never gone back to claim them, giddy with the excitement of moving , wedding, childbirth all at once.

Knowing how wonderfully any oil painting burned, Cora suspected they had all gone into the furnace in the basement. Magical flares, wild spurts of all colours possible, they would have become part of the central heating. No one had thought of rescuing them, including Cora herself.

"Perhaps you could do childminding, that would fit in easily. See what your health visitor woman says about it," Mark suggested. At the clinic, Mrs Murgatroyd had suitable leaflets about fire precautions and general safety and health examinations and forms to fill in.

"It's strange, there was a nice Chinese woman in your road was asking the same thing, recently now, let me see," she fished out another register and gave Cora the address. "Here, it's a Mrs Chow, you can team up with her and see what happens. Let me know how you get on with Mrs Chow and I will send an inspector round to the chosen address before you begin, to start off properly. There are a number of safety requirements to be met, for instance."

Only a couple of doors away, but a lifetime's difference. On the same floor, the equivalent rooms. The floor had rotten boards here and there, covered by plywood and the big front living room was also the bedroom, with a curtained-off section. The husband, a bearded Englishman, smiled as he lay on the living-room bed. It seemed they were not married, with such a difference in possible surnames. Mrs Chow had hinted that he had some vague disability that prevented him from fulltime work, though the state of the flat looked as though truly little money at all was coming in.

There must be a kitchen and bathroom at the back, Cora thought, so perhaps they were short of a room? Their son had the little front room as his own. Kesi smiled sadly and said she would like to be a childminder, perhaps they could combine the caring. Cora knew the inspectors would not pass her own flat (she had already got a booklet from the Post-Maternity clinic,) so this one would be struck off immediately.

There was a postcard in the Post Office window about a jewellery-making business in St John's Wood that needed outworkers. Cora turned up at the block of flats and found a room full of vats of coloured beads on the way to being transformed into necklaces. The rather impatient man told her that she could have a soldering iron (she did have an electric socket to run it from?) and a selection of beads, clasps and wires. She would have to pay a deposit of eight shillings for the loan of the equipment. Come back in two days with the necklaces.

A couple of evenings of charred and almost melting wires showed it was far more difficult than it seemed at first. The pay, at a couple of pence per half dozen necklaces, meant that a worker had to be fulltime, or all the evening and into the night. After a run of such failures, Cora had to return the equipment, show him the ruined necklaces. The deposit was not all repaid, to make up for the supplies she had spoilt.

To make it more embarrassing, another woman arrived with a sack full of completed necklaces and was paid immediately with a broad smile from the businessman. Luckily at that moment Sam started to cry and rescued her from having to stay longer.

"Sorry, I can't stay longer," she ran out of the office, thanking Sam for saving her from further embarrassment. Cora wandered back home defeated.

Even going out cleaning with the baby once a week at their friend Rita's was not enough, though it meant that some more food was buyable each day now. On Fridays she walked round to Mrs Mac's with that day's cleaning money and bought bacon, eggs and bread each time, with a brace of Heinz baby food tins for safety's sake.

The five pounds a week they had to live on, a weekly halter, was choking them both. Thinking of any other quick way to get money, Cora fell back into her previous incarnations, and now an almost ridiculous idea arrived. *Cleaning.* Yes, for other places besides Rita's ? What about cleaning, taking the baby out in the pram with her? It would surely be possible in other peoples' houses; he was a good-natured child, and it would produce something. So, with the bravado of sheer desperation, she wrote out a postcard notice for the Post Office window in Formosa Street:

Desperate for a cleaner? Would you employ a

local woman with a baby? Experienced and with reasonable rates. Phone Cora, Maida Vale 4537

It cost sixpence for the week, so she risked two weeks and hoped for the best, while trying to think something else up. A few days later the phone rang and a foreign-sounding woman with a rasping voice and rather hesitant, said yes, she was almost desperate, and would Cora like to come and see if she could tackle a place that had got rather out of hand? The baby was not an obstacle apparently, and she would pay four shillings an hour. The address was a nearby one in The Crescent.

It grew surreal, as usual. The house was the one exactly opposite their own flat and the apartment on the first floor was the one that Mark used to watch through his binoculars. In fact, Cora felt like confessing to Mrs Gorski that they had already met, in a manner of speaking and that she was sorry for having spied on them, but her husband had been going through a rather strange phase and at that time he was spending entire evenings watching the neighbours, front and back via his binoculars. One evening, a woman had come to the windows after switching their light on and drew the large wooden shutters across, obscuring the view. Mark turned away, defeated,

"It's as if they knew I was here watching them. Got to be more careful."

Viola Gorski was an artist, which was why the entire apartment was in such a mess according to her. Studio work and housework could not mix. Her husband, Norman, was a lexicographer and spent his days ferreting out lost words and following them from one language to another language, beginning with

Early Norse on one side of the world and Sanskrit on the other.

"I do not have clue what he does, my dear, but he has to be left in peace to do it." Viola, for her part was more interested at present in the Song of the Humpback Whale, a free flexi-disc given away with the January National Geographic Magazine. Its ghostly reproach echoed round the corridor. Viola and Norman Gorski, for all their otherworldliness and apparent absent mindedness, were supporters of the new hippy worldview. They were shareholders in several of the new enterprises including the trendy *International Times* newssheet.

But at one small pop-up theatre performance, Viola, who was rather hefty, had ruined her leg tendon. The seats, being trendy, were old vegetable boxes, upturned and as she sat down the side collapsed and the wood shattered, with splinters getting into the back of her knee. As they were the major patrons, there was no compensation, there was no insurance, it had not been necessary; anyway, they would have been suing themselves. She still walked with a limp. So, this was the chapter of arty accidents that had supplied Cora with a chance to clean their flat twice a week, Monday and Thursday afternoons. It could not have been more convenient.

At two o'clock Cora wheeled the fed and contented Sam across the road to the Gorski's to do the afternoon cleaning. Violet Gorski opened the door, looking extremely worried.

"I'm really glad to see you. Had a bit of a disaster." Behind her the black lino floor glittered with silver dust. This was the great problem, Cora could see it at once. The baby would have to stay in the pram for a bit, out of the way of the scattered glitter. It was time for his usual afternoon rest anyway, conveniently. It looked magical as if stars had dropped from a night sky. "Oh, he can go in the kitchen with Theodore, it's almost clear in there. I was doing a different kind of painting, an experiment with extra texture, a collage but all the silver powder has got scattered everywhere. I don't know how it happened. Do you think you could clear it up? Violet looked sadly along her scintillating black corridor leading to other shining floors. An indoors Milky Way. They could have sold tickets.

Cora tried not to laugh.

"A good do with a brush, then the hoover, then a mop and then, if there's anything left, another hoovering will scoop it up. I'll go down on my hands and knees if anything! It's a challenge!" It was so easy to clear up other peoples' problems; she was an expert. The studio shone with its silver floor.

That afternoon's twelve shillings bought them milk, bread, bacon and washing powder. The rest was put aside for tomorrow's food and the gas and electricity meters. On afternoons off the Unequalled Equals mocked with *Baby Come Back* from the kitchen radio with its 1940s sunburst frontage. Woman's Hour, though, came through sensibly at two in the afternoon while babies had their afternoon nap, a chance to be addressed by calm voices with intelligent conversations. Cora took the day's boiled nappies out of the big German pan and pressed them through the wedding-present mangle while listening. Then the nappies were hung over the bath on the line to dry. If it was too cold, they did not dry, turning musty and the whole process had to be gone through again.

A few weeks later in February, a Charles Winchester phoned that he had seen Cora's postcard in the Post Office, and he needed a cleaner, preferably Saturday mornings only, for a house nearby. Mark said he would look after the baby until lunchtime so she could go on her own. It would be a real help, she thanked him.

It was a professional artist's house, something from the nineteenth century, with a proper large north facing studio, immense skylights like a classic art studio. This was situated at the back of a bungalow in St John's Wood, with a contained garden, looped with wisteria, completely peaceful. In the summer it would have wisteria's clogging scent in the courtyard. The house's atmosphere was of late nineteenth century St John's Wood, a world long gone.

At the end of the hall was an impressive life-sized portrait of a young woman painting in a studio. She was dressed in late nineteenth century clothing, an ankle-length skirt with an apron over it. The woman was smiling at the viewer while holding a full palette and a brush. Other students in the studio were visible in the background.

"That's my late wife. We were so happy together, years of contentment and joy. I miss her daily." Charles said, noticing Cora staring at the finely painted self-portrait. "It is her diploma painting, she was at the Slade, one of their early female students." It was such a detailed and controlled technique, something that was hardly seen these days. Mrs Winchester-to-be looked at them with a candid gaze, immortalised forever in her early twenties. Brown eyes with a hint of mischief. So alive that she could (conveniently life-sized) have walked right out and started to talk to them in the hall.

Cora's first impression of the rest of the bungalow was how much the middle classes needed the poor, the working class, to keep up their status. She found there were autumn leaves under the bed, blown in via the patio doors. Spiders' webs festooned bookcases and windows were almost blue with misty dirt. It was a cleaner's paradise; any touch would improve it. The parquet flooring throughout was parched and cried out for polish to give it life again. She asked him to buy a tin or two of Mansion floor polish. Its adverts, strangely, were of a family of mice which took away from its shiny household ideal.

As it was still winter Charles Winchester had closed off the main studio. Its wonderful north-facing skylight, almost a quarter of the ceiling was a severe drawback on a cold February day. Stranded paintings stood on various easels waiting to be finished. One after another, each picture showed vague miniscule figures on horseback travelling across a yellow ochre desert.

"These are all getting ready for my next show, it's in a year's time. I just close the door here until about Easter," he said airily. "It takes too much to heat all this space otherwise. But I'd like you to do a rough cleanout – just the floor and whatever else, like the tables – there's no wet paintings here. I'm painting in the back living room now. Don't worry too much about the stains on the floor, just give it a mop over. Then you can do the kitchen after we have our tea and biscuits." At half ten they had tea and digestive biscuits as promised in the kitchen.

In the side room Cora noticed a jam jar full of coins on the bookshelf above the arty divan with its peasant-weave coverlet. This was his other, warmer, winter studio. Charles smiled at her.

"I've been collecting farthings for ages, once they announced they were going to be withdrawn. They may be worth something one day." It was strange to see such precise saving like this, but it was probably a harmless hobby.

Charles Winchester's paintings stood waiting on several easels around the large professional studio with one impressive easel for actually painting on. A long table was enticingly scattered with several jars of brushes, palette knives, bottles of various turpentines and unguents. Stacks of large tubes of paints lay huddled about. The palette showed a jewel-like dabs of paint already dimpled from use but slowly drying up. Cora fought back the impulse to become an artist again instead and looked at all the enticing equipment as if it was on display in a museum.

She told Mark about the spacious studio, how it was just like an art school and how Charles was really confined to the front half of the bungalow until the weather changed.

"Makes you realise how important Easter is for everyone, all waiting for a bit of sunshine," he muttered. His cough had got worse again and the nights were disastrous as he struggled with incessant outbursts.

29

Cora told Mrs Gorski that she was cleaning for another artist round the corner. Such a coincidence from being an artist, to becoming the cleaner for richer ones. Viola knew who he was and was rather sniffy about him.

"Winchester, yes, Charles had a wonderful change of luck when he changed his artist's signature to Pablo, after Picasso and he's never looked back." He was really dedicated, she said, with a guaranteed exhibition every three years. Luckily, their paths were so different that there was no real rivalry, merely Viola's disapproval. of his lack of experiment. It was as if she could see the groups of his latest pictures, all of tiny figures on horseback against the skyline of an orange desert and matching orange sunsets. Small verticals constructed here and there were fabricated into horses, so far in the distance that there were no trouble co-ordinating horses' legs.

A few weeks later Charles Winchester told her that there had been a strange burglary. Someone had broken in via the kitchen's back door and they had wandered in, but the only thing missing was the jar of farthings. It had happened while he was asleep in the front bedroom. Luckily there had been no confrontation, he had been left safely unaware until the next day.

He pointed it out,

"The burglar must have just emptied the lot into his pockets because the jar's still there on the shelf." Cora felt a chill. Perhaps he suspected her. It was all strange – who would have bothered to take them? It was true there was nothing worth taking in the large studio except several paintings. This was a weird choice. "It's a drug addict, they're after anything these days, I suspect," he said sadly, and she agreed. But she remembered the disappearance of the

Art Deco clock and the binoculars.

Mystery after mystery, these disappearances kept cropping up all round her. From now on and because of this Cora would have to work harder so he would not suspect her, which he had every right to. She did not mention any of this to Mark.

On the way home she tried doing mental arithmetic. There were two hundred and forty pennies to a pound and four farthings to the penny, that meant it would take nine hundred and sixty farthings to make a pound. Even if it had been full up, a jam jar would not have been able to contain all that. Surely it had not been worth the effort. Who would have known about the farthings otherwise and not bothered to steal any of the little silver ornaments and other keepsakes that cluttered the shelves?

Going out cleaning like this meant that their food was buyable each day now. She could walk round to Mrs Mac's shop and buy bacon, eggs and bread each time, with a brace of Heinz baby-food tins for safety's sake. The baby had gradually been drawing apart, managing to wean himself at eleven months. The breasts' milk supply dwindled as he moved onto powdered milk and orange juice or rosehip syrup.

March brought baby's first birthday. An entire year's achievement at last, it was something to celebrate. They got new batteries for the small plastic radio and 'gave' it to him. He was overjoyed, turning the switch on and off and pressing the buttons merrily, something not usually allowed, but worth risking for a few days before he grew bored, as they hoped. The real electric radio, a gigantic wooden cabinet, stood on the high shelf over the fireplace in the kitchen, well out of Sam's reach.

Baby lore got out of date weekly, even daily. As soon as you became an expert on nappy-changing, weaning, teething, colic or whatever, the child moved on to its next startling change. You had to give up what you had just learnt and start in a new state of ignorance in the next step, baby as leader. Cora went to the library every fortnight or so to get some guidelines on what to expect.

"It's not as if my Mum could help you, as she never went through it, because I was past those stages at eighteen months when they adopted me. I was a readymade," Mark commiserated.

April brought Mark's twentieth birthday.

"I'm nearly legal now! Just one more year to go!" he joked. She bought him a tie, which was an improvement on last year's six decorated matchboxes. There were bits of blue sky appearing at last.

Out of the blue, Rick, a lost boyfriend from several years ago, got in touch after finding her book of poems, *Belsize*, in Foyles. Cora was as surprised that it had got into such a proper shop as that and Rick had managed to get in contact through it.

His surprise letter and the enclosed card said he had written to the publisher asking for this to be forwarded and here was the proof and would they like to meet again? The card was Vermeer's *The Love Letter*. She was both of the women or tried to be. The educated, comfortable woman writing at the table in a well-furnished room and the servant woman waiting to deliver the letter after finishing the housework. It was Martha and Mary brought up to date. And the world demanded more and more Marthas all the time. Marys who sat around and wrote letters were not necessary.

Rick was married to Chloe for some years now and had a little daughter and it would be good to have a chat and compare notes. It wasn't. Apart from the initial excitement, the invitation for dinner in Hornsey turned out a blank squib. Rick's wife was a mix of homemaker and career woman, which made Cora feel inadequate from the start. The house was clear, spacious and white throughout, with some good antique pieces of furniture strategically placed. Mark and Rick fell into the usual male gossip about football, random politics and economics while Chloe talked cookery with Cora. A large, almost farmhouse kitchen was the hub of the house, festooned with copper pans and bunches of dried herbs. Chloe produced the wonderful treat of home-made bread, which smelled homely and tasted remarkable alongside a substantial homemade soup. The result was Cora asking for the recipe for the Grant Loaf, which tasted like a Christmas cake with the fruit taken away, rich and chunky.

In a rush of enthusiasm for this new recipe Cora made two loaves as big as house bricks. It was Wednesday, a day off and the sun was shining again. With the baby neatly strapped into the pram and a bottle of orange juice stowed at his feet alongside the spare loaf they set off for Westbourne Grove and the BIT offices. She had thought that the only way of going there and facing those hip and trendy types was by taking a present, the loaf, her only possible treat.

She went along summer-bright streets, bits of litter highlighted along the pavements and gutters, stray dogs eyeing the pram as they approached, looking for anyone to feed or adopt them. A group of out-of-work black men loitered at the corner of Chippenham Road with nothing to keep them going except their group chat, leaning against someone's railings, puffing hand-rolled cigs, trying to make them last. They ogled any woman walking past. Luckily, she was invisible with the pram.

And there it was, BIT, the hippy headquarters, a sign over a rundown shopfront and another sign showing the way up the stairs to the offices. She lifted Sam out of the pram and carrying child and bread managed the shabby wooden stairs. It was a cramped and dingy room, a few plastic chairs with an array of people – a couple of hippies in bright colours and a washed-out old man in a shabby suit. BIT did not really cater for ordinary people; it was set up for the alternative, but like any good outreach organisation, they tolerated a sprinkling of outsiders.

Cora went to the counter where an amazingly good-looking young man stood trying to cope with the problems of the world or at least the neighbourhood. The hippy couple were homeless, girl pregnant and the old man was depressed and suicidal and waiting for a free counsellor to turn up. Otherwise, Giles himself would have to spend the afternoon comforting him and encouraging him to go on living for at least another year, 'See how it goes.' Giles was still idealistic enough not to consider that if the old man killed himself the young couple could have his vacant place to live in.

Cora produced the loaf.

"I just baked this, and I thought it would come in useful instead of money." It was not the best speech, she felt embarrassed here, but Giles took the wholemeal loaf as if it was sacred.

"Too much!" he said, lifting the bread for all to see. "And it's still warm!" She was surprised at how touched he was.

"I came to ask about a babysitter. We can't afford to pay, and they say you advertise that you have a list of volunteers." BIT had volunteers for any situation, gardeners, electricians, babysitters, IT experts, therapists, you just had to ask and any payment of any sort in kind was welcome. There was also a list of crash pads where you had a bed free in someone's place for one night or longer. It was all fluid. Giles found a tattered list of green-and-white striped computer paper and said if they wanted Saturday night, there was a Becky available, she was lucky.

"She's very engaging," he said like a Delphic Oracle. Cora left their phone number and address, with the time they needed a sitter for and hoped for the best.

On Saturday night Becky appeared, a Scots girl dressed in a long brown dress, a dark brown jacket thrown over. Brown hair, brown eyes. Told to come up to the third floor through the intercom, she burst into the room with a swirl of her vast skirts.

"Oh, I'll be fine, and the baby'll be fine, don't you worry now." She turned round. "I used to look after my sister's kids and then all of the street's back at home." She pounced on the plate of dark chocolate digestive biscuits with delight. "These are just my favourites! How did you guess!" Becky then told them that it was only chocolate digestives that had helped her to get off heroin. "I went through chocolate biscuits all the time! Packet after packet and now I'm free of it." They showed her the tea, coffee, milk, sugar and mugs and hurried out. It was too late to cancel now and ask for someone else. They went off to the Lamb and Flag knowing that they had left their baby with a recovering addict but at least there was nothing in the flat worth stealing. Poverty all round did lead to strange choices and sometimes strange freedoms.

The evening's poetry reading was the usual mix of the smart and the shabby, the ramshackle bohemians and the ambitious social climbers. There was a quiet war going on between the newcomers and the old guard who were trying to retain their supremacy. Young men versus old men. Cora was in the middle of this battlefield and, as a young woman she was seen as a novelty, tolerated as an entertainment until they realised she actually had something new to say and could construct a reasonable poem good enough to meet their own standards now and again.

That evening's line-up included Thomas Blackburn, Kevin Crossley Holland and George Barker, all well-established figures. They remained sitting on the small stage as the programme continued, including some new writers. George Barker was clearly heard saying

"Oh no! Not another young poet!" as the young Cypriot Taner Baybars came up on the stage to read from his latest collection *To Catch a Falling Man*. The poor young man had to recoup the audience's attention, as many were already giggling at the rude comment. It was often the case that the older poets shambled onstage, wearing rather crumpled clothes, with greasy hair and smelling slightly of a wine and tobacco mix. They would produce a clutch of folded papers from inside their jacket and often dropped some page or other, causing someone helpful in the front row to have to dash up and scrabble on the floor trying to catch the floating poems. Then the poet would look at various pages, rejecting some there and then, as if puzzled at their own output. Gathering courage, they would also gather speed at this point and then, oblivious to the audience, go on and on without stopping until Billy or someone with enough clout to shuffle them away from their time in the sun went on stage and ushered them back to their seat. Disgruntled, they had to accept this dismissal and would sit down with a scowl.

Mark and Cora got back ready to face a possible mess, both feeling a bit apprehensive now, but there was Becky, watching TV with the sound turned down. Sam had not been any trouble at all, she said. Cora dashed into the bedroom to see if he was still alive, feeling guilty for having left him like this. But he was blissfully asleep and obviously not needing her right now.

Mark was talking to Becky about Glasgow and how she had ended up here, so far away.

"To get away from the scene, really, I had to get off the heroin and there was an offer of a job as a waitress in a hotel and so I moved to London to try and start a new life," she told him candidly. "Then I got to hear about BIT and the alternative movement and became a volunteer. I was going to be a counsellor on the bad trips scene, but that's all gone by the board now."

"What do you mean?" He was interested.

"Well, at first there was a proper quiet room assigned for talking people down from bad trips, we had velvet floor cushions and low lights and soft music piped in, all soothing and peaceful, like. Songs of the whale, that sort of thing. People on bad trips would phone in when it all got bad and they could not cope alone, and someone would be waiting for them and they'd stay and talk and calm them for ages, hours sometimes. Lots of orange juice. We had to phone for ambulances a couple of times when it looked drastic. But it got worse and worse and the helpers got attacked, the cushions got ripped, they vomited on everything and grew violent. Friends would just arrive, dump someone and disappear, leaving us with a near-casualty overnight.

And eventually no one could cope any more, morale had all worn down and all that happened then was that the person would be locked in the room alone until the worst was over, they were just left screaming and crying and gibbering to themselves until it faded away. And then they would be let out, exhausted. It's all sort of over," Becky said. "It's sad and all that effort wasted. There is a food commune though, instead, midday to late evening, sort of a less dramatic place to meet."

Mark was interested in this insider's view right from hippy H.Q. but he had enough sense not to get involved. When Becky had gone he remarked,

"It certainly changes your viewpoint on chocolate digestives, doesn't it!"

30

Cleaning with the baby was a complicated effort once Sam was older than a mere baby strapped into a pram. He was now deposited on the floor at the Gorski's while Cora hoovered the stairs, Then she carried him up and locked them both in the bedroom or bathroom that was being cleaned next. He had to have some toy or something to distract him, though often he wanted to imitate what she was doing and tried to grab the hose of the vacuum or follow the wire to the socket in the wall. She talked to him all the time to distract him and felt she was becoming part of the apparatus herself.

Mark was becoming discontented with their scrappy sex sessions. He told Cora to get a lover to spice up their sex life. Their bodies joined together all right, but nothing else did. She was coldly logical about the idea.

"And what would I do with him then? How do I get rid of him? Just throw him away once he's livened me up? You think we, or him and me, would be just gewgaws to amuse you? And what happens if he and I fall in love, seriously, and want to run off together, where's little Sam in all this, what happens to him?"

It was May now and Mark had a bright idea.

"With this new job, now I'm a real civil servant, I'm going to have proper paid holiday leave soon. I was thinking we could do a week at Butlin's; it would work out almost the same cost as staying here. The food's included and we'd need no heating. They'd have a launderette, that might be free too. And they include a nursery and babysitting." It was a practical dream, it was feasible. Bognor Regis was the nearest, forty-five minutes from London, though Skegness was more famous. Things were getting more hopeful now. They would have to save up for the train fare, but the rest would be easy. It was something to look forward to and Cora thought it would be the perfect summer escape.

But the next week Mark changed tack. He announced he had decided he was now going to have this holiday alone; after all, he was the one going out to work. His responsibilities as breadwinner were giving him problems, he needed this break. No Butlin's for them as planned. In fact, he was thinking of going to France, hitching around as an experiment. He was firm about it. What could she do? He had what little money they had. His wages were paid into that joint bank account that she never saw.

He did not have a passport yet, that would have to be arranged on Monday, it would be about £10. A lot of money she thought, unable to do anything about it. He seemed to be taking a lot of days off work anyway, it was rather dangerous to make things worse by rowing with him about it. She had no winning cards to play. After all, Mark had planned to go round the world with Rhona and Kirsty and marrying her and having the baby had put a stop to all that.

Perhaps it would make a difference and he would come back happier, but she doubted that very much. It was like being an observer of their life from far away. And why he wanted to go to France was never mentioned, it was something else he was imitating from Steve, perhaps.

That summer brought a spate of free pop concerts, starting on Saturday June 7th with a Blind Faith concert in Hyde Park. Stevie Winwood, Eric Clapton, Ginger Baker drew in a crowd of over 120,000 people. They went with Sam in the pram loaded with sandwiches and drinks. Mark's friends called round and walked with them to the Park. Everyone belonged at once, the hopefulness was tangible. It was a really hot day which made it more enjoyable. Time Out's report was that this was a quieter, more thoughtful version of two-thirds of Cream; only music critics would pick holes in it like that. Buoyed up by the general excitement, Cora managed to walk there and back without being fatigued, a total mystery. A carefree afternoon made all the difference.

Now and again Cora found that she was driven further and further out of bed in the middle of the night. Mark lay, arms and legs spread out like a starfish and she ended up holding desperately to the edge of the mattress to foil falling out of bed. Trying with all her might to shove him back to the centre of the mattress did not work, it was impossible. Losing her temper one night, she kicked his shin violently to move him away. He mumbled something in his sleep but did not move or wake up. Cora felt ashamed for having been so mean, but it had to be admitted right now she was almost falling onto the floor. She got out of bed and walked to the other side of the room and shuffled into the clear and now cold side of the bed. In the morning Mark was disconcerted to find her there.

"What on earth are you doing over on my side? What's happened?" Cora said she had been squashed and it was the only way out. Covertly she looked to see if there was a bruise on his left shin, but there seemed to be no trace. It happened a few times again, there was nothing that could be done about it. That weekend the summer night was ruined for both of them, however because of a party down the road, loud music pulsing out into the dawn, followed by a fight in the street and the dramatic sirens of the police arriving. They both lay in bed thinking of past parties which used to be their usual Saturday night routine , and how they met, after all. Now matters had deteriorated so much, like a fork in the road, violence at the party and the pair of them in bed, complaining about the noise.

Early in July Mark sent off his passport application with a cheque for ten pounds. He bragged about it. Butlins was definitely out now, its safe suburban world a miasma. He was all ready to set off on this impromptu summer jaunt abroad. As another treat and a stab at independence on the Saturday afternoon he went to the free Rolling Stones Concert in Hyde Park without Cora and baby.

"We can't ask anyone to babysit, everyone we know wants to go to the concert, daft. And the baby won't be a good idea in all the crowd and the noise. I'll want to stay to the end anyway and then you'll end up being tired and having to walk all the way back on your own. You'll never do it." She had managed to walk there and back last time but now it was suddenly a place for young people with no responsibilities, out in the sun. It was another example of the free and easy world that was opening on all sides, the summer of love that was going to last forever. Music like this was its proof positive, the future was going to be shaped like this.

It was an exciting afternoon and being at the Rolling Stones concert affected Mark, the energy he saw on stage and felt in the crowd unsettling him even further. It was ludicrous. He felt stunted, standing here in the crowd, a married civil servant at only twenty years old. The next week he announced abruptly that he must leave her for a while, to begin again. They would be able afterwards to meet again after a break, almost as new people to each other.

"We are destroying each other more and more. This can't go on, I can't go on like this any longer. We have got to be apart, it's our only way out." Cora, as well as being worried at all this dismantling of their present situation thought this was complete nonsense but was careful enough not to challenge him. She thought that if they could put up with the dull patches the future would improve; doing something too dramatic could destroy everything. And how would they manage the upkeep of two different places to live in? She knew to not make fun of his idea. Perhaps he would go back to living with his parents, that would cost nothing, but it would surely be even worse than living here with her and the baby.

His moods increased in their variety. Cora tried to stay calm and keep plodding on as if nothing was wrong.

Summer afternoon and this time Cora was cleaning the Gorski's kitchen after they had finished their lunch. They often bought French loaves with a crisp crust that fell all over the kitchen floor. She was convinced that the second she left they both had a celebratory dance round the kitchen, scattering crumbs all over the lino and stuffing the sink with tealeaves to block the drains and burning onions in the frying pan with glee. Today Mrs Gorski wanted the oven to be cleaned. Sam was left in the kitchen with Cora.

Kneeling in front of the blackened oven, Cora leant into the dark space and started to scrape off some of the congealed layers of burnt fat. Sam had climbed up onto the small balcony that led off the kitchen and was surveying the gardens on this side of the Crescent. She knew the railings were not safe; he could easily have fallen through the spaces. But the oven needed cleaning and she could not keep dashing across to manoeuvre him away from the edge. Calling out to him to get down and come back here did not work, she would have to go out to the balcony and convince him to stay in the kitchen with her. But it was impossible. As soon as she started to scour the blackened sides of the oven and draw out the dirty once-shiny shelves, Sam had gone out again. The summer afternoon was beguiling.

If he fell off the balcony it would be the end of him, it would be far more serious than a broken arm. But the oven had to be cleaned and here she was on the kitchen floor scrabbling inside it. If he did die, it would be a real pity, a tragedy, she could see the ambulance already and the Gorski's being upset, but it would mean she could walk out of here and start a new life far away, a fresh start. She felt sorry for Sam, but this was what work was like, it was what immigrants did, this all-consuming work that blocked out everything else. It was what you did when you needed money above everything else, just to survive.

Cora was still kneeling with her head inside the oven when Mrs Gorski came into the kitchen and, seeing Sam up on the balcony and realising how dangerous it was to leave him there, called him back into the room and diverted him into the studio

"Come on now, little man, we'll make an artist

of you yet! How about doing some pictures with me?" She led Sam away and set him to painting on a newspaper laid on the studio floor, with a large brush and watered-down paint. He loved imitating what she was doing.

It was only when they had gone that Cora realised how dangerous the situation had been and how she was certainly going mad. Mrs Gorski had just saved Sam's life. Without saying a word, she had summed up the situation. A child was more important than a clean oven.

31

Mark grew increasingly restive this afternoon. All he could think of was sex, sex with the half-undressed girls he saw daily in the park and the streets around. There was no one in the office that was fanciable, and he went back to daydreaming about Ines, his standby fantasy. Stuffing a sheaf of papers into the drawer he went off to the toilets and grabbing himself, masturbated until the release happened, wiping the gloop off as far as possible. Standing there he felt shabby now, this is not how he thought he would ever end up. Walking back into the office he hoped that no one could detect any change in him and that there was no lingering smell to give the game away. Miss Bridgwater, the office manager, looked up as he entered the room,

"Oh, Mr Williams, I was wondering where you'd got to. There's another amendment to the building regulations. We will have to go through the previous versions to compare this year's ruling. I'll leave the new stuff on your desk, you can start it tomorrow, first thing." He sat trying to avoid her eye.

He was a married man; he ought to have constant access to sex, not snatched instants in the office toilets or dutiful encounters at home with a worn-out unenthusiastic wife.

He hoped Cora would not turn up again with Sam in the pram to walk home with him today. He was not in the mood for that sort of public domesticity right now. Sam and Cora were like a Christmas card - all welcome at the right season but increasingly irrelevant at the present time.

Mark went on working with the building's regulation papers. It was a language all on its own, something that Apollinaire would have been proud of. This was his second week wrestling with the instructions, which were to be issued to educational premises under various local authorities.

'Where a Protected route is the only escape route, enclosure at the top floor is not necessary, but:-
If escape is downwards only, Protected Lobby approach (or approach from a corridor of ½ hour fire resisting construction) is necessary at floors below the top. (Approach from the basement may be by:
  (i) Protected lobby at basement level, or
(ii) Protected lobby formed by the staircase itself, by separating the basement stairs from basement and ground floors and from the stairs or floor above the basement stairs by Fire Resisting construction.)
  (a) If escape is both downwards and upwards in the protected route, Fire Resisting separation is necessary between the downward and upward routes.'

It looked like an apt summing up of his present situation, no clear escape but a lot of faffing about. It continued going on about Clearways.

(a)'Where in any room or other space on a floor there is a fire risk which presents a hazard to a Clearway in a corridor, the space containing the hazard must be separated from the Clearway by Fire Resisting construction.'

It looked as though Miss Bridgewater had put Mark on this subject as a way of punishing him for breaking the adding machine the previous week. He longed to go back to inspecting the regulations for history exams with other more interesting material. This stuff was driving him mad.

'A single Protected route as the only escape route is not acceptable.' It certainly wasn't. He needed any possible escape route for himself right now.

He had invented an invisible dog, *Toby*, and walking home these golden summer evenings with the dog, talking to it now and again, was enjoyable. They both waited at the edge of the pavement until he told Toby it was all right to cross the Harrow Road now and they ambled along in the summer rush hour towards the Crescent. They talked to each other in an unknowable harmony, man and dog. When they reached the end of Lord Hills Road he put the imaginary lead into his pocket ready for tomorrow and went up the steps of the iron bridge over the Grand Canal and into Formosa Street. Tonight, Cora and he would make sad love, as he called it, but it was better than nothing.

July became even more dramatic, this time internationally and the media went berserk. The American astronaut Neil Armstrong landed on the moon at 20.18 in the evening in London and on the

21st he slowly got out of the spacecraft and walked on the surface of the moon at 02.56, well after midnight when they were in bed. Other people sat up most of the night to watch it and large screens were set up in Trafalgar Square.

On Saturday dinnertime Cora came back from the almost-restful cleaning at Charles Winchester's to find Mark watching the lumpen astronaut figure on TV, and its strange stumbling on the uneven land. Sam had lost interest but was aware this was important to the adults as both of them sat following the endless repeats and the pundits giving their opinions of what had just been achieved. Cora was not impressed,

"It's called The Sea of Tranquillity. I wonder why." The clumsy lumbering walk of the astronaut was a strange mimic of the stumbling of a toddler, as the over-thick outfit hampered any movement.

"If you ask me, I haven't a clue what they're doing up there, waste of money," Mark said, rolling another cigarette. "There's enough mess down here without going further into space looking for more places to mess up." It was something his parents would have said too, a novel chiming of the two generations.

The next week Mark's passport arrived. He was going mad. Reading about the Bermuda Triangle added to the mix. The Wide World of Magic was becoming more real to him than the here and now, he spent evenings talking it over with Steve until the small hours. And then at the end of July, Mitch came round with a tent ready for the trip to France. He also had five pounds to lend Mark. It was like a game that they were all playing round her, Cora thought.

As August rolled round, it was decided behind her back that Cora and Sam could not be left in the flat alone and that they would also have a week off from cleaning. Mark had been so involved in this trip that the two of them had become an afterthought. They were to stay at the grandparents, it was not possible to refuse. Mr Williams arrived to take them over to Kensal Rise and the comfort of their normal home.

Mark's father drove him to Victoria Coach Station to set off on the adventure before returning home to a subdued Cora but a contented Sam. Beryl was cooking chicken for the cat, and it was pork chops, mashed potato and two veg for dinner for the rest of them. As usual, Mrs Williams had thought of everything and produced a new Mouli Mincer that would grind the meat up small enough for Sam to have some pork and veg too.

But apart from domestic routine there was nothing to do. No wonder the allotment was so important. There was not a book in the house, Cora discovered. The bookcase, which was mostly used to display various ornaments, held only the four London phone directories. One of the new poets had made ructions one night at the Lamb and Flag by reading out the Jones's listings, which caused a mass walk-out by the regulars. It did, however, work on an incantatory or rhythmic level:

Jones, R.B. Grocers, 123 Raneleigh Street,
Jones, R.G. 4 Tower Buildings
Jones, R.H. & N, 8 Preston Street – and so it went on, all the tiny variations balanced against the main repetition of 'Jones.' It made sense as an experiment and could have taught the objectors a lot about the use of the bounce of repetition in the

construction of a poem. He had read about half a page correctly and Cora had checked the page at home, fascinated.

The only books on the shelf were the A.A Guide and The Highway Code, plus the London Anglers' Association members' handbook, which Cora read minutely. The River Thames, South Stoke, between the Leathern Bottle and the Beetle and Wedge was famed for specimen bream. There was a study of fish populations. The Metropolitan Water Board Reservoirs had many rules. Pleas of ignorance could not be accepted. No picnicking or bathing, no motor cars. Not more than one sizeable fish shall be taken away on any one day. No ladies or friends of members were permitted to enter the Reservoirs under any circumstances. This was the 1962 edition, its blurred photos completing the nineteenth century feel with "The Committee Chairman weed cutting at Great Barford fishery, River Ouse."

On the shelf alongside were the previous week's Daily Mails, which luckily had crosswords and other puzzles to get involved in. She could hardly sit and write poems in front of Beryl. Mornings, at 10.30 precisely, they both sat and had milky coffee and read the paper, and then it was a trip to the shops to get something for dinner and then it was ironing or shelling peas or folding sheets or cooking the cat's dinner before their own evening meal after George returned from work. Cora luckily did not have a bundle of nappies to wash these days. There was still the one nappy for the night-time but Sam was more or less potty trained now.

This sort of placid domesticity was easily a way to eat up time and made the outside world into something foreign and almost threatening; you merely dashed out to get supplies and then closed the front door. When the man of the house returned from work he reappeared like Sir Gawain, having vanquished some dragon out there and needing his dinner immediately. Cora was going mad trying to fit in and longing to be alone. Anything would be better than this polished prison. No wonder Mark had wanted to hitch round the world. His mother, meanwhile, was planning on getting new curtains for the front room but had missed the summer sales.

31

By Wednesday afternoon Mark was already on the way to Calais by ferry. After various lucky hitches he blagged his way into Youth Hostels without having booked in advance. On Friday he was in Rouen. A letter arrived for Cora from Mark.

"I will go back to the hostel now. Tomorrow I start hitching north to return to England Mon or Tue. I am unhappy you did not sound happy and I cannot spend Father's whisky £££s cos he didn't sound too joyous either. Lots of love. Mark.".

Mark arrived back in England on Monday. In the afternoon he rang the house from Dover saying he had been stranded so long trying to hitch out of the area without any success.

Beryl answered the phone.

"What's that? You can't get out of Dover? What do you mean by that?"

"I've been trying to hitch out of here since lunchtime, but nothing's happening, lorries aren't stopping and I'm stranded. Don't have any money for the train or a bus. Can you ask Dad to come and collect me? I'll go back to the Office at the immigration centre and stand outside the main door to wait." Beryl was angry at all this and of course had to phone George at work about going and fetching him. It ended up with his father having to drive, right after work, to collect Mark from Dover. They arrived back at Liddell Gardens that evening to a really bad scene, her mother-in-law, losing patience, having attacked Cora. She was seen as the source of all the trouble and the untold never-ending expenses, even responsible for George having to go off after work to collect Mark right now. Cora felt guilty all round and only wanted to be back in the flat alone with Sam, at least that would have been peaceful. Beryl was ill at ease being left alone with her and months of problems burst out,

"We don't know how you got involved with our Mark! It's not as if he was the first one!" Beryl accused. "That baby arrived very soon, didn't he! Don't think we didn't notice!" Beryl was also at the end of her tether, always having to mop up after Mark's abrupt changes of direction and now landed with this rather useless young woman and her child. Cora burst into tears, not able to tell Beryl about all the boyfriends who had left her in the lurch, one after the other. She dashed up to the bathroom and locked the door, the only place of privacy left.

When they returned to their flat. Mark tried to make amends, but it was never the same. The trip to Rouen had been a mixed blessing, it turned out. He said he must be ill. He said he was heading for a crisis. A psychiatrist was suggested by Dr Shanahan.

Cora did not remark that it would have been impossible, on this evidence, to think of the threesome of Mark, Kirsty and Rhona ever hitching round the world. If he could not manage it on his own, in his own country where he knew how the transport system worked, and spoke the language perfectly, how would all three of them have travelled around in any foreign country? There would be all the different currencies to cope with, and various awkward local customs they were not aware of.

Only a large Michelin map of the Le-Havre-Amiens region and the promised bottle of whisky for his father were mementoes of the journey.

Late September there was another Free Concert in Hyde Park, as a finale to the summer. The year was fading away. Mark started contacting various universities and colleges, wherever he could think of. Almost daily, prospectuses were arriving from various teacher training places and universities. Bonny-faced students strolled across velvet lawns and along ancient corridors. Others sat in twentieth century sleek lecture halls. The booklets looked like separate scenes from a film. Soon, as October started, Mark was filling forms all over the place and posting them off weekly. He had one foot in the dream. Cora's birthday flew past.

But at the same time Mark was suffering from hair loss and fits of coughing and flu. He noticed scabby dandruff appearing again, an area the size of a sixpence where his hair was easily pulled away by the comb. He was horrified it could be alopecia. He stayed off work that week feeling really run down.

Going to the doctors was no help; he was too poor to pay all the prescription charges. He managed to pay only for a bottle of special lotion for his hair, which Cora helped to apply over the back of his head.

For the rest of his illness, Mark got by with using a packet of Fisherman's Friend cough pastilles which were strong enough, taken almost by the handful, to freeze the throat and which scorched his tongue as he finished off the packet quickly. By the time Mark had enough spare money to pay the prescription charge, he was almost better.

"They don't have any thought for the working poor, we don't count in any of their allowances. We're forgotten because we're invisible. We are the cogwheels."

32

They reached Bilbao, disembarking after passports were examined by the purser. Several things suddenly made sense - the lumpy men turned into derring-do lorry drivers and the Australians wearing silly bush hats drove off in two adapted Land-rovers labelled "Nomadic Explorations." Gleaming motorbikes appeared on the quay with their now totally covered-up riders, unrecognisable as a human species. Covered in black leather from neck to toe, with shiny crash helmets in flashy colours, they looked halfway into evolving into some exotic wasps or cockroaches. Then they slid away, curving deliciously round road bends with a sexual gracefulness.

A coach was waiting at the dockside with a courier on board. He gave them an account of the Romans first smelting the iron deposits in the area. It developed into a real university-type lecture; meanwhile, the coach had not moved from the spot.

"It's getting on for a quarter past nine and we haven't even left the port," one white-haired man

objected.

"Yes, when are we going to get started! We came to see the place, a trip to Bilbao, not sit trapped in a bus listening to a history lecture!" a woman added. The hold-up was something to do with a logjam in the roads leading from the docks. They glided up the hilly way to the city as he carried on, reaching the nineteenth century as they stopped in the Main Street. The coach parked in the middle of the street where they all-but ran into a branch of Marks and Spencer to look at bargains they could have got at home. Like the Cinderella story the courier warned,

"Back here at ten o'clock, Spanish time, we are off later to a special café. We can't stop for any stragglers. You'd have to make sure to get back to the ship by two thirty by any means, taxis or hitching a lift." Cora walked down the wide central street and then wandered into the largest bookshop she had ever seen. Shelves and tables laden with books stretched into wild perspective-pointed distance. Books were suddenly important, laid out in quantity like this, luxury items and also dangerous. Mainstream books translated into Spanish had gone through a metamorphosis and were worth buying again. The plain authors' names persisted, their titles entirely different. There were classics too, where Jane Eyre remained the same, luckily. John Donne changed to Devociones en Ocasiones Emergentes but the cover photo made him look like a popstar, with long brooding face, and long glossy hair. Charles Dickens was not so lucky, with Una Historia de Dos Ciudades. Of the modern writers, P.D.James had Muerte de un Testigo Experto, with Ruth Rendell turning into Las Llaves de la Calle. Their books spread out across the

world, changing slightly each time they reached another country.

There was an upstairs department too, but to go browsing upstairs as well would have been a type of overeating. Outside, the weather had grown worse. It was freezing and now drizzle was misting shop windows. Buying some picture postcards from a kiosk to prove she was here, the assistant said that stamps were only available from a tobacconist's, there was one around the corner, that way.

Cora found it was such a strange idea to have to buy stamps from a tobacconist's shop, not having to go off and search for a proper Post Office, as in England. But there was nowhere, no counters to write on, so Cora sat on a bench in the main street, semi-sheltered under one of the trees. It was freezing and she drew up the collar of her coat. There were two large post-boxes nearby on the main street that were painted bright yellow. That was the sort of thing that no travel book ever mentioned; the day-to-day items that made up a country and separated one culture from another .She loitered round the main street where their coach waited reassuringly.

In early October Mark had an interview at the teacher training college of Keswick Hall up in Norfolk and he said it had gone very well. His father had taken him there, another day taken off his holidays. Mark said he was going to be OK this time, he knew it. He had been advised by Steve that going in for teacher training right from the start would mean a guaranteed job at the end.

"Look, if you go and get a degree in something

fancy like Ancient History or Latin or even Comparative Literature, you won't be walking into a secure job right in that September. In fact, you'd probably be starting a teaching course anyway, if you were even lucky. So why not do the same as I did, and go in for it right from the beginning as a proper qualified teacher?"

The poetry invitations continued, bringing in a bit of extra money too. Billy became almost her agent, telling her of any opportunities and Cora one evening gave a poetry reading at Ladbroke Grove pub. At the bus stop afterwards she met a young man at the bus stop. He was a designer of LP covers and showed her his folder, with all the fashionable slightly psychedelic whirling colours that marked the new music from the previous pop with its staged photos of the singer or group. Anyone and everyone was part of the new network of possibilities, even someone waiting for a bus on a Thursday evening.

Mark declared that in the light of what they were going through they should start saving for a house.

"Look, if we are going to move somewhere when I turn into a mature student, well, we'll have to get round to buying a house. It'll be cheaper to rent somewhere out of London of course, but we might as well take the plunge. Paying rent is like throwing money down the drain, you get nothing back in the long run. If we look around properly, there's got to be small places that would be cheap. We'll have to start saving on top of everything else from now. We'll have to open an account specially, to make it official."

Cora was already cleaning at four places even as far away as Rita's, her friend's flat near Swiss

Cottage. It was quite a walk, but it was the chance of some quick money in an easy place to work in. As all the family were out, the money was left on the kitchen table and she never saw them; the flat was more or less immaculate anyway. Apart from the odd paid poetry reading she had no other way of raising money. Most of her ingenuity came from budgeting the allowance they had to live on, the unchangeable five pounds.

On one of the December afternoons cleaning at Rita's, the baby pulled down the Christmas tree twice, as he crawled towards the glistening branches and grasped one of them, breaking some of the baubles as they slid off. Cora rearranged them like a window dresser trying to disguise the gaps, although there were so many decorations it hardly mattered. But when he crawled towards it again the next week and the entire tree fell, silver and gold baubles scattering across the carpet, she had to leave an apologetic note and promised to replace them with a new packet of six assorted decorations.

"Oh, it doesn't matter!" Rita said, when Cora phoned up to apologise further. "We're going away for Christmas anyway so the kids will hardly notice. Plus, you can't afford to buy any more ones, don't worry." Niceness also hurt. They both knew that a box of new decorations would cost more than an hour's pay.

Every chance of earning some money was taken up, any opportunity at all. They told everyone they were saving for the move. The Gorskis asked if Mark would varnish their study floor in the spring when the weather got better, and they could open the windows. It was even more potential money for the fund. It turned out that what looked like expensive brown lino was in fact varnished hardboard, which both insulated and gave a smooth flooring right across the entire flat from one window to another. Mark was fascinated when he found this out.

"We can do the same in the future, it looks so expensive and it insulates from any draughts too."

In spite of Steve's advice, Mark went off with his father to Nottingham and Keele for university interviews. Mr Williams had taken yet another day out of his annual holidays to drive him there. Mark came back from the trip feeling a success, he said he had made a good impression all round, plus he was getting more blasé about being interviewed and had even bought Cora a surprise present of false eyelashes. Like big spiders they curled up from the packaging, along with a small tube of glue. Full of enthusiasm she applied the glue and pressed the eyelashes in place. It would make such a difference, a touch of glamour but it was an abject failure. They were so dark and heavy that she could not see out of them. Is that what other women went through to look glamorous, this half-light? She walked to and fro, trying to navigate but it was no use, the eyelashes were a barrier to any daylight and definitely made reading an impossibility.

Mark brought an official civil service notebook from the office for their housekeeping book as a start for the new year. It was impressively entitled E11R Supplied for the Public Service Stationery Office Book 111. While the money piled up weekly in a stainless-steel shaving-brush holder (not silver; or it would have been sold) the weekly shopping and eating did not change. It could not. Cora found that trips to the library 'found' her bringing home cookery books, which she read as literature. Any illustration showed what they could be having. She was living on coloured photographs. Juices and succulent meats, casseroles, sumptuous cakes were all there, page after page, only the ingredients were impossible to get. She was eating books.

Mark's favourite carbonara of beef had been slowly metamorphosising into a rough scrawny stew without any beer in it. Its brownness deceived them enough; at least carrot, potatoes and fried onions were cheap and the aroma of basil scented the air in the kitchen as though something rich was in store. Years later that whirling smell of basil signalled hunger and emptiness for Cora and she tried not to use it in any stew. She kept to Mark's list of things he would eat, a weekly experiment as complicated as any scientific gamble. Though to be truthful these days it was mostly bacon and baked beans, brown bread and fried eggs, simple and with no danger of waste.

33

As he reached two years old, Cora decided to write down the baby's words, as now they were proliferating by the day. The world was pouring into him rapidly. Carefully, she went back, making a list of as much as she could remember and roughly in what order they had appeared:

ma   mammy   daddy   baba   bye-bye   night-night   teddy   hot

And later on, a tapestry of words as the outside world approached even quicker -

No   hoo(ver)   book   clock   on (radio)
rae(radio)   pull (curtain)   light   dark   back
bottle   bac(on)   dog   -oohooh   parafeen

door   clean   din-din bang!   wet   open me shut   bum-bum   gone   stop   see-soon don't!   out   awake   spoon   round & round drink plop!   milk   jump   bo-bos   (sleep) bus   poo-poo   shop   mouse   two   foot sing   tree   that   way   bird   stairs   eye rec(ord)   mouth   top   nose   bed   shoe   paper sock soap   up   nana   grandpa   down   oh-fuck hoo(ver)   head   book   off-on   hat   coat muic(music)   cat (miou miou)   hand   car (peeppeep)   cold   house   like & no-like nice   milk (& milkman noise)   bed   plurals: trowies (trousers)   howies (houses)
He had become his own dictionary.

In February, Billy, who was busy arranging even more poetry readings, dashed round and asked Cora to draw up a poster for his next reading as his usual designer was ill. He bounced up the stairs with his usual enthusiasm.

"I was given your address by that artist in Keats Grove, he drinks in the Freemasons Arms, he's a friend of yours. Can you do it right now, can you?" Billy pranced around the flat talking in shorthand. The baby looked up at him with disapproval, an adult acting like a toddler. As usual there would be hardly any payment. That was how the poetry world functioned; Cora would only get paid by being the reserve poet again for if a poet did not turn up and then she would receive a small fee. The posters were an unconsidered item.

This poster was needed for the last Saturday of February, another poetry reading at the Lamb and Flag, opening at 7.30, entrance fee 7/6d. Poets appearing included: Michael Hamburger, Phillip Oakes, Thomas Blackburn, Bernard Saint, Paul Durcan, Dinah Livingstone. She scrabbled something together, trying to keep vaguely to the usual style and not be too outrageous. Billy needed it the next day as he had to get it photocopied and taken round a couple of bookshops who were growing more sympathetic to poetry.

A week later, a bit of excitement – Sophie turned up with the latest boyfriend, who had given her a lift to Maida Vale. No buses for Sophie; going off-territory needed an escort and private transport; even a taxi was out of the question. The visit would not be mentioned back in the better part of London. By now they and their flat and the baby had fallen out of all possible conversations.

The truth was the baby-mother thing was boring. It was a million miles from the nightly excitement of the pubs, their never-ending playlets and complications. Without even knowing the details, the stink of nappies carried across the ether to the Mag, the Roebuck and the Rosslyn. Also, in a home there would be only one or two people at most; not fifty or a hundred: limited choice with no changing cast of players. And no spare men. No wonder Sophie kept away. It was like walking into a cupboard and being shut in the dark.

She had politely brought a small toy for Sam and a bunch of flowers for Cora. After she had gone, Cora eyed the mixed flowers thinking what a pity it was that none of them was eatable.

34

Steve came round early one evening and introduced Mark and Cora to his fiancée Leanne, just returned from France. He had already gone over and stayed with her in Rouen in his holiday. She was studying Mediaeval French architecture as part of a degree. A sparkling engagement ring was set off by a black silk blouse and black velvet trousers. Her blonde hair reached, glossy and shining, well past her shoulders. Not at all talkative, she did not seem at ease with them and was somehow apart from the conversation. All his evenings at the GPO had gone towards paying for that diamond, its compressed energy pulsing out dashing lights across the room. A couple of days later Steve came round one afternoon after school and asked Cora to try being a friend to Leanne.

"You see, she doesn't really have any friends, that's the problem. And she is rather a deep thinker, which makes it worse. Would you go round a bit and teach her how to chat, to do small talk? It would be a great help, I can't do it."

Cora was not sure of the implied insult – expert at small talk? - but it would be nice to have any contact these days. The house was only five doors away after all, but of course in Maida Vale that was complete separation. Cora still thought that if anyone wanted to hide from the police, this was the one district to go to, everyone was anonymous and untraceable in the large houses that stomped across the landscape.

After a phone appointment (real friends dropped in haphazardly, no phone-calls necessary, ever) Cora and Sam went along the few houses on their conversation lesson visit. Leanne lived on the ground floor with the living room facing onto the grounds. She stood at an ironing board and appeared to be ironing a pile of tea-towels, they were folded and flat and looked like a stack of paper. It did not look like the right thing for a young woman to be doing in the middle of a spring afternoon. Leanne said she had come back this term to finish her degree at London University after studying French cathedrals. There were several coffee-table books with glamorous photographs that she was using as reference works. Her degree exams were drawing nearer. The conversation, Cora realised, was stilted as though it was all done in a foreign language and they could not translate it quickly enough. The pile of paper-thin ironed cloth grew and grew as Leanne continued smoothing away as if in a trance. Sam ignored her politely and concentrated on a toy car alternating with a cloth book that had pictures of rabbits.

They arranged to meet again in a week or so and Leanne said she would like to go to one of the poetry readings on an evening when Steve was on duty at the GPO. Cora returned the few doors home with Sam, feeling slightly puzzled but she could not work out why.

At two years one month now, the baby's words were:
sunshine, window, that way-this way, hello, telephone, letter, street, clean house. He could repeat last word in any sentence, and he could pick out words on radio and repeat (*sunshine* in weather forecast) Plurals ending in 's.'

And in early April fate never stopped its random events; Cora was alarmed, suspicious that she might be pregnant again. She felt faintly nauseous. Getting out of bed, everything in the bedroom went a strangely attractive shade of green. She sat down quickly, aghast.

"Oh no, I'm overdue, three days gone already now. What if it's pregnancy?" She was distraught, whereas Mark was quite calm and soothing, just as he had been the first time. He sympathised,

"Nothing to worry about, love. Remember, I'm going to be a mature student now. We'll be getting that grant as a married couple with a child, anyway, so it won't be too bad, it'll all be settled, you'll see." Cora saw the present difficulties duplicated, going over the same ground again, never being a real person for years yet. A rapid appointment at the doctor's was arranged, she was frantic.

When she told Dr Schofield about the suspected pregnancy and their planned move with Mark becoming a mature student, he was scathing,

"You're not going to get far on £600 a year in Norfolk. It's freezing cold up there, quite different from London. How are you going to manage?" £11 and ten shillings a week and a more contented Mark, plus a cheaper place to live in would be an amazing improvement, whatever the temperature, she thought. Here, Mark was earning just over £15 a week and most of that £750 went on the rent. Luckily it turned out that the pregnancy was merely a scare, after an internal examination Dr Schofield said it was worry and probably an iron shortage,

"Here's some iron pills and eat more red meat. And try not to worry."

Mark was neither pleased nor displeased when she told him that the pregnancy scare had been just that, a scare. He was far more excited at being twenty-one at last, which made him totally qualified to take on any financial transactions, like hire purchase, legally. His father gave him twenty-one crisp new pound notes to celebrate the event.

It was soon after that, right in the middle of spring, Steve had a nervous breakdown, it was not mere depression, it was a complete dismantling of self. He was found wandering round Notting Hill having no clue where he was, why he had gone there, and had even forgotten his name. He was totally spent, with no vestiges of identity left. He disappeared off to some mental hospital in South London and there was no way of contacting him after that.

Leanne called round one afternoon with all this news, shaken enough to need someone to talk to without making an appointment.

"It's Steve! He's left me! It's all over!" Cora put her arms round the slim quiet woman, but almost shrieked, startled as she stroked the girl's golden hair and found it was as coarse as a Brillo pad, not the silken feel expected. This was a strange turn of events; Steve had dedicated so much of the past year on supporting their engagement and he had planned for them to be married soon, bragging about Leanne and how special she was. He had gone on and on about her to Mark and Cora. It was a mystery. And now it had all vanished like smoke, no proof it had ever existed, the ring, the engagement, the wedding, the future.

A few weeks later, however, Steve phoned that Leanne had some of his favourite records and books, he did not want to lose them right now, could they go round and get them back from Leanne's? They could leave any of his things with the landlady of his flat round the corner in Clifton Gardens. It was a stilted conversation, he did not want to talk much, merely to leave this brusque message. His voice sounded different.

Cora told Mark the shocking news when he came back from work and said she could just nip round to Leanne's flat and see what had to be collected as soon as Sam was in bed.

"But I can go in right now, and then see what's got to be taken back." Mark took over at this point and became the go-between the two. He also consoled Leanne, taking back LPs and books from one flat to the other. Cora did not see her again and thought her university course was proving a responsibility as Leanne did not call round again. Exams would be starting in May, it would be a distraction.

As summer rolled in, they went on frantically saving for the deposit on a house and a new timetable began to rule their lives. While Cora and the baby went out cleaning three times a week, plus Saturday mornings without Sam, Mark washed Madame Perpignan's car on Saturday afternoons and cleaned a pub along Shirland Road on Sunday mornings.

Then after Sunday dinnertime he started to clean the stairs and hallway and front steps of a house the Gorski's owned and rented out near Formosa Street. Only Saturday evenings and late Sunday afternoons were left free now in the frenzy of activity. The money mounted up into the account for the deposit on somewhere to live in Norwich. They still looked at shiny things in shop windows that they could not afford, though.

Sam's new words were rain (wet-down-up) – shorter than a haiku! And he could say 'Baroness' clearly now. Other new words were taxi, toilet, wee wee, mummy.
He could point to things 'from nana.'
Says ahah! baba! when he hears one crying.
 Lady. A new word. A warning she did not see.

34

The atmosphere changed. They were both overcharged these weeks, in a ferment of activity. Mark asked Doug and Kirsty to babysit for them. He wanted to go out together for a drink in the Prince Alfred, just across at the corner of Formosa Street. Neither Mark nor Cora had ever been in this pub before and reacted like tourists, amazed at the intricate carved partitions marking its quaint sections round the bar. It was possible to order a drink and sit chatting without seeing or being seen by anyone else.

"It was done in the nineteenth century so women could come in and have a drink privately without causing gossip," Mark said, but Cora thought more of the French Impressionist paintings of couples in private booths. She saw Mark was on edge; quite nervy this evening and it was not really turning out to be a treat after all. He sat rolling a cigarette intently, not talking much. It was worse that they were cut off from any other drinkers after all and they left by the private door of their own booth into the spring street. She did not know what to say to change his mood. He did not react to her chatter as she grew more uncomfortable with the atmosphere between them.

Afterwards they went off for a walk, meandering towards the end of Warwick Avenue where there was a parking space for lorries. They found a bench under the trees and sat in a tense silence. Then Mark said,

" You better know that when we get to Norwich it's not likely I'll be living in the new house with you. It's something you've got to consider." After announcing that, he stood up and left abruptly, as Cora burst into tears.

Mark strode home along the Crescent. Cora really did not have a clue what he was going through. Sometimes he felt genuinely sorry for her but tonight he just felt angry at her frequent changes between a Polly-Anna-ish optimism and an equally childish weepiness. He had enough on his plate right now and tonight he had at least given her an idea that they would have to be apart soon. She would have to face facts soon enough anyway. But he kicked himself for not delivering a truth-telling ultimatum - surely he had made it clear enough they could not go on in this lifeless relationship any longer?

Cora stayed sitting on the bench alone in the dark, tears sliding down her cheeks, sobbing and searching for a handkerchief. From the car park a lorry driver called down from his cab, "*There, there,*" he could help her if she thought she was pregnant, he could get her pills. Family planning as dispended by lorry-drivers. His sympathy was touching, though. At least he had noticed, even if it was a marketing opportunity. He did seem sympathetic.

"No, it's all right," she looked up at him. "That was my husband, he's just saying he's going to leave me and the baby."

"It happens, shit like that. Look after yourself, now." He said from his high-up seat in the dark parking space like an unseen guardian angel. She sat there for a bit to calm down and then slowly followed Mark home.

They circled round each other during the days but had to sleep in the same bed, unless Mark's cough was bad like last winter, when he went and slept on the living-room's spare old bed. He grew increasingly grumpy and irritable, even losing patience with Sam, who merely wanted a cuddle. He turned away. And suddenly one evening Mark was standing, hitting his forehead against the living room wall, so hard that it made a thudding noise and Cora ran towards him, dragging him away and trying to calm him down before any real damage was done. The usual cup of tea, again, the least thing available, which had to mend any crisis.

At the next visit to the baby clinic for Sam's next check-up, after his Diphtheria, Tetanus and Whooping Cough immunisation, Cora mentioned about how Mark started hitting his head against the living-room wall during the week, plus he was going on about leaving her and the baby. Mrs Murgatroyd said it was not a good sign if he was thinking of becoming a teacher if he was carrying on like that, but she also said,

"You must save your marriage" as if it were an object, like a lot of money, which, in a way, it was. If it was a building or a treasure it would be easier to defend, but this was a miasma, there was nothing to hold onto. Ages ago his guitar playing had always upset her. There was something uncanny, creepy, in it and it always affected her deeply. There was a ghastly layer. And now it had come to the surface and she did not know how to deal with it.

Sam's contributions increased. He could repeat hard words like 'allotment,' but said 'cigalette' still for cigarette. He began trying to know colours.
Big & little -big dog, little teddy
ice cream ding ding – the ice cream van sound from the street.
Joined up sentence words.
He could roughly tell what had happened during the day.

35

As usual at a quarter to eight, Cora woke Mark with his morning cup of sugary tea. He turned over languidly and then sat up, leaning on the pillow.
"Oh, I'm not going into work today."
"You're not feeling well? I didn't notice you coughing in the night, though, what is it?"
"I've given up work, given in my notice."
"*WHAT*!"
"Well, I gave in my notice last week, didn't tell you in case you got upset."
"But I'm upset now." She felt chill fear in her stomach.
"I knew if you got told, you'd only try to talk me out of it, and we can't go and get a house in Norwich if I'm at work all the time. So, I've signed on already and they are giving me some unemployment money, and that means it's all going to be all right, nothing to worry about, see?" Cora could see a lot being very un-right and went off to the kitchen to

think over this bad news. There was of course, the mature student grant Mark would get as a married man with a child, at least that bit was guaranteed for September. But this wild jump across a ravine was frightening.

When Mark's father found out about this new arrangement later, he remarked that if everyone who was looking to buy a house gave up their job, the entire country would grind to a halt, but he did not make any real fuss about it, as usual. He had spent his entire life catching up with Mark, even now one or more steps ahead. He had given him some money to pay the train fare.

Arrangements were already being made in the background. Mitch called round that evening with the same tent Mark had used for France and he was also going to take the motorbike away, for safe keeping in his father's garage.

"You can't leave a bike like that out on the street for long before someone notices it's not being used. Those Siamese pipes are a real attraction." He was right. Men often stopped and could be seen staring and discussing the design, fascinated. She had never asked how expensive they were after all or where they had come from.

Summer brought the true value of the gardens into their lives; only the people of the Crescent could use that quiet green space. Cora met the Indian couple, the Ahmeds, in the gardens with their daughter, little Lily, the same age as Sam. The two children played amicably together, sharing a toy rabbit that was on a stick and a bright yellow wheelbarrow. She sat on the grass with them. Mr Ahmed's shirts were always optic white, almost fluorescent in the sun. It got too hot and the toddlers went inside their house which was luckily on the ground floor, that meant direct access into the gardens. There was a central kitchen, with their own room and the rest of the flat was rented out.

As they were leaving, young Lily wandered into the front room, followed by Sam. Cora, going in after him, saw six bunk beds, one chair, no cupboards or chest of drawers. The six men's spare clothes hung from hooks on their bedframes. They must have had nothing except bed, clothes, food, cleanliness, and a job. It was an existence only one or two steps starker than her own. Mr Ahmed had not wanted her to see into the front room, quickly pushing the door close. Smiling and waving his arms, he bustled her along the hall and out of the front door.

Mark was surprisingly calm now that he had left work. He said he planned on going off to Norwich on Monday morning. He was almost a different person, more optimistic. Gathering clean clothes, notebook and important papers like his passport, National Health card and any other proof of identity papers, he packed his haversack and leant it by the living room door. Sam sensed something was going on, in the same way a dog senses it is time for a walk. But of course, he had to be told properly that Daddy was going out for a while,

"We can go downstairs and wave to him, he's got to go and see somewhere." Cora and Sam stood on the wide marble doorstep and waved Mark goodbye, the youngster puzzled and Cora trying not to cry. They kissed and hugged in the street.

"It won't be long, you know that it'll soon be

all settled and you'll be somewhere new," he promised. "And now you can get back to doing some painting too, to fill in the time." And then he walked off towards Warwick Avenue station, ready to get the train at Liverpool Street. Cora stood with the baby in her arms, watching the figure carrying the rolled-up tent and the haversack as he grew smaller and smaller until he disappeared round the corner.

Walking back into the flat, it was suddenly twice the size now that Mark was gone. A few cigarette ends round the flat, in the ashtrays and balanced on the edge of the mantelpiece (his trademark dimps,) a pair of office shoes and two pairs of trousers. Some books and the great grandparents' carved mahogany box. The silver shaving-brush holder was empty, discarded. There was no spare money in the flat.

Their entire routine was ruptured now. He would not be coming back from work after five thirty and there was no need to cook anything each evening. Only Sam's daily pattern and the three day's cleaning afternoons would keep the two of them still pegged into real life. The Baroness had cheerily offered to look after Sam on Saturday mornings, a time which Mark usually spent with him while Cora was cleaning at Charles Winchester's.

They had decided to keep in touch by phone on Tuesday evenings and Cora promised she would say a prayer for him each evening at nine o'clock. He would get in contact via a phone-box wherever he could find one.

Surprisingly, he sent a postcard written that same Monday evening; he had arrived at lunchtime, saying it was now just after eight, he had got a bike from a shop called Dodger's, some bike-hire and repair shop, and now he was going to put up the tent somewhere near a river. So far, all the people he had met had been pleasant. He said he had not had time to be lonely yet. He would phone up tomorrow evening at nine o'clock from a phone box anywhere and she could return the call, it would be easier than him having to get hold of a handful of change to make a long-distance call. This was a change as it had become an unspoken rule that the phone was not to be used, just as the joint account had become unusable without a word being said.

Mark phoned up on the Tuesday evening, forestalling her having to hover near their phone in the bedroom, waiting for his call.

"Thought instead of you worrying about me being late, I'd better tell you I'm over in Padstow."

"Oh, you're in a different part of Norwich? Whereabouts is that?" There was the map of Norwich stuck up on the kitchen wall and she would have to look up where this Padstow place was. He laughed.

"No, silly, It's Padstow over in Cornwall."

"*What! Cornwall?* This was unbelievable.

"Well, it's got boring at this stage, it's lovely summer weather and there's not much more I could do at present and I got tired of hanging around, so I thought of coming here for a break. It's just a pity I can't have you and Sam here with me. The paperwork about getting any house and all that will take time, it hasn't even started yet, there's nothing to sign and I just got worn out chasing from one estate agents to another and getting nowhere, there's nothing else I can do right now. Then the solicitors will take ages." Cora was astounded. This was taking tremendous risks and Cornwall was about as far away from Norwich as you could get. How had he got there? How much had it cost?

The motorbike, surely. You couldn't hitch all that far without staying overnight somewhere on the way and he could not possibly have afforded the train fare there and back. It would have been far too expensive. It looked as though Mitch could have already delivered the motorbike to Mark in Norwich and then got a train back to London? That would make sense.

But for Mark to go as far as Padstow by train from Norwich would mean having to pass through London first, changing to Paddington Station from Liverpool Street and then passing along the entire lower coastline of England until reaching the toenail of Cornwall itself. Padstow was as near to America as you could possibly get. Or what if he hitched all that way? It would have taken more than a day, very tiring, surely, and a great lot of luck. And going by ordinary bicycle would be gruelling and he would be worn out, so it had to be by motorbike. And where would he stay?

Why bother to go there at all? She was too cross and puzzled to work out this new diversion. There would have been extra costs; there always were, with any travel. She had to humour him, this was no time to unsettle things further. Mark said he would ring next Saturday if there was any news then. He missed her, he said, missed her and the baby.

A letter arrived promptly, with his further reactions.

"I was feeling sad and bad after phoning you

yesterday and that made me feel very lonely, depressed and useless. I thought maybe it was selfish but I needed to travel a bit just for a few days. Not being able to find a right place in Norwich was really bringing me down, you must see that. I'm sorry it made you sad and stuff. If it annoys you then that's too bad. I can't care whether you think it's irresponsible or not but I don't want you to be sad at all about it.

I'm glad you're managing anyway (apart from me being naughty) It sounds as though you can't understand me. After a week of no results, I needed this break. I hope Sam is O.K. and not still being naughty but I'm glad he missed me, even if he couldn't express it right. Send your next letter to the same place at college, I can pick it up and when I get in maybe feel a little less lonely than I do now. I didn't think you'd mind just a few days. I'll go now and look around for the guy with his boat again, might get some money. Love and all things to you and Sam. Don't worry and pray that when I get back to Norwich there's a nice big unfurnished flat to let. All love to you both, Mark. There were no kisses though.

Why was he talking about an unfurnished flat now ? What was this all about? They had not saved up and sacrificed so much to go and waste money on rent. It was always going to be a house, or at least a ground-floor flat. The plan to buy somewhere was being changed without her being asked.

Another proper letter arrived now from Mark, at last he had found somewhere in Norwich to live. It was unclear where he had been staying since the days in a tent by the riverbank, but this was an obvious improvement, a room of his own. The letter gave not much more than his short phone call. It looked as though his father had given him money to buy a suit (or had he sent one in a parcel? Unlikely.) This was so he looked professional and smart enough to impress estate agents and the City Hall mortgage providers. There had definitely been no suit packed into his knapsack when he had left last Monday morning. He had never owned a suit, only the tobacco-brown corduroy jacket, and black trousers that were his only formal wear, even when they got married.

"You'd be quite impressed, it's Friday, it's 'wearing a suit day,' looking all official and I went downtown looking extraordinarily posh and scrubbed but found nothing really. I saw the guy I told you about last night and that flat has gone already. The whole supply of accommodation is so tight for flats, not so bad for rooms but as soon as the start of term even looms on the horizon the students hold a kind of stronghold with everything else. They tend to pass their tenancies on to each other, so it all seems to be a closed circle. I went round a couple of estate agents today and one other agency that does flats only.

The estate agents were no help at all, but I think the accommodation agency seemed brighter, offered me a place but it was 5 miles out of the city, so no good. The other hang up they all keep on about is the baby thing and I have to keep lying about still working for the Civil Service. Still, she said to phone in all the time and that I'd probably find something even if only furnished."

The two letters contradicted each other, and Cora could not make sense of any bits of the situation. There were too many ideas here at once and so far, Mark had moved at speed anyway, compared with her own daily plodding along. But there was no reasonable explanation for going and looking for flats when they had planned all along for getting a house; all their money would just be wasted on rent. Why else had they both (and Sam) grafted so hard to save for a deposit? It did not make sense.

Each day when she carried Sam down to the front door, he started to look out on the hall table for what he called 'S' Letter Daddy' which was imitating what she had said – "It's a letter from Daddy." You could probably train children to be bloodhounds if you had enough time.

36

After a pleasantly warm day throughout London, a violent tropical electrical storm erupted in the night in the first Friday of August. An emerald green night sky showed up, livid above the Crescent. Totally scared, Cora crouched on the bedroom floor tapping into the radio, which was merely a series of crackles and wheezes. The BBC was not functioning. One station after another was unreachable and Radio Geronimo, strangely, was the only station available. In between the latest pop releases, they announced that West End theatres were flooded, some had to evacuate their audiences. In the Aldwych Theatre the water was lapping round their feet in the front stalls, ruining the performance of Twelfth Night. Victoria Palace and Duchess Theatre, as well as all West End theatres suffered severe flooding too. cut short their shows Nearly two inches of rain had fallen on London in half an hour. Tube stations were closed, for safety.

"We are going to die apart," she forecast as the

lightning bolts dashed along the street and shook the windows. But amazingly, baby Sam slept contentedly though it all. There was always the extra contentment on summer evenings when a child was asleep and the curtains were drawn against the sunset that still brightened up the room. The contented rhythm of his breathing continued. As the crashes of thunder grew louder and wilder, she got up from bed again. Managing to climb up and stand on the chest of drawers, she hung a blanket across the bedroom window as she thought the glass would shatter with the strident blasts.

Now the room was as swaddled as possible, a cloth cave. There was nothing to do except absorb each strike and hope it was the last. By six in the morning the worst of the storm was over. She was exhausted, worn to a frazzle after hardly any sleep but the baby was O.K. He woke as normal as the morning arrived and the BBC came back on the airwaves full of bad news. Everywhere was new and rinsed, but the gutters in the street here still swirled with rainwater. Central London, however, was still semi-flooded with shops and theatres being mopped out and aired.

But on Saturday morning the Baroness turned up, as dependable as ever, to look after Sam.

"Oh, it was a real scene, wasn't it! Reminded me of the Christmas Pantos we used to be taken to when I was a girl. The devil would suddenly appear on stage with the same clap of thunder, plus green smoke and we would all scream in fake horror. But of course it didn't go on all night. Now, we'll be OK won't we, Sam? We'll build a castle and a farm, starting right now." Cora went off to Charles Winchesters feeling very shaky and nervy. His wistaria in the courtyard had lost branches and his gutters were blocked with fallen blossom, but luckily he had not been flooded. And he was back in the proper studio attending to the new fleet of paintings, groups of Bedouins trudging across their yellow ochre sands. It reminded her of Erena, an Israeli girl living in the same house as Dorothea a few years ago, another translator. Erena had a distinguishing white blaze in her hair, like a collie dog. She said she was doing her Israeli national service, camped out in the desert, when the Bedouins crept up in the night and stole the maps of manoeuvres from where they were stacked under her caravan. Erena pronounced it Bad-ouins. She was held responsible. In all the shock, her hair grew its white spot overnight. And here was Charles Winchester painting endless groups of Bedouins looking quaint and picturesque and being a success.

 Rhona had called round with a stack of more fashionable clothes – a red dress, a long-sleeved red blouse, a swirling purple skirt. Cora tried these new colours on gingerly, setting a new image in place. Then she started to wear the red dress more often. Then it became her only colour. It was like a furled flag.
 Men whistled after her in the street, a new experience. Builders were doing up a house at the end of the Crescent, with a clatter of scaffolding and ladders. The foreman, a handsome Jamaican, stood on the pavement and stopped Cora as she went past with the pram.
 "I've noticed you, one really classy woman. How about we meet after work? We finish here soon." He glowed, bristling with confidence, a white string

vest, almost neon white, a massive signet ring (a fake wedding ring?) on his left little finger.

"I'm a married woman, I wouldn't do anything like that," she smiled. He was certainly good looking. His employees were watching this going on from their ladders and scaffolding and as she walked away, she could feel them all staring. Something had changed.

Mark sent a letter that he had found a room to live in for the time being. So now he was out of the tent near the river. He also had found a convenient telephone box nearby, and she could ring him up on a Tuesday evening, that would be a good idea, wouldn't it? Jotting down the number, it was a sign of progress. He would not be able to guess how much short-change it would take to have a long-distance conversation, it was easier if she phoned him instead. And how were her paintings going now? It was a far cry from when he had forbidden any action there at all. Now it was a form of occupational therapy. But starting a painting did not develop any further, as Cora was depressed now, stranded in space. When he called, she started crying, but Mark said not to worry, things were happening.

"Anyway, I can't go on talking like this because there is someone outside the phone box waiting to use the phone and tapping on the glass. Make yourself a pot of tea, you'll soon feel better, it's not long now."

All summer she desperately sunbathed in any spare time between working, as if at some point of self-colouring everything would change. If she managed to achieve an all-over-goldenness, then their life together would magically change that very afternoon. Mark, of course, tanned easily, quickly, becoming more attractive . She was unaware of how many days he did in fact take off work, sitting perhaps in Regents Park on the au pair's day off, lying in the sun together before slinking out of the park at five o'clock and towards the canal path home.

Perhaps that was why he was so hostile to her when she had gone with the baby and pram to meet him from work a few times on those lovely summer afternoons. It had seemed a good idea, the loving wife and baby meeting the young husband and walking home with him in the mild early summertime through the rush hour.

But he did not speak to her at all and apart from a quick wave and smile at Sam, he did not reply to anything she said. As they walked along the streets it got worse, until Cora was reduced to wittering frantically, only too aware of Mark being totally fed up with her presence. Perhaps one day she would discover he had not been at work at all, but she did not want to investigate that. The fog of the last summer never lifted and of course it was never discussed now. Those deceptions were neatly locked away. Everything was going to be different now with this new life starting somewhere else, with all their saved-up money.

37

It was Saturday morning now and the little group of tourists crossed the Plaza Nuevo, its shops still shuttered at 9a.m Spanish time, its tiles enticingly wet after the council truck had sprayed them with disinfectant-spiced water. Cora could hear a cock crow twice nearby but no one else thought to mention it.

Their special tour of Old Bilbao moved on now to a city café specially reserved for them to eleven o'clock. The Café Iruna was a 1903 temple to Art Nouveau. The walls, ceiling and windows were whirling works of art so that anyone could have sat there alone and be entertained enough by the surroundings. Special coffees and chocolate drinks together with cakes and biscuits were served as they lived like aristocrats for the best part of an hour. Adverts for drinks were set into the tiled walls and arches set with paintings of castles in lush landscapes surrounded them. The bar had a mottled marble frontage and tables and chairs were specially designed, with individual tables topped with white marble. There was a tiled floor and decorative tiles up to head height. It was a public display of luxury. Swirls of mosaic and intricate carvings everywhere, demented life flew round them while complimentary coffees, chocolate and sticky cakes went on and on like the Feeding of the Five Thousand, only this was the luxury version.

Afterwards the courier walked them back across the Plaza Nuevo square, explaining the housing above, a beautiful example of planning from the 1780s, where residential and commercial realities were intertwined. They had an hour and a half left for shopping and sightseeing before going back to the ship.

A Guardia Civil, young man in a green cloak stood near the gangway monitoring them as passport control ushered them back on board. For all the excitement and contrast of visiting Spain it was as if this was their real home now, as they returned to their burrows along the carpeted corridors for the journey back.

This time there were no dolphins as it was night when they passed through the Bay of Biscay, its ultramarine waters the unfathomable colour of night, liquid night.

She went round the block to enter the gardens again through the semi-hidden private gate. The Ahmed couple were sitting on the grass near their house railings while little Lily pushed a doll's pram around the path nearby. They asked how she was getting on, any news? Cora told them she was waiting for news from her husband about college and lodgings.

"There's a lot to be arranged."

"But he is never here, is he? You do not know where he is." Mr Ahmed looked at her, assessing. "I do not think your husband loves you." Mrs Ahmed looked both smug and sympathetic. You have fallen off your perch and we have not. You will not be able to jump back, we know that. You must have done something wrong. People like us will have to be apart from you. If your husband had a really white shirt none of this would have happened.

But there was a development at last. Mark had found a house, a small two bed terrace house in the middle of the city. Cora would have accepted anything right now, stranded in a flat with no connections except the Baroness and Mark's second-hand friends.

The summer continued with Cora and Sam

going out cleaning on Monday and Thursday afternoons at the Gorski's, Wednesdays off, Fridays at Rita's, then Saturdays at Charles Winchester's – they could pay their way as long as Mark sent the cheque for the rent and the Baroness looked after Sam on Saturday mornings. However, she found an angry note stuffed in the letterbox demanding payment of their milk bill.

Apparently, Mark had not paid the milk bill over the last six weeks and it was now a small fortune. As her cleaning work earned just enough to feed Sam and the phone bill and the gas and electric meters each week, she had no spare money. Giving the milkman a week's money she promised to get the rest of the money as soon as possible or pay extra for as many weeks as it took to pay off the debt. There was no jewellery to sell; the binoculars and little silver clock had disappeared long ago.

There was one way out. The sewing machine! An entire business plan jettisoned, the toy-making finished. She put a card in the Post Office window yet again and a week later, luckily, a man appeared and the machine was sold for six pounds. She had to knock off ten shillings because it did not have a case and this customer might be the only one. The five pounds and ten shillings covered the milk bill and the crisis. Cora hid the spare notes down the spine of an old prayer book, with the bill paid and one extra pound over. If they needed a sewing machine in the future, it would have to be on H.P. or buying a similar cheap one from a junk shop. Perhaps Mal would let her use his new machine for any toymaking if any opportunity cropped up in the next few weeks, but that was unlikely.

The cheery orange lentils had gone - all the jars were now empty as they jogged along the days, raiding each resource for possible food.

Across the road, in her studio, Mrs Gorski was also reaching the end of her tether. Having totally run out of ideas for art, she had taken to cutting up a book of old Ordnance Survey maps. It was a type of desecration. Bits of the Home Counties scattered round their feet, neither use nor art, lost completely. These showed the country in the reign of King George the VI, long before most present roads, trainlines or houses changed its landscape. These narrow strips were all over the studio floor as they fell off the trestle tables. Viola was gluing them in random stripes and then painting stark black shapes over the resulting collage. It was like swirling Chinese characters on a newspaper background and was not working out in practice, so that Viola was now distraught. Cora found that the strips were firstly not able to go up the hoover (they blocked it) and that they had to be returned to the table for further use. It was hopeless.

The extra pages of a lost green-field England strewed across the floor and Sam caught some of them, scrunching the pages in his tiny fist like an infant emperor.

And even Charles Winchester was affected by the malaise now. When Cora turned up on Saturday morning after handing Sam to the Baroness, there was a shock awaiting, the usual calm shattered. She had always depended on the peacefulness of his studio to revive her. Charles opened the door and stood there, with a black eye and the side of his face bruised. He was ashamed of looking like this.

"I fell, last night," and then he turned away and walked back into the hall. It was obvious he did not want to talk about it. But it was strange; it was a bungalow, and the possibility of falling was limited. There were a few rugs, but he had not mentioned tripping over one of them. Perhaps he was a secret drinker, or perhaps already the ravages of old age were beginning to attack his sense of balance. Somehow his dignity had to be kept intact, so Cora did not question him when they shared their usual cup of milky coffee and digestive biscuits in the little kitchen, trying to act as if this was normal. She would see how he was next Saturday and take it from there. She did not like to ask if he had been to the doctor's or the hospital, or even if there was anyone likely to call in during the week. It was as if she was his only visitor.

37

End of summer, the first scattered leaves gathered at the edges of the gardens. Long shafts of sunlight reached across the living room carpet, a last message of light as autumn began. Steve called round one Sunday evening early in September, some time after Sam had gone to bed. He had timed it well. Cora was obviously glad of a visitor after an almost solitary week and he was good company, although this time she could detect a slight change in the atmosphere between them. It was difficult too, because they had not met since his breakdown that spring. He had lost weight, his face looked sharper, more chiselled.

"I've changed jobs, I'm teaching English to

foreigners, it's less responsibility as they're all adults. I realised I'd got too involved with the children at school, all their problems at home, that sort of thing, just got feeling too worried and ground down with it. Maybe a coward's way out, but I had to do something to improve things for me instead. And you, how are things going on, about the house and everything? Any news?" he asked.

"Well, it's almost a 'no comment' situation. I don't understand it. Here I am, I'm supposed to be an intelligent woman, but I might as well be one of those princesses in a fairy story, trapped in a tower and with not a clue of what's going on, waiting for the prince to climb up their long tresses, which of course I haven't got. It's like a jigsaw, I can't get it right."

"That's because you haven't got all the pieces." Steve looked serious. There was a tension in the air. Cora began to enter a strange territory, like Adam and Eve and the Tree of Knowledge. "You probably could judge better if you knew a bit more."

"Perhaps," she said cautiously.

"I can tell you the lot, if you want." Cora nodded agreement. The atmosphere changed, taut. Top diving board time.

"Well?"

"Mark is living in Norwich with Leanne. They've been there all along, everyone knows except you, he had us all hiding it and covering-up for him. When he went off with the tent and his haversack, Leanne was waiting round the corner and they got in a taxi with the budgie in its cage and they both ended up on the train to Norfolk together. I've felt uncomfortable about it all summer once I found out about it. I met Rhona on her way here one day and she told me the full story. They've known all along.

And apparently when he went off to France last summer, he was looking up Ines, that au pair he had the affair with, she came from Rouen. Don't know what happened about that, looks as though it led to nothing, luckily for all concerned. Strange, though, as Leanne and I were in Rouen in July, only a few weeks before Mark. Wonder what that was all about, like crossed stars.

I know Leanne has some money of her own, that's what has kept them going all summer. Her father's in charge of her allowance, there's some investments, she told me all about it when we were together. I think she might be well off, really, in the background. Since her parents divorced, she's had a regular allowance and she'll come into money when she's older. The flat along the Crescent belongs to them, Leanne and her brother, it's not rented."

The shock did not show at first, there was a delay-point that she had acquired over the years, an almost animal-like facility that allowed her to escape from awkward situations without disclosing her true feelings. Because, having launched this thunderbolt, Steve merely left as if it had been just any social visit and she was left to take it in. The September Sunday evening was beautiful with a slow sunset already turning the sky peach colour. For a second, she could see how difficult this all was for Steve; Mark had taken on most of his personality, taken over his girlfriend and was now taking on the same training college place too; it was almost a complete impersonation. It must feel spooky to have someone replace all your past identity so quickly.

But then the walls and ceiling started to move,

to close in threateningly. She went into the bedroom to make sure the baby was all right and to reassure herself that something was real and unchanged. The flat began to whirl around, and she felt in danger - so much so that she fled upstairs to the Palmers' and burst into their flat, crying,

"Mark's left me", snuffling and weeping. They reacted wonderfully, sitting her down on the sofa and Mrs Palmer produced a glass of brandy, which was supposed to help, but Cora was past caring. Mr Palmer was kindly and advised her to get to know her rights from the proper authorities the first thing on Monday when offices would be open. They sympathised but could do nothing that would really help, it was late Sunday evening after all. She sat on their black plastic sofa looking at the display cabinet with its unused best china tea set and collection of wine glasses, the framed Constable "The Hay Wain" over the imitation electric fire, family photos on the mantelpiece scattered among small glass animals; all the ordinary homelike things she usually despised; they were wonderful, ordinary and safe. They were beyond price.

Even Cora realised that she could not sit here in the Palmers' flat snivelling for much longer, the baby might wake up and need her. Thanking them both for their kindness, she went downstairs, realising the Palmers were not so bad after all, in fact they were normal backbone of England Londoners who usually kept themselves to themselves. She had misjudged them and had expected too much of them. Salt of the earth, that was it, salt of the earth.

Mark had managed to weave truth and lies so well together that she could not unravel the weft from the weave.

A wall of bits of reality and unreality barred wherever she looked. It made her unsteady, unable to make any decision, puzzled at her own reality too. Like acid it was eating into her.

Back in the flat, casting about wildly for someone to contact right now, anyone in fact to talk to, she remembered Stan, a rare sensible, sensitive man whose parting message at the end of their affair a few years ago had been,

"Whenever you need me, just phone me up. Whatever and whenever, you can depend on me." It had not stopped him from marrying a classic English Rose, but he had given her their new phone number. Sunday evening: he would surely be at home. Rose answered the phone. Not a good start.

"You want to speak to Stan? It's rather late. We are just finishing a dinner party here, he is in the hall with our guests, saying goodbye." Rose went off, obviously miffed at this interruption.

Stan appeared at the phone, puzzled and at a loss for words. Hearing all about the problem he backtracked amazingly quickly and merely told her not to do anything stupid. All his kindly and friendly persona had disappeared and he did not seem overly concerned, brushing her crisis aside.

"Got to go, our guests are about to leave right now. Good- bye and look after yourself and the baby."

She phoned up the Williams's and said that Mark had left her and was involved with Leanne in Norwich all this time. Grandpa seemed not to really believe her and merely told her not to do anything stupid. (Suicide? Drunkenness? Running away? Not many options available really.) He would call in some time during the week, probably Wednesday. Cora knew he did not like being alone with her, he was always ill at ease in her company and would not be able to talk easily. She would have to put up the living room curtains again if he appeared with Beryl or was that game well over and finished by now. There was nothing to save.

Running out of people to talk to, Cora tried the Samaritans, which was as desperate as anyone could get. But a voice to speak to would perhaps stop the sliding walls and the galloping nausea. She reassured the counsellor that this was not a suicide call, it was all about being in a mess with no way out and no one and nowhere to go to at this time of night.

The lady at the Samaritans was a friendly voice in the midst of nothingness. She was obviously delighted that actual suicide was not on the cards, just an ordinary deserted woman and child. It was bad, but not disastrous, a crisis, but a slow one.

"You will come through this, even though you don't think so now, and from what you've told me, there's a lot of love floating about in your situation right now." Perhaps the new Cora had translated everything into this new space that she herself did not actually understand and the sweet middle-class lady, in the middle of the night was only too eager to take up this ball and run with it. "Do ring me up again if you need to, we are here to help you further if you need." She did not have the authority, she said, to give legal advice but on the quiet, off the record, yes, taking up the option of a house, even elsewhere and alone was probably much better than staying here in a third-floor flat without a garden in the middle of London.

"You have the future to think of for your little son," she gurgled sweetly. Such a nice person, it seemed wrong to leave her there alone, dealing with all the broken and bereft of London and trying to breathe new hope into them. Her voice sounded blonde and she probably lived in South Kensington, perhaps she could cope by not really having experienced these extremes, just as doctors were always supposed to remain healthy whatever germs and ailments were doing the rounds.

Over the small hours Cora looked at the bits of information that had filtered through. Steve was right. It was like holding pieces of a thousand-piece jigsaw without having any idea of the picture on the lid. If Mark had gone off with a tent - she had seen it – it was surely a small one-person tent. It looked like one, but how was she to tell when it was all rolled into a bundle? There was no way a couple, however much in love, could stay in a tent with a budgie in a cage. The bicycle he had acquired would have to be parked nearby too.

And if Mark was registered as unemployed and drawing benefit, he would have to give an address different from here in London and a tent would not be applicable. And what about Leanne? What was she living on? It looked as though they had fixed up somewhere to stay right from the start, a shared room at least, or a furnished flat. They could not have started off by wandering round looking for somewhere to pitch a tent in a strange place or looking for somewhere to live right there that first afternoon. Staying in a B&B would have to be booked in advance too, or even a hostel. And there was the ruddy budgie, Harold, to think of too.

All those letters about being lonely and looking for somewhere were fantasy. There were twenty-two letters, all versions of the lie skilfully done, how lonely he was, how he missed the baby and herself. She had kept them all as some sort of lifeline and now it showed that they were all false. So much had been happening and at such speed too, but how had she been so gullible? It showed how rabid she had been, the envelopes were torn open as she had grabbed at them, read them rapidly and then stuffed them into the sideboard drawer. She had never read them logically, one after another and searched out the clues and lies. They were like letters she was not supposed to read, especially now that she could see the deception beneath them, its secret embroidery.

But Mark had said he had managed to arrange a mortgage on a house after all, via the City Council, a new project for encouraging young couples to become houseowners. He had found a suitable little terrace house at last. He had not sent any photo or any of the estate agent's details about this one and Cora was left out of the arrangements. But at least something was happening, however secret Mark had kept it from her.

38

She woke still crying, in a hammock of tears after an almost sleepless night. As soon as any possible office would be open the next day, Cora phoned up the Council office in Norwich about the house. She had to get the number via an operator, not having any of the paperwork herself and having no idea of the right names or phone numbers. The long-distance phone call was an extra expense, and she was not supposed to go behind Mark's back about the mortgage. Ring again tomorrow, the woman said, as Cora did not have all the necessary information, like the reference number of the application or even the address of the new house. The next day an official said it was being arranged that there could be an advance from the City of Norwich of £1400 for twenty years at a six and three-quarters per cent option, whatever that meant. Mark had all the paperwork, obviously, over in Norwich and there were no duplicates.

She had become an intruder into her own life.

Having done that, Cora thought about checking up on their Trustee Savings Bank account for the deposit for the house. How near was it to the finishing line? Had that gone through? With so many barriers falling down now, she could ferret into anything. The bank clerk was unhelpful as only someone obeying rules can be unhelpful. He was polite but firm.

"That account is in Mr Williams's name and I cannot divulge any details about it. It is bank policy."

"There should be about two hundred pounds in the account." Cora was crying now. "But I'm his wife, we've saved up all the money together, it's for our new house, well, the deposit and so on. He's gone off, I'm here in London with a baby in a flat and I don't know what to do."

"I am sorry," he persisted, "but that is the rule, even if you are his wife. As this account was opened in his sole name, it is counted as your husband's asset alone and I can't tell you how much is in the account." He relented enough to tell her that money remained in the account and had not all been withdrawn. "That is as much as I can tell you and I really shouldn't be telling you this, but as you seem to be a special case I can go this far." It was the sound of a rigid rule cracking under the influence of her anxiety. "This is only because I can see you also have a joint account as a couple." If he had looked further, he would have seen that she had not signed any cheques for well over a year; it had been used only by Mark. She had been quietly effaced from their joint account. He would have the cheque book with him right now, wherever he was.

Mark and whatever he was up to was there in Norwich, totally safe behind an official wall of secrecy. She could only hope that the mortgage agreement from the council office meant that he would actually have placed the deposit in their hands. Never to have questioned what name the new account was in, she had assumed it was in their joint names too. And so easy not to have ever thought of it; she had taken so much for granted, so much so that she had easily been edited out of her own life and as far as the bank was concerned, she was a complete outsider, a stranger asking awkward questions. Unhappiness would have to look after itself.

She put down the phone. Mark could be living on the money, the sky his limit until the September grant came in. Leanne was not likely to be doing any work, she was not a working sort of person. She would never be sent off to work as a waitress, shop assistant, clerk or chambermaid. Class was all; like an Indian caste system, there was a reverse type of untouchable; the middle classes who were clearly above any effort when unemployment happened. They were paid without question, too posh to be interrogated and too posh to do work beneath their station.

It would have taken several weeks to go through the conveyancing work at any solicitors, she realised. That meant the house was chosen and a deposit paid well over two months ago. No wonder he had been able to go off to Padstow to celebrate in June, long before the August Bank Holiday, with all the details settled It meant that Mark had an address to give them that was not a tent by the riverside. No official letters had come here to Warrington Crescent. He must have been living in a furnished flat for all that time.

So, all the rest was invention and subterfuge, while Sam and herself went out cleaning to pay for their own upkeep. Looking round the flat again, thinking of the future, Sam and local schools, a constant up-and-down-the-stairs life she thought that anything would be better than this for the future. Life on the ground, for a start, would be a wonderful freedom for any child. All the traipsing up and down to play in the gardens would become more wearing as he grew older. And as a teenager, he would become totally untraceable.

She burst into uncontrollable tears in the launderette in Formosa Street and a kindly neighbour followed her out. The woman took her and Sam home to a basement flat just a few doors away along the Crescent and calmed her down, a helpful anchor to reality. The house was next-door to Leanne's flat, they were as near as that. Tea and biscuits worked their usual medicine plus the realisation that neighbours did exist.

The builders were still at work at the house nearby. The day after, now a lost person, Cora stopped, almost in tears again and nearly fell into the boss's arms. He was standing on the pavement, white vest as optic bright as usual, athletic body, smiling gold teeth. Something made her go up to him,

"I should apologise, but I'm all over the place now. My husband has left me, so you were probably right, intuition, you must have guessed something was in the air." He put his arms round her and gave her a warm hug.

"You don't have to worry; I could take care of you and the little one. Where do you live now? I could come round to your place and help you to sort things out." The workmen nearly fell off their ladders trying to listen in. Although any sympathy was welcome right now, a vision of Grandpa and Grandma stopped her. Their disapproval, this man's anonymity; Cora had to stay with the structure that was left of the family and not start messing about with handsome Jamaicans, however rich or helpful they might seem.

"We're still here for a few days, dear, you know you can call on me if you have any problems with money, like, I'm still here." A moment of sanity fell. He was surely married, and she would be lucky if he even made her a proper mistress, most probably he would be a modern white slaver and she would end up like that poor prostitute over in Ladbroke Grove, with a kid in care, or in a back room.

It was worse than being a widow; now she was easy meat for whoever was clever enough to trap her. For the rest of the week whenever Cora left the house she had to walk in the opposite direction, going round the entire block to avoid the decorators' ladders and their smart and attractive, tempting boss.

38

Earlier in July, Rhona arrived one evening with a selection of clothes for Cora to choose from. Cora was scared stiff, hearing a strange noise as Rhona let herself into the flat with a key. The sudden clicking of the key, opening of the door and the sound of a footfall was frightening in the silence. Cora was angry when she saw who it was. But Rhona was almost amused, not apologetic at all.

"Oh, didn't Mark tell you? He gave me his key so that I could call in now and again, have a look at how you and Sam are getting on. Just a way of taking care of you both, he asked me specially." It made a terrible kind of sense, to check they were not starving, or Cora was not lying in a drunken haze with a sick Sam toddling about needing care. But at the same time, it was a complete insult implying Cora was not a competent person and had to have a minder. Rhona was trying her best, but it should not have been arranged behind her back like this.

"I thought you might like some of these, bright colours for the summer, you need a change, just look at these! Some of these will fit you, I'm sure. Just try these on, choose what you like. You can always give the rest away to a charity shop." She fished a handful of clothes out of a bag and held them up. A red dress and red blouse stood out from the rest of the clothes. It was only when the shock broke through everything that Cora had a sudden urge to wear red at all times, unlike her usual plain dark colours. She became larger than the situation, larger than the world. It was the same experience as just after Sam's birth, when she felt stronger than the entire universe, capable of solving all problems. It all changed. Everything sparkled, it all lived, each brick and stone. It was almost being able to see through walls It was like St John must have felt, experiencing so much that had no words to shape round it, trying to trap as much as he could, as it swirled away into space.

>   Mind: I'm worried
>   Heart: Just relax
>   Mind : But I'm totally lost now
>   Heart: Just follow me
>   Mind: But you've been there before
>   Heart: Trust me, you'll love it
>   Soul: If you two would shut up, I'd show you the map
>
> - Unknown

A sudden impetus, Cora knew that Sam and herself had to get to a church right now, this minute. It was a sunny afternoon and Sam was happily able to walk these days too. They strolled along to the church at the crossroads of Warwick Avenue and the Crescent - St Saviour's – for Cora to pray about the situation. She did not know where the nearest Catholic church was; this one would have to do instead; it was a hallowed place after all. The building was dark and silent, with no lights on. But here and there, the stained-glass windows spattered the benches and the flagged floor with multi-coloured lights. Sam climbed up to the pulpit, exploring. The place was deserted but there were two women who came towards her who said they were retired nuns from South Africa, visiting London. They shook hands, which was a friendly gesture. Cora spluttered,

"I had to come here, had to; there was a draw like a magnet, I had to. There's times when a church is the only place to go to." They realised what was happening to her.

"You are having a spiritual rebirth.", one said in the tilting South African accent. They wanted to give her all their English money as they were leaving that day, but all three realised it was wrong to cross money with faith. Birth; rebirth. They were absolutely right. They parted with promises of prayer, which after all was international and above any borders of space and time.

When Cora was born, her mother had nearly died, and Cora was also at the point of death. But Mrs Finch managed to throw a couple of drops of water over the baby in a frantic shortened version, thinking she was dying too. In the middle of the panic the midwife, Margaret McLoughlin also baptised her in another attempt as the baby spluttered between life and death. By that time, Mr Finch had rushed off and got hold of a priest in the hospital and Father Garvin performed the actual baptismal right there in the labour ward.

Three times baptised; three times between life and death, balancing between two worlds. Perhaps this had come back again, as Cora teetered between the here and now and the great beyond that was now so tangible. She veered, balancing skilfully between the two worlds. That was what the two women had recognised in her. The three of them respected each other no – it was four – the child was included too.

All that summer, the Baroness had been taking care of Sam on Saturday mornings so that Cora could go and clean at Charles Winchester's in St John's Wood. Without her help the two of them would not have been able to eat and continue to keep any slight existence going, like paying the milk bill. No more Observer on Sundays; the library and the radio were the only access left to all ideas and news. When Cora told the Baroness what was going on, she was immediately sympathetic and understanding.

"Oh, I do sympathise!" The Baroness said, putting her arm round Cora right there in the street. "My husband was a rotter too!" This startled Cora out of feeling sorry for herself. The larger-than–life, comical Alice in Wonderland-ish Baroness had been through this extreme test too. A marriage, Brompton Oratory or Chelsea Registry Office? Or perhaps a country church in the Home Counties, somewhere classy. An arch of swords as they came out of the ancient stone church; her in a long white gown, white silk handmade shoes, bouquet of white roses, him in a morning suit, perhaps even a top hat, dashing husband. No mention of children. Perhaps that was the trouble, that was why he cast her off, or had cast off in different directions and she had ended up living cramped in one small back room of a house which she would once have considered her entire town residence.

All contained in that one word 'rotter.' Other people had experienced this mad pit of twisted wires and electricity, of violin strings and black mud, of seeing the everyday world as a foreign land. Outsider without a map or language, watching other inhabitants meekly go about their normal lives. The Baroness had been through this. Here was proof that it was possible to come out the other side, but preferably without ending up wearing several layers of dresses, droopy cardigans and stockings that permanently fell down.

At this point the yellow-painted wooden radio became an absolute lifesaver. It had always been a regular BBC Radio Four background fount of information, from one news broadcast to another. But now Cora craved music non-stop. Radio Caroline was still around until eight at night and all the pop songs rained down consolation, though it was difficult to tease out whether they helped to heal or if they cleverly extended the pain into something exquisite and fascinating. They appeared like invisible doctors, the Chi-Lites with *Have You Seen Her*, the Four Tops and their heart-breaking *Walk Away Renée*, Marvin Gaye's thumping *I Heard It Through the Grapevine* and the far milder *Rainy Night in Georgia* from Brook Benton. They all dashed in like stretcher-bearers towards a casualty.

But best of all, the skewer turning exquisitely and turning again and again in the pain, was Smoky Robinson's *Tears of a Clown*. Cora put the radio on at full blast, louder than it had ever been before, the floorboards in the kitchen soaking up the vibration. Up on the wide kitchen shelf over the unused iron range, the radio dealt out a fragmented prescription for pain. Sam trotted in now and again, not really liking the row. She sank into the music as if it was a vat of honey. It was not acknowledged how all the sympathy and understanding came from the American black soul like this. They were all in the kitchen, trying to console her from far away. They understood, they had been in this pit before her. Here was the music that went with it, a small hint of an escape route.

At the same time, Cora would have been happy if someone had rattled on the door, a cross neighbour complaining about the noise, someone to talk to and fall into tears in front of and to end up having a cup of tea with. But instead, she was with the guy who sat in a children's playground, sad that his woman had left, the trees reminding him of their love, their initials drawn in a heart on one of the trees.

Charles Winchester's house was apart from the present century and a respite from the city outside. His large collection of books, mostly on fables, legends and spiritual matters, many of them Celtic tales, spread across several bookshelves. Like at the Gorski's, Cora knew the titles and authors of all the books after dusting the spines regularly; Arthur Waley's *100 Chinese Poems*, Lao Tzu, the Upanishads. None of them had been any practical help in his spiritual search. It was as if he had followed a private course of study. She told him how different she felt now.

"It's like coming out of a dark tunnel and into an almost blinding light. It's as if I'm seeing all the world as if it has just been washed and I've never seen it before." He told her that what she was going through was exceptional.

"It is as if you are in the same state as St John, when he was writing the *Apocalypse,* where he is trying to drag the unreachable down to earth." Cora understood what he meant, with Jesus long gone and no one to talk to about it, St John grappling with language, almost strangling it, trying to describe the indescribable.

"It's like a deep night's sleep can be the soul's transference between yesterday and tomorrow, but you can't say how it works." This was all that the drug culture was attempting to do too, with disastrous results for whenever it went wrong. Already, casualties and misfits were accumulating with all the social pitfalls of drug misuse, yet the constantly hopeful all started on the same disastrous journey.

For the atheists there were the attempts of William Blake who hippies were attracted to and were reclaiming for themselves. But for those of the coldest logic, it was *Through the Looking Glass* and the easier *Alice in Wonderland*, written by a mathematician after all. The world was made of layers and layers and it was quite feasible to spend an adequate life at the outer edge. But once the travel into deeper layers happened, an enrichment occurred that could never be lost again, whatever happened years later.

Charles was wrapped in nineteenth century wordiness, yet one could see the searching soul looking out – and missing the goal time after time... He gave her his book of poems, *One Man's Anthology*, privately printed, a proof of his spiritual searching:

I move on the water, I walk on the sea
Over sea that is sleeping, from a ship that is sleeping,
Containing the dreamers that dream in their sleep,
My spirit is walking alone to the glory,
The glory, the fringe of the infinite still
Of the moving, immutable Word of Creation,
The Word that encompasses time – and is breaking
The ship of my spirit: the vision is breaking.

Cora could not work out if it was utter twaddle or the

profound thoughts of someone specially gifted. She kept the book nevertheless and could not throw it away.

Later in September Mitch called in, a bit embarrassed now the truth was coming out. He admitted he knew what had been going on but excused himself with,

"But I went to school with him, I've known Mark for longer than I've known you." Cora was wonderfully past caring now. She could say what she liked, there was nothing to save. No need to be polite at all. Other peoples' feelings did not have to take precedence anymore. She snapped,

"So, if you knew the murderer for one minute longer than the victim, you'd support them? You don't mind being complicit in someone else's betrayal like this? What a strange attitude to morals you have!" He looked his beautiful deep dark look at her, but it no longer worked its magic. She saw him as a painting, an arrangement in white and black. The luminous dark olive eyes were just an arrangement of light and dark from now on.

Different people reacted in surprising ways. Cora met Madame Perpignan in the hall and began to tell her what was happening.

"Come in, my dearr, let us talk this through." Madame was disappointed. "Ee was always so pleasant, all the times 'e washed my car, so pleasant."

"Ah, yes, he always would be to other people, you wouldn't know." When Cora told Madame the full story so far, she offered her a glass of sherry and

Cora thought, why not, though it was years since she had drunk any spirits, especially in the middle of an afternoon. Sam sat on the deeply piled carpet with his latest toy. He was used to ignoring adults by now.

Madame Perpignan leant across and said dramatically, in her usual thick French accent,

"Thees othairr woman, well I can tell you – it weel 'appen to 'er." Cora could not see Mark ever leaving Leanne in this sort of mess, or ignoring her, not beautiful Leanne with her long fair tresses and winsome smile and quietness, but knew it was a kindly meant remark. Madame Perpignan was the ult in worldliness and sophistication, always dressed in sleek black costumes, pearl necklace and diamond earrings, she brought a Parisian view to the situation.

39

As if in a home-made Agatha Christie mystery, Cora got hold of all the letters she had saved, all stuffed haphazardly into a sideboard drawer. Was there one thrown away, might there be one missing? It did not really matter, there were twenty-four, some loose papers too and she laid them out like playing cards, putting them in date order. Thank goodness she had kept most of them complete with envelopes. It was amazing to look at them now, torn at the edge, opened rapidly, so eager for any connection.

Each one had been immediately read, desperately consumed for the latest news and then flung aside. She had never followed the story from one week to the next. Perhaps she had not wanted to see the truth. And here it was, like a neon sign.

The first was merely a white postcard, sent that

very first evening in early June, saying Mark was just going off to put up the tent somewhere. He feared feeling empty and lonely though had not yet had time to miss them both. He had got a bike from a place called Dodgers. It all held together so well, it was all exactly as expected, apart from his having the money to buy even a second-hand bicycle. Where had that come from? But with the new omniscience, how on earth were the girlfriend and the budgie in its birdcage all supposed to fit into the small tent? They had to be indoors somewhere.

The second letter, sent in a self-addressed and stamped envelope she had given Mark beforehand, contradicted everything already written. Had she never noticed this? She had consumed each letter so greedily and never looked at them again, always on the lookout for the next one instead. And she certainly had not challenged him, though it was all a mist now, perhaps she had done, and Mark had managed to waffle out of it.

This version said that he had so much trouble finding somewhere to stay and that the first night he met some guy and stayed in his front room somewhere by the river, a house with a long garden with roses. They chatted about poltergeists while listening to Pink Floyd. The guy said he could go back the next night too, but Mark said he didn't like to overstay such generosity and was determined to find somewhere to camp. He found a place by the river near the university to set up the tent. But he had to be careful because there were many young country skinheads on the council estates nearby who could prowl around. Where were Leanne and the budgie in this story? Where was the bicycle?

Mark said he left his backpack in the railway station's left luggage while he went round accommodation agencies.

The next letter was an absolute hand grenade.

She remembered this one all right, when Mark had phoned up one evening in mid-June sounding rather superior, like a sneaky schoolchild. He was in Padstow. That was over in Cornwall. Again, where was Leanne and the ruddy budgie in its cage? They would have to leave the budgie with someone and then, did they hitch all the way from Norwich to Padstow? But if they had gone by train, how on earth had they paid the fare there and back? Even if, as more likely, they had gone with the motorbike and sidecar, there was still petrol and food and lodging to pay for, as well as having to travel right across England to get there.

He said he was painting some guy's boat in Padstow (another convenient 'guy' turning up) and had spent the payment on going to the cinema (alone.) Where were they staying, just turning up at the spring weekend at the start of the holiday season with no accommodation previously arranged? It did not work out whether - as his letter claimed – he was alone and even more so if they were a couple. Meanwhile, of course, Sam and herself were left behind, going out cleaning in order to support themselves. But in the long reach that relationships could have, the cinema over in Padstow played *A Whiter Shade of Pale* in the interval and that had freaked out Mark completely. It was the first record she had ever bought. That bit was probably true, their special song from the weekend they met had remained significant.

On the evenings when he did not phone, she

had promised Mark that she would say a prayer for him each night at nine o'clock. He said this music had happened precisely on the dot. For once, Leanne must have wondered what was going on. Then there was the letter giving the address of his new lodging, a Flat 1, which seemed strange if it was supposed to be a shared student house. And, even more bizarre, Mark wrote that he had made a loaf, 'The bread turned out very light' and he had given some to Mrs Thing upstairs and would have a chat with her. This unnamed woman did not sound like a student. He also said he was very depressed, ' locked in my room.' The weather was bad and he could not work on the sidecar of the motorbike. Later on, it turned out that Mark and Leanne had rented a flat in the same road, on the lower floor, with the landlady living in the top floor. It looked like he had given a false address at first, a student house directly opposite. And every one of those 'I am feeling lonely' letters had been written with Leanne being around.

"Like a cup of tea, dear?' No, she would most probably call him Darling.

"Yes, anything to go with it? Did we finish the bread after all?"

"You're writing to her again? I thought you sent her a letter on Monday?" It would have been something like that, Mark could not have stolen away to compose a letter alone, and most of them were on proper Basildon Bond with their trademark light blue envelopes. Though, as student time approached, a few envelopes contained foolscap pages from a notebook. But nothing had been truly private, plus he'd had to post them and also there would have been the:

"I'm just popping out to post this," unless

Leanne was again also with him as they walked into town past the nearest post box as he posted it.

All the time Cora could not work out how so many expenses were being met from Mark's unemployment allowance. He was paying the rent on their flat in London and sending a pound note now and again. But how he was managing to pay the rent on wherever Leanne and himself were living, plus buying a bicycle (however second-hand,) their trip and stay in Cornwall as well, plus whatever they needed on food and rent was a further mystery.

Cora remembered that Steve had mentioned once that Leanne had some money from her family, she had an allowance from her divorced father or remarried mother, who had moved to Scotland.

"There's money in the background. That's why I went out doing extra work at telephone exchange, I was trying to put some money aside for getting married later, after buying the engagement ring." Cora wondered where that flashing diamond had ended up now and how much it was worth.

Mark told Cora later that Leanne had gone to claim unemployment allowance in Norwich. But Leanne, of course, was too delicate and posh to go out to work and had seamlessly transitioned from university student to unemployed young woman.

"We've made an arrangement already that she goes onto my grant as the wife's part and you can go onto some welfare arrangement. It's all been settled; you've just got to go to the unemployment offices and make a claim. And don't insist on making a claim on my part of the grant, I'll end up working in a factory on a conveyor belt and if you force me to do that, I'll just kill myself." So much for the new woman.

I am a spare wife and here is the spare child and please can we have something to live on.

One by one, like a pack of cards, it all fell into place.

The Baroness admitted, sadly,

"I saw them both in the Gardens with Sam once when you would have been cleaning on a Saturday morning and I thought it was strange. They were sitting on a bench together, deep in conversation, in their own world. Sorry I didn't tell you then, but I wasn't sure if it looked suspicious, you see."

Maura arrived from Hampstead and took her out for a quick drink in the Warrington Arms while the Baroness babysat, telling Cora,

"We were all here, all the time, but he didn't let us through. Lies are fun, but they can get as addictive as any drug and you could say he just ended up at the mercy of his own choices. The news about your breakup has been the talk of The Rosslyn for the past fortnight!" That was fame indeed. Traces of past Saturday nights, random connections, confidences shared, possibilities and dead friendships. Now, friends were clustering round like a gang of angels.

Kirsty and Rhona confessed,

"He wanted us to say he was visiting us all the time, but we said we couldn't be used as an excuse, because we liked you."

Kirsty added "And anyway, you don't have to worry, none of his other girl-friends were as good-looking as you." That was a bit of a bombshell - so there were even more others that she did not know about. Ines, Emma and Leanne were bad enough without adding even more.

The Gorskis took a world-weary view of the

situation. Theodore, sitting at his gigantic desk surrounded with its mountain of papers said,

"Well, then you can do the same later, you can have an affair too. And so, you can go on." He looked calm as if dispensing the wisdom of centuries. The evil see-sawing of this outline shocked and disgusted Cora. Was this how they had managed, was this how long-established couples carried on together? It was a vile view. Their image as the sophisticated European couple had its tatty edges like this. She could not respect them now and all their apparent intellectual credentials.

40

Mark came back at the weekend using the motorbike this time. The flat was glistening with white electricity and even he noticed it and stood gawkily at the living-room door. The flat was pristine, shimmering with silver. Cora was absolutely high. He stood with 'muddy' shoes at the threshold – he could feel the difference. She could see bits of dry red clay falling off his shoes onto the floor and then fading away as he stood there. It was her place now; he was the interloper. Cora was glowing. Mark was no longer controlling her reality. When it had all collapsed like this she sprang back into life. The air cleared, dancing with life like when dust motes are seen clearly in shafts of sharp sunlight.

They sat in the kitchen with the first cup of tea, Sam reaching up to his Dad eagerly and clambering up onto his knee. Mark told her calmly that there was more news; Leanne was pregnant.

"That's all I've got to tell you, that's the lot.

There's nothing more to tell you." At this, Cora erupted, shouting it was a sin against their baby, discarding their own child for a new one. She battered at his chest, livid at the betrayal of Sam more than herself. How could he replace one child with a brand-new strange one? How could he split loyalty like this?

Mark tried to excuse the change of circumstances as if it was a logical change from his point of view, having a brand-new pregnant woman on his hands.

"She's not like you. She doesn't want to do anything. She just wants to have a baby, that's enough for her." Leanne had missed the degree exams in May, obviously. Her stay in France for the Comparative Literature and Culture degree was all wasted time now. Intelligent enough to talk to, but nothing else. The perfect woman. He could mould her into whatever shape he wanted to have. Maybe that was where the traces of clay came from that Cora could see spattered on his clothes. But she was not dislodged from the euphoric state she was in, even after this new disclosure. She remained whirling outside in a new space.

They had wild sex on the floor.

"Do you realise the floorboards are a forest?" Cora whispered, nibbling his ear. "We are in the middle of a forest from the last century, or even before. All these floorboards were growing, live trees, a hundred years ago. I can see them." He agreed, once she pointed it out, drawn along in the tow of her new awareness. But she could actually see the forest and its leaves, it was not imaginary. She could see through everything now, like clear glass. A sense of euphoria changed everything now, Cora was like a liberated animal being freed into the wild.

Mark caught some of her new awareness. They became totally reckless, giddy; even more so than when they had first met. Mark fetched his motorbike, parked further along the Crescent and suggested they go out for a last Saturday night round London. Kirsty and Doug were roped in for babysitting. It was bizarre. The pair of them were like careless teenagers suddenly let out for the night. They careered round London, like dizzy tourists whirling through a jigsaw of Saturday night crowds in Kings Road, Chelsea, Soho. Sidling round the young Saturday-night revellers, not worrying about swerving round corners, Cora could have reached out and touched them on the various crowded pavements. It was like one wild party with the two of them circling happily round its edges. Part of it. Alive, young again, in the thick of it, Saturday night itself. They were both young again, free and with all this world before them. The motorbike gave them this galloping freedom. When they got back, elated and giddy, Doug was dozing, his head lolling against the back of the chair but Kirsty was as alert as ever.

"The baby hasn't woken at all; we were quite lucky tonight!" Sam was in a puzzled state, he thought all was settled well now. Daddy was back, the atmosphere changed. Getting out of his cot (easy to drop one side down now,) he toddled round the bedroom and tucked them both in bed that morning.

But Mark returned to Norwich early on Sunday morning, going off by motorbike now. He did not say where the ordinary bicycle and the tent were kept these days. Probably in the garden of the student house where he and Leanne had a room, or the proper furnished flat they were renting. Mark had been running two truths at once; proclaiming extreme loneliness, while living with the new love of his life who was apparently expecting his baby in February. Always, according to the letters he sent, it was somewhere too small to house Cora and Sam. And of course there was not enough money to support them there. If they had gone up to Norfolk, Cora would have had to immediately start working somewhere to support the two of them. And leaving the flat in Maida Vale empty would be a risk too; she was trapped, continuing the four sessions of cleaning a week, plodding on with the sturdy help of the Baroness.

Cora took out all the letters Mark had sent, not that it would be much help now. It was like playing a messy version of solitaire. There was this new layer, the expectant Leanne to factor in with all the protestations of loneliness from Mark and his heartfelt messages to Sam. Now, like a proper detective, a new Miss Marple, Cora went over the letters again, gimlet-eyed; the protestations about being so lonely while living with a pregnant girlfriend were a level of deception that was almost genius. It was getting as intricate as the Dead Sea Scrolls. She started again, reading between the lines and through the paper itself, reaching through to the expectant Leanne. It would be waste of a lifetime trying to figure it out. And all the time, as Mark wrote these heartfelt letters, Leanne would have been sitting in the same room and perhaps walked with him to a post-box on the way to the shops.

But she was fascinated, especially as, tidying up

their books and papers to pack away for the move, she found a stack of Mark's notes, and a notebook, a rough diary, with odd words and phrases inserted in code. It was a mixture of his varied reading material with quotations from several books. The code was a rough version of taking the middle letter of any word and then scattering the other letters on alternative sides of the central one. Except that was not the same for each one. It was obvious that the important bits were the ones to keep secret in case Cora had ever come across his writings, and here it all was, still unfathomable.

She got some scrap paper and started bit by bit. It all led to here. Picking up a note from April last year, it said:

"Went to opticians to OK new frames. *Nipopt sool. Nil deis. Rity sembarro shunarbo kin I. Dolkin I. The same one. Vag relet-Kzrsit??"* Was that "inside Try embarrass and gave letter-Kirsty?"
Namet donffed wokot sowell ese chegotter motooorio.
"So we'll see together tomorrow?"

*Salo nidest leary etch fin serpent dirked amen rusheeld.*Trying various mixes, Cora almost gave up, tempted to leave his secrets where they were. It was a personal crossword, but no answers would be appearing in any newspaper the next day. Here and there, however, a word did emerge from the mist but it only hinted here and there at bits she did not know:

Sunit taly naniffed. Solay ninta fray Mulhearn.
Minust laty inffaned unrabosh tranter difficult

But wait, was that aborshun ? And the one before, that said *shunarbo*, wasn't that the same, aborshun almost? Abortion - hadn't Ines, the au pair, had hers done before she went back to her parents in

France? Mark had mentioned (and how on earth had it turned up in conversation?) that St Albans, not that far away, was more liberal. And that would have included the North Finchley house that Mark had been working on. All this must have come about when Cora's first visit to the Family Planning had been arranged. Or was it when a friend of Mal's had gone off to Hemel Hempstead also in a bit of a fix?

Three pregnancies in three years; he was certainly fertile.

There was a notebook with list after list of books Mark was reading, almost a complete university course in alternative worlds. He must have taken his own writing, the great saga, to interviews and kept it apart with his few belongings. No wonder Mark was frequently so off-course and moody, his mind was completely elsewhere. Head in the clouds, feet at work and body unhappily married.

A Guide to Glastonbury's Temple of the Stars, The Sky People, The Way of the White Clouds, The Genesis of Religion, The Once and Future King, Out of the Silent Planet, these books all jarred against the photographic research of Muybridge and his pictures of horses and their influence on Degas and other painters...

There was also the map of northern France from Mark's trip and she remembered now that Steve and Leanne had gone to Rouen too, last summer. Steve had mentioned (he knew everything) that Ines lived there; poor Ines after her affair with Mark, the rushed abortion and the mysterious return home. But on the back of the map, which he had used as a type of diary, he merely wittered on about traipsing round various Youth Hostels in the rain and various strangers he had met, nothing about what he had been up to. She bundled the loose papers into a box from the grocers, although Mark had already effectively discarded them and, after looking over that summer's letters again, burned them in the fireplace. There was nothing to keep now.

41

Lying in bed, relishing the quiet rest of an autumn morning, Cora was grabbed at by Sam. He was insistent she should get up right now and go into the kitchen. He had some strange authority, as though he was the adult and she was the child. To humour him, she got up and he took her hand, leading her to the kitchen window in silence. They looked out at the dawn as the light nurtured the bricks, the roofs, the grass. From being a misty grey, they watched as colours flooded back into everything. It was like watching the Creation. Sam did not speak. He was totally in control of this, insistent, showing her something important, something she needed to learn. How the two-year-old knew the exact time of sunrise and its effects was another mystery, and how he had become an adult, in charge of her. He had never wandered into the kitchen on his own before, so how was he drawn to this now? Sam stood at the window, holding her hand. The slow release of sunlight was like a general love to all the area as more and more houses lit up in the spread of light.

Gradually some people came into the gardens walking their dogs and children ran past. The ordinary day had begun again. And with that, Sam reverted to being a toddler and they pointed people out and then had breakfast at twenty past six, well before their normal time.

At the end of September, homeless, winsome Sarah turned up yet again, looking for a place to stay. This time she was not suicidal, merely looking for somewhere to live. Cora knew there was little time left here in the flat, so did not even care when Sarah produced her new boyfriend Chris and they seamlessly moved in. They made a diversion to her sadness. The double bed in the living room became their home, with the single bed, as usual, kept as a sofa substitute. Sarah confided to her,
"While you were in hospital having the baby, Mark was making advances to me. I thought you ought to know that now." It was irrelevant, but showed that Cora's suspicion that March week two years ago was accurate, though she could do nothing about it at the time. They had few belongings apart from clothes and Chris's guitar, which he practised on all the time. Trying to capture the Dylan chords exactly right, he spent most of the day getting the record player onto slower and slower speeds, tracing escaping notes carefully. It was not too bad; at least it had an underlying tune.

The next weekend when he arrived, Mark was not in a good mood. Leanne was cross with him for betraying her by having sex with his own wife. They had had their first row.
"It looked as though I'd lost both of you. She was really angry when she found out about us. Was going to call it all off." Cora, acting as a strange

mediator in the circumstances, said he should not have told Leanne about it, but he said it was about being truthful and putting everything on the table; but really it was a form of boasting. He felt invincible now. There was nothing more to hide; he could relax. At last, his two women knew about each other. Cora was out on her own, re-formed, a different shape and whirling with an energy that was all around her these days.

Mark did not get upset about Sarah and Chris being in residence, in fact he saw them as keeping Cora company and distracting her from his own actions. Then, in the living room he found a cube of resin, looking like an Oxo cube left on the top of the sewing machine. He held it up in front Cora, waving it in her face, full of righteous anger.

"That's all I need! Drugs here! Just because I can't be here all the time, things definitely get out of hand. So, you're involved in drugs now?" Cora stared at the cube, puzzled, thinking of gravy adverts. "I thought you had more sense than this!"

She protested that she did not know what it was. Mark said authoritatively that it was Lebanese Red. How did he know that, she thought? He's far more involved than I've ever been, to know what it looks like.

"I didn't notice it there, Chris has not mentioned anything like that, but honestly, it must be Chris or Sarah's." It was a parody of the usual TV police raid, she thought, being accused by your husband of being a dealer and saying you did not know what the stuff was doing in your flat. They had not been smoking stuff here in the flat, there was no smell at all. She knew immediately that it was Chris, and his absences were about dealing and getting supplies. He often asked her for a penny to do his I Ching for the day as if it sanctified what he was up to next.

The shock, however, that Sam might have found it - it was just at his eye level – brought terrifying thoughts that she would be quickly declared an unfit mother and he'd be taken from her.

Sam had already caught head lice from Chris. In the last two nights, Sam had been restless, whimpering while still apparently asleep. She found out what was wrong on noticing little specks of blood on his pillow. Looking at his hair, minute shining silver eggs and a few wandering lice showed the problem.

"Oh, it might be from Chris, if you're worried," Sarah said, unconcerned. "He's really lucky, he doesn't need to wash his hair often, he has dry skin, that's why." It was clear she did not care either and might be infected herself. So much for Chris's long dark curls and his winsome face. Cora dashed out immediately to the chemist's and had to buy a lotion that smelled so strong that anyone within a couple of yards would have known she had the lice too. The bottle's instructions gave them a fortnight's exclusion from real contact with anyone else, but she was past caring by now.

She did not tell Mark where the headlice had come from, pretending it was from another child in the park. She was in enough trouble as it was; now the flat was crumbling into little pieces and Mark was triumphant. He did remark though, as if to add to the mess,

"While you were in hospital with the baby, and

I was here alone with her all that week, Sarah kept approaching me, it was most embarrassing. I had to fight her off. I thought you should know that now, seeing as she's living here these days." It matched almost word for word what Sarah had already told her.

The September term at college had started and Mark had other things to do right now, with his new identity as a student. Not only was he going to the same college where Steve had been, but he had gone off with Steve's girlfriend and made her pregnant. The shift of identities had been complete. On Monday morning Mark returned to Norwich on the motorbike, keeping up his self-righteous stance and superiority, leaving Cora and Sam to stay lice-ridden and living with a drug dealer in the flat.

On September the eighteenth Jimi Hendrix died. It was all over the radio; his music was played all day as if it was a royal death. It shocked all the underground network as well as ordinary pop-music lovers. They were all upset, he had reached into their emotions and stretched them further with his turbulence. And now he was gone. Chris's mother wrote to him. He must have already given his mother this address; not a good move from an official point of view, but Cora was past caring.

Chris read it out,

"My Mum's really worried now, she's sent me this warning, 'Don't die like Hendrix.'" This implied she knew he used drugs and she could not do anything about it now, wherever she lived. The entire druggy world had tumbled into chaos. The Club 27 started about then with the deaths of the 27-year-old Alan Wilson of Canned Heat and Brian Jones of The Rolling Stones. The sixties' underbelly was showing up now and Janis Joplin was going to follow soon after.

Cora remembered what the babysitter girl from BIT said about changes in the special room they had set up for bad drug experiences,

"It was designed as a really soothing room, walls in a sort of light grey, and an oatmeal-coloured carpet, all restful, with no bright colours. We used to have velvet cushions in there, but they were destroyed, sick all over and that sort of thing, soft music too, to help people with bad trips. And there was a voluntary helper or adviser on duty to talk them down." But it had become so overused, the clients so violent, and the volunteers so worn out that these days anyone on a bad trip who called in was just locked into the room until the worst was over, having to recover alone, "They're going through heaven knows what, now," she said, sadly. "These days we just leave them in there, screaming. The dream is over."

Not distracted by Sarah and Chris in the midst of all this, Cora went on packing away any possessions that could be put aside. Getting old grocery boxes from Mrs Mac's she collected random books and papers, plates and winter clothes, all disappearing daily. If Sarah and Chris were not around, only a few cups and plates and a tin-opener would have been enough to get by on. Sam's toys had to stay out so that he could carry on as near to normal as possible in the circumstances. He was the only oasis amid all this upheaval, intent on his little circus merry-go-round and setting out his farm animals in make-believe fields.

42

The Baroness gave Cora a small Willow Pattern teapot as a goodbye gift. They parted like mother and daughter, with regret on both sides. The teapot would obviously have been called an export reject; the Willow pattern people were blurred. The blue transfer had jarred, so that the prosaic normal design shifted and the entire drama of the couple on the bridge wavered and the two lovebirds were indistinct above the waving blue trees. It was like a film version of what was happening here and now. They knew they would never see each other again.

On Saturday. Mark arrived back to help with the move on Sunday afternoon as his college term had already started and he was happily established in this new routine as a student. George and Beryl turned up to say goodbye and help with the departure, George taking down the last of the boxes and Beryl bringing sandwiches and a new thermos flask with coffee as well as a new toy for Sam.

Sarah and Chris had been quietly sent off to stay out of the way while the grandparents were around, but they had been given the spare key to be able to get back into the flat once they had all gone. Sarah and Chris could hardly be thrown out into the street. They were left to squat with the lumpy double bed and the carpet.

Cora had ordered a van for £25 last week. Mark was cross when he saw it arrive, looking down from the window as it was parked below them.

"Where on earth did you get that? It's far too small. Honestly!" He was angry with her.

"It's an ad in the Kensington Gazette, see,

here, it says 'Long distance 1/6d a mile anywhere, inclusive of return journey' So he said it was £25 to Norwich, and I booked it for Sunday 4th October and here it is. Seemed the cheapest, you see."

"All I see is an extremely small van. We'll most probably have to leave things behind, more like." Cora was past caring now. There was nothing to be sentimental about, she thought, they might as well leave the lot except the big kitchen table. Furniture, the wooden witnesses of all that went on. All their emotions absorbed in silence; that was the value of antiques; what they had been through. They were so different from pieces of joined-up wood.

The lorry driver, Leo, solved the problems immediately like a real pro. The double mattress went over the cab, its frame stacked against one of the van's walls and the rest of the furniture was easily shuffled around the rest of the space. The other bed was left behind and apart from the table, chairs, and sideboard, the wardrobe helpfully was easily dismantled. The mangle also was taken apart, and as much as possible of the gas stove taken to pieces. The rest was books, clothes, crockery and pans, with the cot and a small pushchair. There was plenty of room after all. It was the moment to start off. Mr and Mrs Williams waved them goodbye, disappointed that a family nearby in London was not going to be possible, however much they had done to help out.

Mark had only disclosed at the last minute that his parents had added an extra hundred pounds to the deposit for the new house.

"Mum said it was because they thought it might be a way of securing some safety for Sam, it would cover the solicitor's fees and things like that."

Their kindness was endless.

Mark, Cora, and Sam sat up in the front of the cab with the driver. Leo was easy-going and even produced a gigantic thermos flask of coffee in contrast with the one given by Beryl. It tasted strong and sweet.

"Oh, it's made with Camp Coffee, you know, the bottled concentrated stuff. It sees me through times when I need a drink and can't stop and find a place to park." They swapped biscuits and cheese and pickle sandwiches. Sam had banana and rosehip syrup in a bottle and after looking at the city streets whizz past, he fell into a comfortable sleep, lulled by the rhythm of the engine.

The magnificent pram, now an embarrassing responsibility, a wounded animal, was abandoned against one of the trees, where it leant like a drunk. Wheels askew, it had lost all its Mayfair Norland Nanny image and would never hold a child safely again. It stood, a stranded drunken aristocrat among the piled up black bags, many of them already torn by stray dogs, cats or rats, with vegetable peelings and scraps spilling out across the pavements. It was an amazing testimony to the power of the dustbin men and all the secret people who served the city; withdrawal of their labour showed how much they really did each day.

Each basement area along the Crescent had scribbled notices on pieces of cardboard from besieged basement tenants, pleading with other residents upstairs to not place more rubbish in the bins, which were already overflowing. Daily they had to spray the areas with disinfectant to disguise the smell of rotting refuse right outside their living room window. Light-blue pools of Jeyes Fluid showed their attempt at keeping the worst of the stink at bay.

In spite of the outlook all along the Crescent, a siege of rubbish, Cora was delighted at the proof of how valuable dustbin-men were to a neighbourhood, to a city. It was a show of power by the invisibles that kept a city ticking over and who no one wanted to acknowledge even existed as real people. Steve had pointed it out.

"That's why they have West Kensington, it's kept as a cheap place to live in, right in the middle of all the salubrious residential areas. The middle classes need their support workers within easy distance, all the cleaners, window-cleaners, child minders, they need them within walking distance, for convenience. Then you don't have to pay them more, because they'd need better wages to be able to travel in from the outskirts. It wouldn't look too good to see them being bussed in like real slaves. You can sometimes see people-carriers in the early mornings, though, packed with contract or agency workers already. Otherwise, they'd have to live in the same house with the family, up in the attic like in Victorian times." It made horrible sense if you thought like that.

They were being driven away from all this mess into an unknown place. So far Cora only knew Norwich as a lacey design of black lines on the map stuck on the kitchen door. She had not seen the house of course, Mark said it was a lovely terrace house, she'd love it, and she was in complete ignorance of what was going to happen, merely that it would be better than all this, a house on the ground and a handkerchief garden. There was not even a photograph, apparently.

43

They left the second-hand double bed and both of the keys with Chris and Sarah, leaving them squatting in the empty flat. It was the least they could do, postponing a real decision, not able to actually throw them out into the street. There were enough difficulties to be going on with, without causing dramatic scenes on the doorstep. Mark told Cora at this point that he had not told her he knew the entire building was going to revert to the Church of England Commissioners soon, from the lease that some gangster held, which was probably coming to an end next year. It was unclear, of course, whether they would have been rehoused somewhere near, or just given a notice of eviction and have to find their own new place to live. It was yet another precipice they had managed to escape.

It was telling that Mark. Cora and Sam had to keep a distance from each other because of the headlice. So far Mark had escaped, as Cora and Sam continued to stink of the strong lice-killing lotion.

43

Petula Clark was singing over the intercom in the cabin. I used to wash nappies to this song, Cora thought closing the door and going on deck. The sun, at last, began to shine on the sea and the sea began its short dancing steps. The sparkle on each wavelet danced like sequins turning towards light.

I am in it at last. I am in the TV advert, only I can't see it properly because this time I am in the ship, being content in a sunlit sea. How strange. Then, I could see far more, the wide ocean, the liner, its decks, the shimmering wake as it cut its way into the contrasting dark. And I am just walking into the living room at this instant with a cup of tea, or, well, something is in my hand, and worries crowding my thoughts, and my legs won't work, I am stumbling across the room with fatigue or malnutrition ,or whatever it was, and on the television there is this transcendent scene, the liner going off into the velvet distance leaving its scattered white footprint behind. I am so tired and only this flat and this street exist and there is only eight shillings left until Thursday. And Mark is pulling away from me again, I am shredded and yet able to move about and talk as if normal.

'You could use a cruise with P&O'
But there is this ship, silver, going off into the distance, further up the television screen until it fades out at the top into a black dot. In a couple of hours' time the advert will be on again and I will be standing here again, with washing or ironing or a cup of tea or the baby crying and for a couple of minutes I will gather some hope from that image across my life.
And now I am on that ship and writing this.
The dots of sequined light make a morse code, a silver braille as if the ocean was talking to itself knowing we will never understand it or crack its code. Like the dolphins welcoming the ship, playing in the turbulence and diving under the ship to reappear at the side - they are in their own medium - they understand it. We are privileged to be even this far or this near, able to skim across the surface edge of their world. It has taken so much research, effort, ship-

makers, steelworkers, riveters, to reach this far, this surface beneath the black glittering surface is unknowable, for all our efforts to understand, to infringe, to dive. Sunken ships show the failures going down into the depths too.

At the end of the cruise they approached the white cliffs, not of Dover, but of Portsmouth. It looked so easy, the ordinariness of white chalk edges meeting the sea. It must have looked the same to any invader, especially the Romans. At school she had translated Julius Caesar's Latin version of this same instant. It looked as if it was all going to be so easy, so simple, clear. But once back on land the old distractions and rules took over again and she would be ordinary, the belonging taking over.

To stay on the ship was not an option. They emerged from the ship early in the evening and walked down the gangway to a waiting coach. Hauliers steered away from the ferry terminal apart from the assorted private cars and made their way along the motorway to their warehouses and business parks, aiming to reach London easily, well before midnight.

From here the passengers could see the group of cleaners at the dockside, waiting to tidy up their places. Dressed in overalls, they sat and stood round a picnic table, having a last cigarette before starting the shift, the unseen helpers of the glamorous surface. The coach then decanted its passengers into smaller district vans and they dispersed to their original pick-up points. It was carefully planned. The tour was over, it had all been achieved. The woman staggering across the living room and seeing the P&O advert had been vindicated.

The van left London and started to pass

through the edges of Walthamstow towards Epping countryside and scattered towns of Newmarket and Thetford. They were soon in the flat-lands of Norfolk. By mid-afternoon they entered the edges of Norwich and progressed from the larger houses with long gardens at the end of Unthank Road to a more built-up area. Cora kept asking if that was like the house? Or that terrace? Or that one? There seemed to be no other example in all of the eastern region as they drove past. Sam had luckily drifted off to sleep after another drink of rosehip syrup and a rusk.

It was warm for this fourth of October as they arrived at a sun-baked red-brick terrace house. Spears of Golden Rod stood tall in the cobbled back yard, growing up amongst the paving stones. Children from the street came out of their houses and watched as various bits of furniture were lifted out of the lorry and onto the road outside the house. There was not going to be any privacy here, they were the entertainment of the street's quiet Sunday afternoon. Chairs, mangle, bed, sideboard, stood, almost embarrassed in the open air. The lorry driver was efficient at setting out the furniture and Mark reconstructed the cot. It was beginning to grow dark already and Leo wanted to get back to London, his job done. The wedding-present Cannon stove and mangle nestled together in the quarry-tiled kitchen. There was already a stove left there but it looked fragile next to the gigantic cream monster, waiting to be attached by a gas service man during the week. It had taken the efforts of the two men, Mark and Leo to move it each time.

At one instant when they were alone together, Leo, the driver, said to Cora quietly,

"It's a good house, a really good house you've got here," summing up the situation tactfully. Mark left at the same time as the driver, as though he did not want to be left alone with them and Sam and Cora were left alone in a darkening autumn house which had no gas or electricity. The excitement was over and here was real life, an empty house, their belongings scattered around in a semi-clean building. They had brought supplies of milk and the usual baby food. Sam could always chew on a couple of rusks or have a mashed banana as no cooking was possible yet. He sat on her knee having his bedtime bottle, but he stopped and looked at her,

"I want my Daddy live in my house."

No one thought that the little heart could be broken, that the child could be feeling as great a loss as herself; he was merely a pawn in the game. The sexual revolution emphasised that everyone's access to sex should be free, it was a personal right to self-expression. Selfishness was god, passion was paramount, what you felt was the supreme way to live. Babies and children with all their plain daily repetitions were in the way of all the adult dreams. No one looked at them in the middle of all these dramas while the adults rearranged and went their separate sexual ways. Her tears fell on his hair as she waffled on that Daddy would be coming back soon, he lived very near-by and they would be seeing him very soon.

Changing all the old rules about constancy and belonging, Mark now wanted to stay like that mad dash round swinging London, always on heat and not wanting to be pegged down by dull daily responsibilities. Yet he was going into the exact same circumstances all over again with another baby.

Perhaps being a student with all the emphasis on self-development and following his own interests was so different from going out to work that it would manage to paper over the drawbacks this time with Leanne.

There was a torch, and she lit a candle, placing it in an empty saucepan for safety in case it fell over. She would have to go to the electricity and gas showrooms to register and pay a deposit tomorrow, Mark had left some money towards that and gave her the addresses.

"And first of all, you'll have to call into the solicitors on Monday morning and sign the mortgage agreement right away too," he added as he left. " It's on Theatre Street." In the half-dark she made the bed and collapsed into it, her mind racing. She got into bed after the cheese sandwiches and cup of water, exhausted in the pitch black, her last thoughts about the Golden Rod growing in the little courtyard outside the kitchen window. She was in the middle of Cider with Rosie whether she liked it or not. It was almost the countryside here.

Next morning as soon as they could, Cora stocked up the pram again and they set out for the city. She knew things were bad when she kept smelling chocolate in the air. Hallucinations could follow trauma, people could have these false realities, she knew that. Stopping a passing postman, Cora asked where Theatre Street was, for the solicitor's offices.

"It's along here, through the rest of the park, it's on your right," he said cheerily. Then, gathering courage she asked him if he could smell chocolate or was she imagining it. The next stop would be having to find a doctor's and registering for some psychiatric help. "Oh that!" he laughed," It's that chocolate factory over there, it's Rowntree's, it spreads all over in any breeze, depends on the weather, you'll soon get used to it." And so, restoring her health and sanity he continued on to the main road past Chapelfield Park with his sack of letters.

It was awkward at the solicitor's, as after signing the mortgage agreement Cora had to ask where the Social Security Centre was, saying she had to register for Child Benefit. Mr Harris drew her a quick map and shook hands as the process of buying the house was concluded now. He was quite proud of how rapidly they had completed the conveyancing.

What Cora had not told him was that she had to go to the unemployment offices and claim right away for any financial support. Mark stated he was not going to give the pair of them any money after the next month's mortgage instalment. It was like standing at the top of a waterfall; the drop could be fatal now. He said,

"There's nothing left. What do you think I'm going to do here to produce more money for you? You'll have to go and sign on to get some money now. We've sorted it all out about the grant, so you've got to see about something else for yourself and Sam." The mature student's grant that Mark had been awarded was also designed to support a wife and child, but had been hi-jacked by Leanne, for more convenience. There was also the rent he had to pay on the proper flat that they had probably been living in all along. That first flurry in June of him mentioning getting a flat, instead of buying a house, was probably a crossover from acquiring their own one. No student, however mature, could afford to rent two flats at once. The only thing to be grateful about was that the loving twosome had not squandered the money that Mark and Cora, and even Sam, had saved for the deposit.

It was a strange experience, to admit to a clerical officer that your husband has gone off with a new woman and made her pregnant and here is the discarded wife and child wanting some money. Plus, they had turned up from London this week. It sounded as though all three adults had cooked up some plan on how to defraud the welfare system and the taxpayers here. Her big wedding ring shone uselessly on her finger. The officer was non-committal, neither blaming nor gushing with sympathy. It was a process of signing here and here and an inspector would call round in a few days' time and the claim would be going through as soon as possible. Messy life had become a sheaf of papers with ticks and boxes.

As she pushed the pram back through the new city, Cora wondered how she could raise any money for the week or more before the claim went through. They only had one pound and ten shillings to live on for the foreseeable future. The wedding ring! What about pawning it? Ian, an actor in Hampstead had told her his unusual method of putting money aside.

"Each time I've got a bit of money, after a good run with a show, like, I go into a pawnbroker's and exchange the watch or signet ring I've already got and pay up for a more expensive one. Then I've always got something to fall back on in the case of any lean times."

She looked at the wedding ring, assessing it. It was gigantic and solid gold. A foolish choice. Going into a phone box, she leafed through the trades directory and found there was a pawnbroker in the centre of town discreetly situated in a side street. After a couple of mistakes, she found the right place, the three golden balls sited above the doorway showing its identity. That part of the counter where pledges were made was in a separate corner, a plain booth with a hatch. The pawnbroker took the wedding ring, turning it over in his hand, feeling the weight, then he produced an old ledger for her to sign.

Signing the pawnbroker's register was a trip back into Victorian times. It could be redeemed if she paid more than this price back in the future. The man gave her two pounds, which would see them through a week's basic food. It was a knife-edge again, but she was used to that.

Later in October, as her birthday came round, Cora had forgotten her right age and found the entire year had been lost without trace in the wall of lies. Sam and herself still had random headlice. Mrs Murgatroyd had made up for her initial carelessness long ago by sending advance information from London about little Sam moving to a new address; the country was more concerned what happened to a child than its own father. The local children's nurse, a Miss Brown, called in with the only nit-comb in Norwich. She held it up. Its steel teeth shone in the October afternoon light. Sam thought it might be a new toy.

"Don't lose this, it's the only one and I'm responsible for its keeping, or I'll have to provide another one out of my own wages." Even amid all this chaos, Cora was now responsible to all the inhabitants of the city.

44

Sorting things out from all the bundles of clothes, curtains, shoes and of course the heaps of books in cardboard boxes, Sam joined in as if it were a game, which of course it was, in a way. It was a parody of any Christmas morning, excitedly opening presents. And here, a small paper bag fell out of one of Mark's discarded shoes. It was quite heavy, and Cora opened it with curiosity. A plastic bank moneybag hidden inside showed a collection of small brown coins. Farthings! The missing farthings from Charles Winchester's studio collection. It was the same as that instant in *The Magus* where Nicholas Urfe had found the discarded cigarette packet. Items, so innocent in themselves, could lead towards the mists of deceit and evil. The tiny coins fell out onto the floor and scattered across the room - to Sam's delight - as if grateful to see daylight again.

The universe-wide illumination had faded away as completely as it had arrived. She had come down to earth as rapidly as she had ascended in September. The world was as ordinary now as it had ever been All that omniscient strength had gone. Cora had fallen down a sterile rabbit-hole now and all the spiritual awareness had gone. Like Charles Winchester she was as locked-out as before, with only glimpses of that other-worldly existence, an outcast once again. There was no proof it had ever happened except she could remember Charles Winchester's jealousy and the two women from South Africa in the empty church and that shock of recognition from them both.

A strange memory surfaced about Mateus Rosé; a bottle of wine they had been given as a wedding present. The wine came from Portugal, only across the border, it was so near. It was so tempting to go right across now, right into the magic courtyard on the label. So long ago, yet Cora could remember the drunken experience after their wedding, how easily she had gone right in there, zooming in effortlessly as drunkenness gave such wild powers. It was so easy, listening to Jimi Hendrix after so many drinks in the pub and later back in their own room with the others. She went into the palace, into its cool rooms. Life was going to be like this.

She had, of course, got it completely wrong. On the label at the back of the bottle, the little palace stood, not above a flat stripe of lawn but above a lake.

It reflected itself on the water delicately. But on the label on the front of the bottle, the little palace was set in front of a lawn. There were two truths as usual, each apparently as real as each other.

Unusually Cora knew what to do now. These modern inventions could serve old purposes. Thanks to the internet, thanks to so many peoples' ingenuity the little palace was available and pressing the right buttons she went through the central dark doorway and into the compressed space of the square courtyard.

The past was waiting, transformed, calm, a taunting immortality.

She was staying at her grandmother's in St James's Road, a summer evening and she was lying in bed at the age of seven, with the book of Jeannie Harbour's beautifully illustrated Hans Andersen's stories. There was one picture about the Princess and the Swineherd. Of course, he turned out to be a real Prince in disguise. At the almost-end, it said 'he went back into his own little kingdom and shut and locked the door.'

She progressed through the dark doorway and went through. Time could be shaped however you wanted it to be, though it took an effort. It was like picking a lock and she easily slipped inside the little palace balanced between time and never.

Acknowledgements

The one person who should be acknowledged here is The Baroness, Lady Louise Banks. Her reassuring personality, never unwavering, was far more of a benefit than we realised at the time. She deserves this recognition and is the only real person named in this drama. Her warmth was our treasure and the little teapot still exists, with its faded Willow Pattern, the lovers transformed into birds above the bridge.

Printed in Great Britain
by Amazon